I0699078

WORTH THE RUSH

BEA BORGES

WORTH THE RUSH

BEA BORGES

Copyright © 2024 Bea Borges

All rights reserved.

No part of this book may be reproduced in any form or by any electronic or mechanical means, including information storage and retrieval systems without written permission from the author except for brief quotations used for book review or promotional edit.

This book is a work of fiction. Any similarities to real persons, living or dead, is coincidental.

Any use of this publication to "train" AI technology to generate text is expressly prohibited.

ISBN: 979-8-9917080-0-5

Cover Design by Summer Grove, @summerrgrove

Formatting by Robert Harrison, Seneca Author Services

Developmental Editor- Melissa McGovern, Memos In The Margins

Copy and Line Editor- by Kat Wyeth, Kat's Literary Services

This is for those managing their grief after loss.
You may not ever feel completely healed.
The right person won't need you to be to love you right.
XO, Bea

Content Warning

Hello readers,

As swoony and light hearted as Worth The Rush is, there are some themes and occurrences that could be triggering for readers. Both main characters are dealing with grief and loss in different ways. I have done my very best to handle these instances with care and respect. I hope if you choose to read, you'll feel that way as well.

If you believe any of the warnings listed below would be damaging to your mental health, please take care of yourself!

XO, Bea

+loss of a friend, off page
+pregnancy loss, off page
+explicit sex
+drinking and mention of struggles with alcohol
+cheating, not between the main characters

+mention of grooming
+mention of emotional abuse/abandonment/neglect
+high risk situations

IVY

"**F**light 877 to Denver is boarding now. All passengers on Flight 877, please proceed to gate sixty-five for boarding," a woman's voice announces over the intercom.

Finally. As little as I want to be here at all, we've been delayed twice. Which puts me two and a half hours behind schedule. I stand and grab my carry-on bag before getting in the A line. First class would have been much more enjoyable, but apparently, I'm on a "budget" until I learn to "make it on my own." What Sullivan Rutherford, *dear old dad,* fails to acknowledge is that I've been on my own from the time I could walk. Probably before then, but that's a story for another time, *preferably in therapy,* and I have a plane to catch.

I say a quick hello to the neatly dressed attendant behind the desk, swipe my phone over the red scanner, and hear it beep.

"Have a nice flight," she tells me with a smile.

"Thank you," I reply. She doesn't need to know this flight

was not my idea, and as much as it looks like I'm willingly getting on this plane, I didn't have much choice in the matter. No, telling her *that* would probably lead to either a very uncomfortable silence or a call to Airport Security. Neither sounds like something I want to deal with at the moment. I'll keep all that frustration inside until it gets to be too much, and I end up making an impulsive decision. *No, Ivy. We aren't doing that anymore.* I scold myself silently and take a deep breath.

"I'm sorry?" The woman in front of me turns and looks at me. *Okay, not so silently.*

"I didn't say anything," I tell her with a polite smile, gaslighting the shit out of her. She gives me a confused look before turning to face the front of the line again. I really need to work on keeping those inside thoughts—*inside.*

"Speaking to yourself out loud is a completely normal reaction to trauma. About 25 percent of adults participate in it."

At least that's what my therapist said when I told her I was alone a lot growing up and then again during my failed marriage. So here we have it—a trauma response? Check. A failed marriage at twenty-seven and enough baggage from it to last a lifetime? Check, check. Enough room in this overhead compartment to fit my bag? Probably not, and I doubt all my emotional baggage would fit either.

"Hello, welcome aboard flight 877. We're so sorry for the delay, everyone," one of the flight attendants greets us as passengers step onto the plane.

"Hello," I tell them with a small wave and try my best to smile. I know it's not their fault we've been delayed or that I'm here in the first place. *I am practicing being patient.* I make the long journey back to my seat. My seat must be in the last row of the Pacific Ocean instead of the LAX tarmac because I stand in the aisle with my ass in everyone's faces for what feels like forever. As I inch my way through the cabin, I search until I find my assigned seat. Right next to the bathroom. *Great.* I roll my eyes and barely fit my bag in the overhead compartment. I double-check my ticket, and dear lord help me, I'm in the middle seat. Sighing, I address the man in the aisle.

"Excuse me, sir, I'm right in the middle there," I say, pointing at my seat. "Would you mind if I squeezed past you?" I pour the last bit of patience into my tone. He looks up at me from the TV show he's already playing on his phone, removes his headphones, and takes a little too long raking his beady eyes up the rest of me before reaching my face.

"Not at all," he tells me, leaning back in his seat and spreading his legs further apart. "Go ahead," he encourages with a condescending smile, and I swear he fucking winks at me. *Gross.* I stare at him. I may not *personally* know this man, but I *know* him. The men who get handsy when their flirting attempts fail, with their heads so far up their asses that they think there must be something wrong with me if I'm not ready to jump into bed with them. His mother probably told him he was *such a handsome boy* one too many times in his formative years. Unfortunately for him, he's about to find out that even on a good day, this isn't behavior I tolerate, and the patience I have worked so hard to maintain throughout today has run out.

ALDER

"We need to land. Now," I say into my headset, sitting in the cockpit beside my co-pilot. The sound of the blades overhead and classic rock fade into the background as we turn all our attention to the task at hand. Dispatch received a call this afternoon that a man had decided to hike up the mountain without checking the weather. Now, he's stuck up here, and the storm is bearing down on us ruthlessly as Nate, Griffin, and I focus on getting him home safely.

"We can't land," Griffin surmises.

"We don't have the clearance, and we don't have the time before things really start whipping up here," Nate tells me. *Shit.* I make a split-second decision. I'm going to have to rappel down to him.

"Take over," I tell him, already moving backward to let him grab the control.

"It's not a good idea, Alder," he tells me while I unbuckle

myself from my seat and make my way into the cabin. He sighs, moving into my now-vacant seat.

"It's all we've got. Get me as close as you can," I say, clipping into my harness and securing it to the aircraft. I connect my rescue strap for our patient and run through my mental checklist twice. My supply pack, which will be our lifeline in case things go south, is secured on my back.

Our patient was able to make a call for help eleven minutes ago, so we're operating on the assumption that he's still unharmed. "All clear, Nate! Just a little closer!" I yell, and Griffin slides open the door until we hear it lock into place. Blinding light and air so frigid it steals my breath mixes in with the snowy mountains in the distance.

Feeding myself some slack, I swing my legs out into the wind and onto the slippery tops of the skid. Taking in a lungful of freezing air, I swing my body out until I'm facing Griffin. Leaning back into my harness, I wait for his all clear. Nate positions us just above where I need to rappel.

"Go." I hear Griffin's order, and as I look down, I feel muscle memory take over. Bending my knees, I push myself away from the aircraft while letting my line slide through my hands, sending me toward the ground. Years of training, experience, and discipline combine as I lower myself. The wind has picked up significantly in the last fifteen minutes. I'm descending swiftly while adjusting to the force of the wind and the sway of the helicopter.

The sound of crunching snow fills my ears as my feet plant into the ground. Out of the corner of my eye, I see movement; turning toward it, I see a man crouched over. He's only wearing a long-sleeved tee and a pair of jeans. His shoes are basic tennis shoes. He isn't prepared for this kind of hike or the harsh weather at all.

"I'm s-ss-so sorry," he says through chattering teeth.

"It's alright. You did the right thing by calling for help," I tell him because he did do the right thing. Should he have prepared more before setting out? Yes, but he realized he was in a potentially dangerous situation and made the call. Some men would have been too prideful and decided they could find their way down on their own. "We're gonna get you out of here, and you'll be back at the resort with a hot drink in no time. What's your name?"

"Th-that sounds good. I'm Shh-Sean," he says, walking closer.

"Okay, Sean. Nice to meet you. I'm Alder, and we're about to get to know each other real well. I'm going to slip this over your head and strap you into the harness. It's going to feel like you're sitting in my lap, and that's exactly what we want. Once we're secured together, we can get the hell out of here," I instruct him. "Ready?"

"Ready," he confirms as I slide the sling up and around him, settling it over his hips and tightening the straps of the harness over his shoulders. I ratchet him up off the ground and get myself into position. "Alright, boys. We're locked in and ready to come up," I say into my headset.

"Copy. Starting the pulley system now. Hang tight," Griff responds.

"We're going up, Sean. Hold on," I tell him as we're lifted into the air. Immediately, there's too much movement. Sean glances around nervously. We're swaying. A lot. More than usual. More than I would like. I remain calm as we lurch with only fifteen more feet to go. We lose a couple of feet, and our ascent comes to a standstill.

"Alder." Griff's voice is calm, but I can detect a small flare of panic as he says my name.

"Yeah, Griff?" I ask.

"The pulley stopped working." His tone is practiced. Flat but urgent. That's unfortunate. We need to move. And fast.

"Copy that," I say into my comm.

"You can't make the climb with him attached to you." Nate chimes in.

"Thank you for the vote of confidence, Nathan." I throw as much sarcasm as I can manage behind my words.

"What do you want to do here, Boss ?" he asks me. *Think Alder. Think.* I run through our options, and I don't like any of them, but we have to keep moving. There's no way Sean can make it on foot long enough to get to a safer location down the mountain.

"You're going to have to take us down like this—at least to lower ground. Find a place where you can let us down and land." I relay my plan to my crew, and then to Sean, I say, "I'll rappel us down, and we'll stay clear for landing. Once Nate lands, we'll take a helicopter ride to the hospital to get you checked out and make sure you don't have frostbite."

"That's at least three full minutes with you guys out in this wind," Nate speaks into my ear.

"They can make it," Griff affirms. I reach into my supply pack and pull out a wool face mask and three packs of hand warmers, thankful I always keep it rescue ready.

"We can make it," I agree. "We're going to have to. Just go. Now." And then we're moving.

"I'm going to put two of these in your shirt, and I want

you to cross your arms over your chest. I'm also going to put this over your head," I yell to Sean. "This isn't going to be pleasant, but we have to beat this storm." He nods at me, and I do as I told him I would. The wind is painful now anywhere my skin is exposed. It feels like needles pricking my face where my goggles don't cover. I see where Nate will land and say a silent prayer and a thank you that we're almost out of the elements. We're slowly lowered down until I'm standing.

"As much as I've enjoyed this connection we've shared, I'm going to untether us so we can move away from the landing site. Okay?" I look at Sean, who nods at me and, through chattering teeth, says, "Kkkkay." I unhook myself from Sean and move us a safe distance away so Nate has enough room to land. Once the helicopter is on the ground and it's safe, I help Sean into its open door. Nate and Griffin take on Sean's weight, and together, they get him in. After securing Sean into his seat, I make sure to pull in the rest of the rope manually. I add a note under Griff's logged events in the flight manifest while he shuts the door.

Turning my attention to Sean, I say, "Well, that was one way to get the blood pumping. Next time, just ask me out, Sean," I tease. "I'm assuming you didn't think a helicopter rescue would be necessary when you started your hike today," I say as I get my medic bag to check his vitals. Griff grabs a blanket, throws it over his shoulders, and sits back in his seat.

"Acc-tually," he starts, "I was hoping to be engaged by...th-the end of the day," he tells us, still stuttering slightly as he warms up. He pulls a small box from his pocket. "I was trying to set up a sunset proposal before heading back to our cabin rental for my girl, but I guess Mother Nature had other plans."

"No kidding. Are you still going to ask her to marry you?" Griff asks.

"Oh absolutely, I'm locking her down the minute I see her." His voice is so sure. I check his vitals, and after seeing his blood pressure and checking his fingertips and toes, it looks like he may just end up with some altitude sickness. He calls his girlfriend, soon-to-be fiancée, and he hands me the phone to relay the information about the hospital we're arriving at, then I give him his phone back. By the time he's off the phone, we're almost there.

On the hospital's roof I hand him off to a team of doctors, passing his chart to one of them. Marigold Levinson, head of general surgery, is among them.

"Isn't it a little early in the season for you to be playing hero, Alder?" she asks, her dark-blonde brow raised, voice teasing.

I place my hand over my chest. "Never, and who's playing?" I ask with a wink and step out of the helicopter, looking over my shoulder at Nate and Griffin. "Nice work out there."

"Never a dull moment with you around, Alder,' Griff says, getting out and walking toward the hospital doors. "See you guys later!" he calls.

"See ya, Griff!" I wave.

"No offense, man, but I'm really hoping I don't have to witness your heroics again for a while," Nate tells me, and I chuckle.

"You can pretend our love doesn't mean anything, but I know the truth," I tell him solemnly and wave. "See you around, Nate. Get some rest, and don't forget to tell Sarah how heroic and handsome I was today," I remind him.

"I'll be sure to mention it," he tells me with his middle

finger raised and an annoyed head shake. They've been married for two blissful years, and now they're expecting their first kid in just a few months. I'm still laughing when I turn around and see they're starting to wheel Sean inside.

"Thank you! I won't forget this or you saving me today," he yells.

"The pleasure was all mine. Maybe next time you decide to take a sunset...or any type of hike, you check the weather before starting out, yeah?" I say it lightly, but he knows I mean it. Safety isn't a joke to me. Making sure people are safe is one of the biggest reasons I do this job.

"Of course. I will. Thank you again," he says and extends his hand to me.

I take it and shake. "Now go get the girl. She's probably so worried about you that you'll get her to say yes pretty easily," I tell him, and he chuckles. His team takes him down the hallway, and I walk the opposite way to the elevators. Once inside, I let my shoulders relax and take a few deep breaths to center myself. My blood is pumping so hard I can still hear my heartbeat. I ride the elevator to the bottom floor and walk out to the lobby. The storm is just starting to make it into town. Luckily, we were able to beat it here. I know the roads up the mountain will be clear by morning, but there's no reason to risk it tonight —even though being in my own bed sounds really great right now.

It looks like I'll be hitting up a hotel room tonight or possibly crashing with one of my siblings. That's just another great thing about living up the mountain from a small town filled with your family. Being one of four gives me options. I send a text to the sibling group chat that I titled The Holloway Heathens.

ALDER

Guess who just saved a hiker from what was surely imminent death?

Texts that highlight my heroics are my favorite texts to send. The alternative is bleak and brings down the vibe considerably.

ALDER

Here's a hint: He's got a great ass and a charming personality too.

ALDER

Fine! I'll tell you. It was me. Your favorite brother.

BABY LO

Are you ok? Are they? I thought Rhett was the favorite.

RHETT

Atta boy! Proud of you! Correct, Baby Lo. I am the favorite.

ALDER

I'm fine. The hiker's fine. Actually, he's getting ready to propose to his girlfriend in the hospital as I type this out. Rhett, you are absolutely not the favorite.

KNOX

👍

What a typical Knox response. I roll my eyes.

WINNIE

Mare texted me. She said the guy was lucky! Sounds like he was lucky you're good at what you do!

I'm not surprised that her best friend already stole my thunder.

ALDER

Aww, Win. You're gonna make me blush. When are you leaving my less handsome, less fun, not favorite brother for me again?

RHETT

Alder.

ALDER

Oh, shit. I'm so sorry, Rhett. This isn't how I wanted you to find out.

I laugh as I picture his face reading that one.

WINNIE

RHETT

You're not as funny as you think you are.

ALDER

I may not be as funny as YOU think I am, but I'm definitely as funny as I think I am.

ALDER

PS: Who wants to host me tonight? I'm stuck in town because of the storm.

KNOX

Not me.

He may be brutal, but Knox will always tell you the truth.

RHETT

After the last comment you made about my FIANCÉE?

ALDER

I'll take that as a no.

RHETT

So, he isn't just funny. He's smart, too. 😼

The jokes on him. I see my opening.

ALDER

You'll never convince Winnie to stay with you if you keep highlighting all my best traits, Rhett.

RHETT

🖕

I laugh. Picking on my little brother is so fun these days, knowing at the end of the day he's happy and in love.

BABY LO

We have a couple of rooms left at the hotel.

ALDER

Thank you, Baby Lo. You're my favorite.

BABY LO

Duh. I was being modest earlier. I'm everyone's favorite.

WINNIE

True. You're the most precious.

RHETT

100%

KNOX

Affirmative.

I roll my eyes, but it's the truth. Lo, Baby Lo, Florence

Holloway, is the fan favorite of the Holloway bunch. Being the literal baby of the family, twenty-three to my thirty-six, it's actually a miracle that she isn't an insufferable brat. She's the opposite. Responsible, generous, and the sweetest of us all, she's also the self-confident woman we all knew she would be. Announcing to my parents that she wanted to run the Holloway Hotel by herself right out of college had us all concerned, not because we didn't think she could do it, but because no one wanted to see her fail. She's proven that all our concerns were fruitless and has blown us all away with the improvements she's made to an already flourishing business.

ALDER

I'll be by in a little bit. I'm not on call for the next two days, so I'm going to AJ's for a beer before turning in for the night since it's right across the street. Anyone care to join?

RHETT

We can't, we're busy.

WINNIE

Busy with what?

RHETT

We're busy.

I can read between the lines. There aren't many nights that Rhett and Winnie aren't "busy."

ALDER

That's fine. I'll see you guys for dinner in a few days at Mom and Dad's.

BABY LO

I'm heading home now before it gets too bad out there. I left you a key at the front desk.

KNOX

Hazel and I are already home, but she says, "Hi!"

His message has a picture attached, and I smile at my phone screen. Hazel is the most special two-year-old in the world.

ALDER

Hi, Hazey baby!

KNOX

I make it to my truck as the last text comes in and send a goodbye to the family group chat.

ALDER

Okay, getting ready to drive. Love you all

It's only a ten-minute drive from the hospital to downtown Silverthorne. I park in front of the hotel and cross the freshly snow-covered street to AJ's. The town has been festive since Thanksgiving passed two weeks ago, but this is the first big snow of the season, and there's something about Silverthorne at Christmas. I personally have a harder time getting into the merriest of spirits when December rolls around, but I've worked hard to get where I am, and that is something I remind myself to celebrate often.

The lodge is a big part of that. When I decided to invest in the old ski lodge, I never would have thought that a few years later, I would be a part owner. Now, I am, for all intents and purposes, a silent partner, but able to take care of the day-to-day running when needed. After the most recent shift in ownership last week, I'm anxious to see whether it will affect my silence. I don't know much about my new partner, only that he's sending someone here to run the hospitality side of things.

I push open the heavy wooden door that leads me into the bar, letting some snow and cold air in with me. I look around the old brick walls and hanging green lamp lights over the tables. It's a slower night tonight for a Friday, but I'm not complaining. I'm just looking to get one beer and then get some sleep. The rush from our rescue earlier is wearing off, and I want to be in bed *before* I crash. I make my way to the polished live edge bar top, taking in the way the grain and natural shape of the tree has been showcased. Then I drop onto an empty stool.

"Hey, Alder. What are you doing in town so late?" Buck, Winnie's uncle and the owner of AJ's, asks.

"Hey, Buck. I'm stuck here until the storm passes. Staying at the hotel for the night because your niece's fiancé wouldn't let me stay at their place tonight."

"Not surprised. He's pretty greedy with her, isn't he? What is he, in love with her or something?" he asks, and I laugh.

"Right. Maybe he should just marry her or something." I wink at the older man behind the counter, who's beaming. When Rhett asked Winnie to marry him a few weeks ago, there wasn't a single person in town who wasn't beyond thrilled. That being said, Buck was the happiest, and he's been flying high ever since. Having raised Winnie and Colt after their parents passed, it's evident that all he's ever wanted for them was happiness, and by some miracle, my wonderful, charming, hot-shot little brother just does it for her. Who would have thought?

"Well, what can I get you tonight, son?" Buck asks.

"I'll just have whatever IPA you have on draft."

"You got it," he says, grabbing a glass from behind the counter. I glance around as he gets my beer and sets it in front of me, then moves on to someone else.

I thank him and turn to spot Colt in the corner chatting with a giggling brunette. He waves at me, motioning for me to come over. It's not a surprise to find him in the bar, seeing as he spends most evenings here and his uncle owns the place. It's even less of a surprise to find him here chatting with a beautiful woman. Colt likes women, and women like him. I shake my head a little and feel cold air at my back as I wave back at him. I lift my glass to my lips, feeling the slight burn of hops hit my tongue.

I hear the scrape of a stool down the bar from mine and look over. I almost choke on my beer. I've seen quite a few beautiful women before. I've been with plenty of them. I like women, and I like sex. If they're game to keep it casual, then we're both going to get a lot out of the exchange. The woman sitting on the stool to my left, though? She's stunning. An absolute smoke show. With her cute little nose stuck so high in the air like she's looking down on everyone around her, and the rigid set of her back, she looks like she should be sitting on a throne. Then she speaks.

"Can I get a vodka tonic with lime when you get a minute, please?" she asks in a raspy voice that makes that drink order the sexiest thing I've ever heard.

I wasn't looking for anything other than a beer tonight, but now that I've seen the woman sitting next to me, you'll be hard-pressed to find me looking at anything else for the rest of the night.

IVY

What the hell have I gotten myself into?

That seems to be a running theme in my life. A cycle I can't break. One I can spot coming from a mile away but am destined to repeat. Two weeks ago, I was sitting in the sun on the Southern California coast. Well, I wasn't sitting exactly. More like *lounging* on the beach. I'd had a little too much champagne to drink that I'd spent a little too much money on.

After my ex-husband of less than a year announced his new engagement a month ago, I'm embarrassed to say I went a little off the rails. Like *crash Daddy's boat* off the rails. I mentally wince, thinking about that night. What's worse is, it's not because I'm still in love with him or anything. In fact, I would go as far as to say I was *never* in love with him. Our marriage wasn't really so much a romantic entanglement as it was a business deal. No, it was because he announced his engagement to *her*. Margot Moreau; stunning, long legs, cool haircut, French, seems super sweet to your face and then sleeps with your husband, bitch. What a piece of shit. The both of them, but Noah? Noah James could fall off the face of the earth, and I wouldn't bat an eyelash. I built a five-inch thick, reinforced concrete wall around myself, but somehow it still stung. The human condition is fascinating.

I've never given much thought to how my life would go. In the state of Colorado, under a constant cover of clouds and snow, there is a small mountain town named Silverthorne. With a population of 4,769. *Okay, someone has to take away my access to Twilight.* I think it's safe to say I'll stick out like a redhead in a snowstorm. Which is exactly what I am at the moment, so that's not even a metaphor. The wind picks up again, and I can't see out my windshield. *Shit.* Snow. Snow. More fucking snow. It's everywhere. There's no getting away from it. It's been coming down steadily from the moment I landed in Denver. Thankfully, for just a few moments, the flurries start to slow, and the faint glow of civilization I've been heading toward for the last thirty minutes is getting brighter and closer.

The Edgemont Ski Resort and Lodge, my purgatory, will have to wait a little longer. There's no way I'm making it up the mountain in this. It's already dark and as careless as I am with my own life sometimes, I won't risk somebody else's trying to make it to the top of a mountain in the middle of a snowstorm. I think back to the conversation I had with my father a few days ago.

"If you think you can continue on the way you're going and then waltz into,"—I have never *waltzed* into anything in my life. I am not a good dancer, despite the many lessons I've been subjected to—*"being the CEO of my company, you are sorely*

mistaken, Ivy." I can still hear the disappointment and contempt in his voice. It's not hard to detect when that's all you've heard your entire life.

It's always been the plan that one day, I would take over our family business. I'd move back home and take my place on the board for Rutherford Industries, specifically as a creative head in our new branding. Since my small stint on the other side of responsible the past month, Sullivan Rutherford has decided I need to *"gain some first-hand experience"* before handing over the proverbial reins. Really, I think he would find any excuse to keep me away from the business. Away from him...but I've had my eyes set on this job and the life that comes with it for too long to give it up now.

Focus, Ivy. I don't have time to dwell on my personal issues. There are more urgent ones at present. Like not sliding my shiny new parting gift, which was parked and waiting for me at the airport, into a ditch. And how I'm going to create two new streams of revenue over the next three months so I can leave this place. I need to get back home. Back to my life. This is just an unfortunate stepping stone to get me where I'm meant to be.

Silverthorne looms before me. It's hard to see it fully with the conditions being what they are—it's the middle of the night and snowing. What was supposed to be a scenic drive from the airport this afternoon turned treacherous because of my flight delays. Having grown up in Northern California, I've driven in the snow before. This is different though. This is a blizzard. Or, well, it feels like one. I feel my throat tighten. *Do not cry. Do not cry.* I can't afford anything else obscuring my vision right now.

There! I take the exit a little fast, having almost missed it, and luckily, this road will take me directly into downtown where my destination will be. I can't wait to take a hot shower and curl up in a bed. I'm exhausted from more than just today. I drive down the main street and notice that it looks as picturesque as a snow globe. Lights and decorations litter the buildings and lamp posts. I check my GPS to make sure I'm in the right spot. I had to google if there would be anywhere to stay tonight. This place is the only one. And I don't mean the only one available. I mean the *only* one. I pull into the parking spot with a sign that reads Holloway Hotel Customer Parking Only, the words barely visible, and slowly roll to a stop. I breathe a deep sigh of relief. My hands and back are sore.

I didn't realize how tightly I was wound up until now. I look out into the dark night, squinting even though it doesn't help. I can't see beyond the building I'm parked in front of. Three months. I can do this. I will do this. I send a quick text to Sienna, the only friend I have who will care where I am. I'll call my father tomorrow. I straighten my back, tug my beanie down over my ears, and step out into the freezing cold night. *Fuck, that's really cold.*

Walking into the lobby, the first thing I notice is how cozy it is in here. The plush brown leather sofas have a few fuzzy cream throw pillows on them, and the amber light that's filling the space is inviting. I look up and see a staircase with a black iron banister leading to a small sitting area that has a few shelves filled with books. Yes, it's very cozy, and making a tally in my mind, I mark this hotel as charming. I'm not sure why I do this, but it's something I've always done. A quirk I've had so long that I don't remember when it started.

The snow that was clinging to me outside is starting to melt, and I pull my hat off. I look at the big clock on the wall. 8:47 p.m. *Okay, so it's not the middle of the night.* It only feels that way then. There are paintings on the walls of what looks to be this building before it looked like this, perhaps in its original form. I spot another room with a lit-up bar, but no lights are on in the main area.

"Hello, welcome to the Holloway Hotel. I'm Marilyn. What can I do for you this evening?" A pleasant voice breaks through my thoughts. I turn and see an older woman standing behind the check-in desk, looking at me expectantly.

I clear my throat, not sure how my voice will sound after being alone on the road the past few hours. "Hi. I was wondering if you have any rooms available. I just got into town and was heading to The Edgemont, but..." I trail off.

"But driving up the side of the mountain in the dark during a snowstorm sounded like a bad idea?" she supplies, finishing my sentence and thoughts perfectly. I smile. She gets it.

"Exactly," I confirm.

"Well, I do have a few rooms available, and I also commend you on not throwing common sense to the wind and deciding to ride out the storm here in town." She beams. "Will a king room work for you?" She holds up a key. Not a key card. An actual key. That is...charming.

"That's perfect. I would have taken a closet with a throw pillow and a towel to cover up with," I say, accepting the key.

"Luckily for you, that won't be necessary. Your room's up the stairs, third floor, fourth door on the left. I hope you enjoy your stay."

"Thank you. Is there anywhere I could get a drink? I saw that there was a dining room when I came in, but it looks very dark in there. I'm praying that's just because the vibe is really dark and moody or that there are vampires that hang out in there after a certain time of day." I ramble off without thinking how strange I must seem to this complete stranger. She doesn't know that fictional vampires are always just a thought away for me. I don't drink very often these days, but I'm too keyed up now to sleep, and a nightcap sounds good.

Marilyn doesn't miss a beat. "No vampires tonight; you can try back next week though. Unfortunately, we closed the dining room early because of the weather. Most of our staff has gone home. I live in town, so I volunteered to stay," she tells me. "If you're really needing a drink, you can go to AJ's. It's right across the street, and Buck will probably still have the kitchen open." I'm not sure which part of her response trips me up the most. Her playing into my bit without so much as blinking, that there's a bar within walking distance, or that its owner's name is *Buck*. I think it may be the name.

"Thank you. I think I'll head over there before I settle in for the night." I turn and give Marilyn a little wave.

"Tell Buck hi for me! Have a good night!" she calls as I walk toward the glass door and back out into the whiteout. I pull my hat back on my head and tug it down. Stepping off the curb, I see the bright neon sign for AJ's. Overhead are strings of lights, and on every shop door, there seems to be a wreath, a bow, or a fully decorated Christmas tree. It's very charming, but as adorable as it may seem, I'm not looking to fall in love with this sleepy little mountain town. I'm looking to prove myself in order to finally have something that's mine, and no one can take it from me.

AJ's Bar is warm, so I already like it in here. From the rustic wooden door to the stunning wooden bar top, it's obvious it's been crafted with care. I note the exposed brick walls and wooden floating shelves that display sports and other memorabilia. My quick survey of the room tells me this is most likely a local hangout. Everyone here seems comfortable and familiar. I feel a small pang in my chest. I've never had a place like that. I've spent time in plenty of bars, but none that I felt comfortable in. Or with anyone I felt comfortable with.

There's quiet chatter floating around the room, and checking the mental tally in my head, we can add this bar to the charming column. I walk straight to the counter, ready to have a drink and call it a night. The bartender is older and moving a bit slowly, filling a glass with beer. I internally tell myself not to sound like I've had the last couple of days that I've had. It's not this man's fault. *Patience, Ivy.* I remind myself.

Sitting down on an empty barstool I ask, "Can I get a vodka tonic with lime when you get a minute, please?" Hoping I sound friendly and not like I'm in a hurry. I remove my jacket, then, after debating it for two seconds my hat, running a hand over my head and through my hair that I'm sure looks matted and greasy. I set them both on the empty stool to the left of me and lift my head to take a look around the bar. I don't get any further than the seat to my right, where a pair of icy-blue eyes are watching me. They're attached to a face that could be a priceless work of art hung in a museum.

A sharp jaw covered in stubble that I can almost feel running my finger over. High cheekbones and pouty lips. His hair is dirty blond and messy. I run my eyes down his throat to wide shoulders, and that's when I notice his clothing. He's in some kind of jumpsuit. Red with a patch on the shoulder. Then I see the reflective band around his elbow, and over his chest is another patch in the shape of a triangle. Alpine Search and Rescue is embroidered around a red plus sign, signaling someone in the medical field.

I realize, too late, that I've been ogling this stranger for far longer than acceptable. I flick my eyes back to his face and find him smirking at me. *Kill me.* The bartender has my drink and sets it down in front of me. I turn my attention to him, and hopefully, the dim lighting in here hides my blush.

"Just the one drink tonight? Or do you want to open a tab, hon?" he asks. Most of the time any term of endearment annoys the hell out of me, but this man exudes wholesomeness.

I reach for my purse. "Just the one tonight should do it. Thank you," I respond.

"Add her drink to my bill, would you, Buck?" The voice comes from the man beside me that I just visually catcalled. *Wonderful.*

I turn toward him to politely decline. "That's not necessary," I tell him.

"*Necessary?*" he asks quietly. Almost to himself, then lifting his eyes to meet mine, he stares at me as he speaks. "Probably not," he agrees thoughtfully. I start to turn back to my purse when he speaks again. "I can think of a lot of things that aren't *necessary.*" He pauses, smiling. "But I still enjoy doing them," he tells me, picking up his beer and taking a drink. I watch his throat as he swallows, then his tongue as it peeks out to lick his lips. I don't particularly care for beer, one tick in the *not-my-type column,* but then why do I wish it were me licking the bitter liquid off his lips? Probably because he's hot. Like stop-and-do-a-double-take-in-the-streets hot.

Still living in the delusion I've found myself in, I lean onto my elbow, cradling my jaw into my hand and angling myself toward him on my stool. I wonder what other things he enjoys. What he finds *necessary* and what he finds indulgent. Is he a list maker? A rule follower? *Why do I care?*

"What's another?" I ask, my curiosity getting the best of

me. He faces me and mimics my body language. Pointedly and playfully. He takes up so much space, and when he turns on his stool, his knees brush against mine. I feel the brief touch go up my spine, causing goose bumps on the back of my neck.

"Talking to strangers in bars," he says, and I have to think back to the question I asked him before responding. "Although, after you looked at me for as long as you just did, it started to feel necessary." The right side of his mouth tilts up, and I spy a dimple. This man having a dimple seems unnecessary. He's got enough going for him without that fucking dimple.

"I'm worried that you may have a selective memory. It was *you* who was staring at *me*," I tell him.

A few small lines form between his brows as he scrunches them down in disagreement. "I observed a beautiful woman sitting down in the seat right next to mine. Staring feels like too strong of a word," he says.

"Staring may *feel* like too strong of a word, but it doesn't change the fact that you were doing it," I quip before taking a sip of my drink. *Mmm that's good.*

His answering chuckle is a deep rumbling. I swear I can almost feel the comforting vibrations in my chest. I take another long drink. I don't even know this man, but I want to curl up on his chest and purr. That's an unsettling thought...and visual. I shake my head.

"What thoughts are you getting rid of when you do that?" he asks, infiltrating my brain. I choke on my vodka tonic. *Oh god, that burns.* He pats my back gently and hands me his napkin. *This is fun and not at all embarrassing.* I'm not usually this off my game. I'm blaming it on the past couple of days. "That bad, huh?" he asks, and I feel my neck start to heat because, yeah, that bad.

"I'm sure you're a really nice guy, but I'm not interested in sleeping with you," I blurt out. I'm lying, but I'm trying to put my best foot forward here. I need to refrain from making the wrong choices I always seem to make. Like going back to this guy's place. I don't need my first night in town to be making a mess that I'll have to clean up later with a local. Although, I can almost guarantee I would be having the time of my life getting messy with this man. Better to rip the Band-Aid off.

I'm prepared for him to be frustrated, for him to tell me I'm a tease. I'm prepared for him to call me a bitch or pretend I'm ugly. I'm not prepared to be startled by his laughter. Full-blown, head-thrown-back laughter. I stare at him. Confused. "I'll take that as my cue to leave then." I sigh, grabbing my drink and reaching for my coat.

His laughter slows, and I can tell he's trying hard to hold it together when he retorts, "Who said I was planning on sleeping with you?" *This is embarrassing.* Did I misread his attention?

"Listen, I'm sorry if I offended you—" I start, but his hand coming to rest gently on the counter next to my arm halts my words. He's not touching me, but I can feel the heat coming off his arm.

"I'm not offended," he informs me, still smiling. "And for the record, I do want to do things with you." He lowers his voice, and I lean forward to catch what he's saying, a wicked grin on his face. "I want to do a lot of *unnecessary* things with you." He drags out his words and they hit their mark, if their mark is between my legs. "*Sleeping* isn't on the list, but—"

"There's a list?" I cut him off this time, and his eyes get shiny.

"An extensive one," he murmurs.

"Do you make a lot of lists?" I ask. "You seem like the type to make a lot of lists."

"I do..." he confirms before asking, "What's your name?"

"That's none of your concern tonight, boy scout. I'm not looking for anything after tonight. I don't plan on being in town for very long," I tell him.

"Well, I guess there goes my plan of trying to lock you down and get hitched next week," he says with a grin.

"Funny," I tell him and take a drink.

"I'm *technically* only in town for the night," he says, and that bit of information has my ears perking up. *So he's not from here?* I finish the rest of my drink and give him a small smile. I'm about to make a decision that may haunt me later, but he looks too good to pass up. What's the worst that could happen?

ALDER

The drive up to my cabin was exactly as expected this morning. *Other than the visions of last night that are embedded into the forefront of my brain.* The road crews cleared the roads early enough that I could make it home before the sun was fully up. Leaving the redhead's bed this morning was harder than I thought it would be. I'm kicking myself for not getting her name. It's going to eat at me all day. A smile tugs at my lips, thinking back to her telling me she wasn't interested in sleeping with me last night. So blunt and to the point. She was lying, but I found her directness uniquely sexy. Not only did we have off-the-charts chemistry in bed but out of it as well.

I'm contemplating turning around and going back to her room at the hotel and attempting to get her name again. Maybe my sweet baby sister will break the rules and get it for me. I'm off the next couple of days, and my only plans are our family dinner and snowboarding. A family dinner that I can't get out of even if I wanted to. When I moved out here to the middle of nowhere, I was under the impression I would have fewer unan-nounced visitors and family check-ins. That has not been the case. At least once a week, I get someone coming to knock on my door to check on me.

"Just dropping off a lasagna, I made extra and was going to freeze one, but then I just thought I would bring you one."

"Hey, bud. I just wanted to come up and have a beer with my brother."

"Alder, I was out for a drive and thought I would come say hello. How are you, dear?"

As smothering as it can feel some days, I'm thankful for my supportive family, and I also understand that I had a very rough go of it a few years ago. No matter how much ground I've gained, it's hard to forget the depressive episode I went through after losing Ray.

I close my eyes and bite down on the inside of my cheek. Thinking about my friend and all the plans he made. A life that he never had the chance to live. The guilt has threatened to eat me alive in my weakest moments. It's one of the reasons I don't drink more than a couple of beers anymore. I rarely drink at all. I've discovered that when I find myself too far down into a bottle, I also find my mental health even lower. Training like I have, as hard as I have for my Alpine Rescue Certification... losing ground for a few hours of mind numbing doesn't seem worth it.

I put a pot of coffee on and walk out onto my back deck to take in the view that is my backyard. I can see all the way to Kettle Peak today, since the storm has cleared out. My mind wanders as I survey the wintry landscape. Green eyes and lips I can still taste play in my memories. I can hear her raspy pants and moans in my ears. I don't usually like being told what to do, but last night, I couldn't find it in me to care.

Distant ringing pulls me from my daydreams. *Who would be calling me this early?* For a second, I let myself think it's the woman from last night. A woman whose name I don't even know, so I'm not sure how she could be calling me. Maybe I'll call the hotel later and beg Florence to help me. I walk inside and just miss the call. The lodge? I hit the number and wait for our operations manager to pick up.

"Hello, thanks for calling The Edgemont Ski Resort and Lodge. This is Jack speaking. How can I help you?" His voice is warm and friendly as always.

"Hey, Jack. It's Alder. It looks like I missed a call. Was someone trying to get a hold of me?" I ask, hoping it was a mistake and nobody needed anything from me today.

"Alder! Yes, I called. Kirk is out today with the flu, and I'm hoping you can fill in for his classes. The new hospitality manager is here, and I want things to run as smoothly as possible. I know you have the day off, but I already called Cal, and he isn't able to make it in." He says this all in one breath, not stopping until he relays all the information. I can tell he's stressed and desperate. I sigh, resigned to the fact that my day of playing catch up on laundry and possibly a visit down to town to stock up on groceries is officially derailed.

"What classes do you need me for?" I ask. *Please, not the kids' class.*

"The kids' classes. At nine, we have the 9–12 year olds, and at eleven we have the 6–8s," he confirms. I blow out a breath. Of course. I really want to tell him no.

"I'll be there," I agree.

"Thank you! You're a lifesaver! I have so much to keep

track of today, and I want to make a good impression. Stop by my office around two so I can introduce you. Thanks again, Alder!" he rushes out before hanging up, and before I can tell him that meeting some asshole from California who wants to turn *my* lodge into a luxury spa is the last thing on my list. The previous man I shared the lodge with sold his half of the business to someone in California who's never stepped foot here. Now, I have to add that to my list of things to get in order. I run a hand down my face. This serves as another reminder that things change so quickly.

I look around my home. It's nothing fancy. An A-frame log cabin nestled in the trees about three miles from the lodge. It's small and rustic. Not like the sprawling ranch you might see if you visit my childhood home, but the view out the back glass windows is really the draw for me.

Looking out and seeing the snow-covered mountains, I'm reminded that *this* is why I live here. Like a hermit in a secluded cabin. Which half of the time I am. Being outgoing is something people have come to expect from me, and even though it's such a large part of who I am; I love a good karaoke night; I also love coming home *alone*. I don't bring anyone except for my family here. That's not to say I don't take women *other* places, *their* places, though I haven't done that for a while. Not before last night, and if I'm being honest, it felt more like I got taken somewhere. I grin, thinking about her taking control.

Rolling my head in a circle, I decide I'd better get ready. It's seven thirty, and I'll need to get all the gear ready for the classes I've been roped into teaching. If you can even call it that. I would venture to say maybe two kids from each group will be paying attention. These kids are enrolled in classes so their parents can drink Bloody Marys at breakfast. No judgment; it just quickly becomes fifteen screaming kids all falling over their skis and snowboards, complaining that they don't want to be there.

Three hours later, and I've made it through my first class with the older kids. It went better than I thought. The smaller kids should be here any minute, and even though I may not want to teach this class today, they are always adorable. Decked out in their snowsuits and some too small to get down the smallest bunny hill. They make me think of my niece, Hazel. She's the best thing to ever happen to our family. The fact that she's even here is a miracle. The day she was born is one I'll never forget, but the chain of events that surround her birth reminds me that even the most dire circumstances can bring something magical. I chuckle softly. I never would have thought that my older brother was as soft as a kitten until he had her. That softness is reserved only for her, but I still get a kick out of seeing it.

I look up from where I'm standing at the bottom of one of the bunny hills. *Here come the littles*. I can see them now. They're running down the hill toward me. The excitement is written all over their little faces, and it's infectious. I can remember being this excited the first time my parents brought us here.

"Hey, guys! Be careful coming down the hill!" I call out, trying to get their attention. They all keep running. Smiling and shaking my head at them, I turn to grab the bag of tiny goggles, readying myself for the next hour. I take a sip of coffee from my thermos and turn to see one of the smaller kids in a bright-blue jacket fall near the top of the hill. They start to roll. *Shit*. Last time that happened, the kid threw up. I toss my cup and make a break for him. I've run halfway across the hill when the kid's dad gets him stopped.

A flash of purple to my right catches my eye, but it's too late. I try to slow, but I'm going too fast. The momentum I've gained running combined with the snow is going to carry me right into them. We collide.

A startled gasp registers in my ears as the side of my body makes contact. My hands instinctively reach for the purple ski suit and grip at the waist, turning them with me, so I'll take the brunt of the fall. I land flat on my back shortly before a body slams on top of mine, effectively knocking the wind out of me. We stop moving, and I hear a husky groan coming from the person I've taken out. A knee slides up the left side of my body and then firmly pushes into my stomach, making it hard to catch my breath. The sun is so bright, even with my goggles on, I can't open my eyes. I open my mouth to apologize, but before I can, a raspy, *sexy,* too-familiar voice cuts me off.

"What the hell? Do you tackle guests to the ground often?" she asks. There's my confirmation that it's her. My redhead—*my?* No, *the* redhead from last night. Her breath smells citrusy, like lemons? Oranges? I would answer her, but I don't think she's really looking for my answer. I decide I'll give her one anyway. I feel her shift, hair grazing my cheeks, and then a shadow is cast over my face, giving me the ability to see again. Only when I do, my ability to speak disappears. I'm looking up and into those unique jade-green eyes that I spent last night getting lost in. The most beautiful face I've ever seen. A face I spent a lot of time kissing last night. I look up at her purple beanie. Her *purple ski suit?*

That's a lot of purple.

"Excuse me?!" Her raspy voice borders on indignant. *Oops.*

I must have said that last part out loud. "'That's a lot of purple'? Is that all you have to say to me after you just plowed into me?" She's clearly pissed, so I bite my tongue to keep my ill-timed joke to myself. "You could have seriously hurt someone. Did you think to look where you were going at all? Exactly where were you going in such a hurry anyway?" She is absolutely laying into me. Question after biting question.

She's verging on sounding like a spoiled brat. Which is familiar territory working here, you see a lot of rich brats. None have ever provoked such an immediate reaction in me as the woman lying on top of me right now though. *The same woman who was on top of me with far less clothing last night.* I can feel my eyes crinkling at the corners. She doesn't know it's me. Not with my goggles on. "Why are you smiling?" she asks in an annoyed tone. *Am I smiling?* "What the hell is so funny about this?" Her green eyes narrow into slits as she chastises me. *Stunning.*

I clear my throat and slide my goggles up onto the top of my head before saying, "Well, I didn't want to interrupt. It felt like you really needed to get all that out, but it seems that you're still lying on top of me, princess,"—her eyes flare at the pet name that slips out—"and don't get me wrong...I'm thoroughly enjoying this tongue-lashing you're giving me." I wink, and her expression turns deadly. "I personally don't mind you being there, but you sound upset with me at the moment. I usually like women on top of me to be enjoying themselves. So if you wanted to get up, I could properly apologize for *plowing into you* and start my next class."

She makes an irritated sound at that and scrambles back, enveloping me in her cinnamon and citrus scent. I am once again blinded by the sun as she takes her shadow with her.

"Search and Rescue?" she questions. It's not a nickname I've gotten before, but I like it when she calls me it. "What are you even doing here? Did you say teaching a class?" she huffs out, planting her hands on my chest for support while she stands, causing my mind to flash back to the night before. *I wouldn't mind that happening again.* I need to get that thought out of my head immediately. I don't sleep with guests. No matter how beautiful or fiery or—no. It doesn't matter. She's off-limits. I may have made that decision last night, but that's only because I didn't know she was a guest yet.

She moves to the side, and I stand beside her. I dust off my pants and look over at her. She's gorgeous. She has her arms crossed over the chest of her purple suit. Her left hip is cocked to the side, and the set of her mouth tells me she's still riled up.

"I don't hate the nickname. I've been called worse than 'Search and Rescue,'" I comment.

"So was the getup you were wearing last night part of your pick-up routine? Do you prey on innocent women who get stuck in town often?" she asks in the same bratty tone I'd like to...*no.*

"Innocent? I think it was you who wanted to hear about my *unnecessary* list," I challenge.

"I remember it being you who mentioned that *list,*" she counters.

"And I remember everything on it that we didn't get to last night."

"That's not the point, hotshot. What are you even doing here?" she asks again.

"I fill in as a snowboard instructor for the resort," I answer. I don't tell her that I'm a part owner. I've been a partner in the resort for the last ten years. "My full title after all the courses and training I've done is an Alpine EMS Search and Rescue pilot," I elaborate, then apologize. "I'm sorry I ran into you. There was a kid, one I'm responsible for, rolling down the hill. I was worried they might get hurt," I explain. At this, she softens a little. "I didn't see you, though I'm not sure how I missed you in this getup," I add without thinking. *Shit.* Wrong thing to say. She's pissed again.

"Yes, yes. 'That's a lot of purple.' I remember," she says as she waves a hand in the air. "I thought you weren't going to be in town very long," she accuses.

"I did say *technically*. And technically, we're not *in* town," I tell her. "You didn't exactly say you would be here either," I shoot back.

"Right." She half laughs and shakes her head, her red hair falling over her shoulders. "You said you had a class to teach?" She looks over my body then, and I feel exposed even in three layers of snow gear. "So, I'll let you get to that. I have other things to do," she states and walks off toward the lodge without a backward glance in my direction. I should tell her that I don't just teach classes here, that I own this place just to see her squirm, but last night and this morning have been the most fun I've had in months. I shake my head and smile again. *That purple ski suit.*

IVY

Coffee.

I'm in desperate need. Water and something vitamin-rich is probably the answer to the never-ending trivia game, "What Does Ivy's Body Need Today?"—a game I play frequently. But I want coffee. Living with low blood sugar is moderately annoying and sometimes tedious, but it could be worse. At least it's manageable. Something about me should be.

After waking up alone, I finally bit the bullet when my third alarm went off and made the rest of my drive up to the resort.

"Have a safe trip up the mountain!" Marilyn called as I exited the hotel this morning.

"Thank you, Marilyn. Have a good day!" I replied with a wave, rushing out. I was up at the ungodly hour of five fifteen this morning after last night's exhausting, but in the best way, escapades. I was surprised, and oddly bothered to find the other side of the bed empty and the sheets cool with how early it was. I sigh. Well, it's not like I didn't remind him multiple times that this was a one-time thing. I guess I'm just not used to men listening when I speak. He seemed to though.

I'm reminiscing as I make the drive to my cabin. Thankfully, the main roads have been cleared, and the snow has stopped. In my experience, more times than not, you hit it off with a guy only to find yourself wildly disappointed later that night. Last night, though; I bite my lip at the memory. I saw stars, fireworks. The instant intellectual connection I felt with him absolutely translated into a physical one. I see a sign letting me know I've made it to my destination. The Edgemont Ski Resort and Lodge welcomes you! The email on my phone said that I would find my cabin key under the welcome mat. I drive past the main building until I see cabin number four, my new home for the next few months.

Walking inside, I note the cozy couch in the living room and the reading chair in the corner by a wood-burning fireplace. I don't have as much time to look around as I'd like. I throw one of my bags onto the bed in the back bedroom and grab out the article of clothing I'm most excited to wear. I dress in my favorite ski suit as quickly as I can before running out the door. It probably isn't necessary for touring the property, but I love it, and it's my favorite color.

With renewed determination I decide it's good that I won't see the man from the bar last night. Even if the conversations we had last night, between our other ventures, were the best I've had in years, I shouldn't be disappointed. That's not why I'm here. Silverthorne is a stepping stone.

Now I'm walking into the main building here at The Edgemont Ski Resort and Lodge, caffeine and sleep deprived. It's going to be another long day. Lord, help anyone who crosses my path.

"Hello, welcome to The Edgemont Ski Resort and Lodge," a friendly voice calls as I walk in the double doors. "What can I do for you today?" the man asks.

"Hello. I'm Ivy Rutherford. I—"

"Ms. Rutherford! Yes, hello! I'm Jack, the operations manager here. We were expecting you last night. Did you make it here okay?" the man interrupts. I may not have made it here last night, but I can't complain about the pit stop.

"Define...okay." I smile.

"I'm guessing that means the weather hit you then?"

"It did. I stayed at the charming hotel downtown though. I just made it up here this morning," I tell him.

"You must be exhausted. Would you like to start our tour later today?" Well, that is a tempting offer, but the sooner we start, the sooner I can get a feel for my task here.

"I'm here now, so if you're up for it, I'm good to go," I say.

"Of course. Let me grab my radio, and we'll head out," he tells me, reaching behind the counter and pulling out a small walkie-talkie. He clips it onto his belt and extends his hand to me. "It's nice to meet you." I take his hand and shake. It's warm, like his smile. Jack is...undeniably attractive. With slightly graying sideburns and a crinkle-eyed grin, he's probably a good ten to fifteen years older than me.

"Down the hall over there are the offices," he says, pointing behind me. "I can show you those when we get back from walking the grounds."

"Sounds good. Where to first?"

"I thought we would start with each variety of cabin we offer and go from there."

"Perfect. Lead the way," I say, gesturing toward the glass doors.

After Jack's small tour, I walk the property on my own, looking for inspiration as well as anything that can be improved upon. It's beautiful here. I didn't want to admit it, but even in my sleep-deprived state this morning, I found this resort to be incredibly charming, just like the other places I've been in the fourteen hours I've been here. The cabins are all so picturesque, mine included.

From all that I've observed, this place runs like a well-oiled machine. I haven't seen any unhappy guests. The lodge is simple and tasteful. There are a few things that need some updating, but that was to be expected. The vintage feel of the Edgemont is special. So I plan to lean into that. Starting with a gift shop. The missed opportunity to have branded merchandise for sale is the biggest issue I've come across.

It's nearing lunchtime, but I need to check out a class that's being offered. My stomach growls as if it just heard me thinking about making it wait for food. No coffee, no sleep, now no food. My body is going to be so pissed at me. I don't need to check my blood sugar level to know that I'm cutting it close. I'm walking down the back steps of the main lodge, looking out over the bunny hills. The snow is so bright out here. I spot a group of small children and walk toward the bottom of the hill where they look to be heading. Some more gracefully than others. I chuckle to myself as I watch a couple of them pick up some speed.

I'm midway to where I saw the group starting to gather, and I'm jonesing for a coffee so badly I think it's giving me a headache. That or the lack of food. I glance back at the cabin, contemplating if I can make a quick enough run. Could I make it back in time for this class if I hurry? Probably not, if I'm being honest; I'm not much of a runner. The question becomes moot when I'm hit. Hard. By something hard. And warm? I feel hands on my waist, twisting me around, and then we're falling. Am I being attacked? I land chest-to-chest with my assailant. I'm not sure if that's the right word yet, but I'm readying myself for a fight if I need to. The air rushes out of me in a harsh groan on impact.

This is absolutely not what I need today. Sitting up, I bring my right knee up and press it into my—attacker? But when I get a good look at him, I can see it's the man who was standing at the bottom of the bunny hill with the kids' gear a few moments ago. What the hell? The class instructor? He's caught me at a bad time, and I'm not known for biting my tongue. I go to lay into him when he blurts out maybe the last thing I would imagine him to say.

"That's a lot of purple," he says, a little dazed, after my initial *What the hell?* I see red. I'm not even sure what I'm saying after a couple of minutes, but then he smiles at me. What the fuck is wrong with this guy? And what's wrong with me that I might find the very firm body beneath me attractive? I'm beyond annoyed. At him, this situation, but ultimately, myself.

Hungry, in need of caffeine, in need of sleep. The perfect storm that he isn't prepared for.

After I let loose on him, he slides his goggles up onto his head. And are you kidding me right now? The man from last night? "Search and Rescue?" The nickname slips out. "What are you doing here?"

He speaks, and even though he's right in pointing out that I'm still on top of him, the smug way he does it puts a bitter taste in my mouth. Not to mention, his breath smells like coffee. He brings up my outfit again, and I want to shove him back to the ground when he stands after me. We both dust off the snow that's sticking to us. I'm ready to leave now. Not just this resort. I'm ready to leave Silverthorne. I'm ready to leave Colorado. I'm not meant to be here.

"So, was the getup you had on last night part of your pick-up routine? Do you prey on innocent women who get stuck in town often?" I snap.

"Innocent? I think it was you who wanted to hear about my *unnecessary* list," he accuses.

I cock my hip out and fold my arms over my chest. He's got some nerve. "I remember it being *you* who mentioned that list."

"And I remember everything on it that we didn't get to last night," he says suggestively. Oh, believe me, so do I, action hero, I think, and then snap myself back to the present.

"That's not the point, hotshot. What are you even doing here?" I redirect him back to my original question.

"I fill in as a snowboard instructor for the resort. My full title after all the courses and training I've done is an Alpine EMS Search and Rescue pilot," he answers, then says, "I'm sorry I ran into you. There was a kid, one I'm responsible for, rolling down the hill. I was worried they might get hurt," he tells me, and I thaw. Slightly. I hadn't seen the kid falling. "I didn't see you, though I'm not sure how I missed you in this getup," he comments, and any thawing his earlier explanation caused is frozen solid once again. Jerk.

"Yes, yes. 'That's a lot of purple.' I remember," I say, flinging my hand in the air. "I thought you weren't going to be in town very long," I accuse.

"I did say *technically*. And technically, we're not *in* town." He gives me his flimsy reasoning. "You didn't exactly say you would be here either," he accuses right back.

"Right," I huff out. "You said you had a class to teach. So, I'll let you get to that. I have other things to do," I bite out, turning on my heel, and make a beeline for the main lodge. Shit, shit, shit. Not only is Search and Rescue a resident in Silverthorne, but he'll be here at the lodge, seemingly under my employ. Coffee. Immediately or this day will be going from bad to worse quickly.

Inside, I walk down the hallway that Jack showed me earlier and find a freshly brewed pot of coffee. Thank God. I think an espresso machine will be my first act of service as the hospitality manager. I take a sip. That's pretty good. I grab my jar of candied grapefruit peels I left in here earlier and look around. It's quiet back here. Walking further down the hallway, I spot a cozy-looking office with an extremely large window— and a couch. I'm not sure which office is mine, but after I see that, I know I'm moments away from sitting there. I just need to sit down for a minute. Rest up for the staff meeting in about forty-five minutes. I sit the jar beside me and lean back into the plush cushions.

Voices getting louder rouse me from sleep. Sleep? Oh, shit. I've fallen asleep. It doesn't matter how many times I tell myself an alarm doesn't need to be set. It always does.

"I haven't seen her since I showed her around this morning," I hear a man say. Jack, I think. "I'm going to check the front desk," he tells someone else, and I try to clear my fuzzy thoughts.

"She wouldn't have gone out on her own, would she?" another voice calls. A voice I have become intimately acquainted with when its owner was telling me dirty things last night, and it sounds like it's getting closer. I sit up. Shit. Not again. Fatigue and fog still cling to me, but I stand up anyway. That was a mistake. The room spins, and my vision turns to static. There's a breeze. Inside? I hear someone curse. Then warmth and a scent that's comforting and familiar wraps around me. It all goes black.

It could have been seconds or minutes when I come to. I open my eyes to meet a pair of blue ones. Really blue. Pale, like I imagine a glacier would look.

"Those eyes are the prettiest shade of blue I've ever seen," I blurt out. Shit. That's going to be a thing.

"Yeah?" His question comes with a raise of his dark-blond eyebrow and a smile. Ugh, is that a fucking dimple out again? "Thanks, princess." He calls me that again, and the attraction fades slightly into annoyance. "How you feeling?" he asks, then adds, "We should probably stop meeting like this."

"I'm fine. Thanks for breaking my fall," I rasp. Well, doesn't my voice sound nice and breathy?

"Again," he adds, and I narrow my eyes.

"Yes. At least this time, you weren't—" I'm cut off.

"Plowing into you?" he asks, using my earlier words against

me. The look on his face and suggestive tone elude to more than an innocent run-in. I squirm. Realizing I'm still lying across his lap, I sit up. The motion once again makes me dizzy. Warm hands gently grip my shoulders, and that's annoyingly comforting. "Easy there," he murmurs.

"Okay, let's not speak to me like I'm a feral animal," I reply between clenched teeth. His deep, relaxed chuckle skitters up my spine. He stands and slowly pulls me to my feet. "Thank you," I relent.

"Anytime." Hmm...

"Have you seen a jar with orange strips in it?" I ask while looking back at the couch. He steps to the side and bends to pick the small jar off the floor.

"This?" he asks and holds it out to me.

"Yes." I open it and eat two sugar-coated citrus strips. This isn't the best thing to get my blood sugar up, but it'll have to do because I forgot to grab a juice. Or eat anything. After chewing them quickly I look over at him staring at me. Then I remember that I don't know why he's back here.

"What are you doing in here?" I ask, a little accusingly. His head tilts to the side before answering.

"In my office?" He pauses. "I wasn't sure I needed a reason. I am curious why you're in here, though, not that I'm complaining." He's teasing me, but shit. This is embarrassing. "And not to sound like one of the three bears, but it looks like someone's been sleeping on my couch," he says in a way that has me clenching my jaw. I couldn't have chosen anyone else's couch. I try to think of something to say, anything that would let me save a little face. Footsteps in the hall save me from my floundering.

"Ms. Rutherford! There you are! It looks like you've met our—"

"Snowboarding instructor," Alder cuts in. "We met briefly this morning." he says to Jack and then turns to me. "Have we met before? I feel like we might have," he asks me pointedly. I scowl and also flush with a fresh wave of annoyance.

I pretend to think for a second. "Sorry, I don't think so. Must not have been that memorable," I claim as innocently as possible. The reality of our current situation is that I got my socks knocked off last night, and he absolutely got his world rocked.

"Alder, this is Ms. Rutherford, our new hospitality manager," Jack says, walking into the small office. I look back to Alder, and he's looking at me, both brows raised in surprise now. Well, it looks like we're both a little caught off guard.

"You're the new hospitality manager?" His question doesn't give me the impression he's happy about this development. Well, back at you. I clear my throat and stick out my hand between us.

"Ivy Rutherford," I say my own name and hate it.

"Alder Holloway," he replies, retaining eye contact while taking my hand in his. His warm, calloused hand wrapping around mine sends a pulse up my arm. I feel lightheaded again, and it's not from the low blood sugar.

"Nice to meet you." Thankfully, my voice comes out much steadier than I feel. He smirks. Damn, and there's that dimple I can see through the scruff on his face.

"Nice to meet you too, Ivy." My name on his tongue makes me think I'd like to hear him say it again. How unfortunate that we'll be working together. I pull my hand back, and my fingers slip through his. The sensation fades, and I don't know whether it's my blood sugar returning to a normal level or the loss of contact, but I'm slowly feeling less fuzzy.

"Now that introductions are out of the way, how has your day been, Ivy?" Jack cuts through the tension I'm feeling, and I'm grateful for it.

"It's going really well. Thanks, Jack. The property is beautiful, and I'm excited to implement a few ideas to increase revenue and improve customer experience," I tell him. His smile turns worrisome, so I rush to reassure him. "Everything you've done here is great, and I'm not looking to come in and mess up anything anyone has worked hard on. I just have a few ideas to add to what you've already created." He seems slightly mollified by this.

"That sounds great, Ms. Rutherford. We can't wait to hear more," he tells me, and I believe him. Jack is a charmer, but I'm not interested in anything more here. He may become a friend, and that's really all I'm in the market for.

"Please, call me Ivy," I insist, and we smile at each other in camaraderie. Alder's throat clearing has us both turning back to him.

"Well, if that's all you need me for today, Jack. I think I'll be on my way," he says this to Jack without looking at me. It gives me a chance to study him. It's probably a bad idea. He's as gorgeous as he was in the bar's dim lighting. That feels unfair. Wavy dark-blond hair and a jaw that could cut fucking glass. The scruff on said jaw is—unfortunately, still very attractive. Broad shoulders, and how tall is he? How had I not noticed last night? six foot three? six foot four? He's really not my brand of heroin, but I have a feeling this man is everyone's drug of choice. *Shit. I'm thinking in Twilight references again.*

"Are you sure you don't want to stay?" he asks Alder. He sounds confused, which makes me feel confused. Why would he want to stay for this?

"Nah, I need to get going," he replies.

"Of course. I'll see you in a couple days. Thanks for filling in on your day off," Jack tells him.

"No worries," he says easily, then dips his chin at me. "Ivy," he says my name instead of goodbye. *I like the sound of my name coming out of his mouth too much.* I nod my head and give him a tight smile.

"Alder. I look forward to working with you," I say, and he grins at that. Looking amused as he walks out his office door, my interaction with him leaves me feeling unsettled, fidgeting with the lid on my candy jar. I'm not sure what's amusing to him, but I have a feeling I wouldn't think the same.

# ALDER

The drive down the mountain still requires my full attention, even though road crews have cleared the main road since our last snowfall. The anniversary of Ray's death is today, and I'm not looking forward to spending all evening with my family like I usually would. I love them and know they mean well, but insisting I come down for dinner tonight, knowing that I would rather be alone, is getting to me. Compacted with the fact that my second run-in with Silverthorne's newest resident has left me with feelings I'm not interested in dissecting. I'm not in my usual fun-loving state.

I pull onto the evergreen-lined drive, all dusted with snow. It's scenic, and I'm fortunate to have grown up the way I did. Along with two loving parents and siblings who would do anything for me, I grew up in a beautiful home in a beautiful state. Some people dream of leaving their hometown, but I've never felt that way. I like where I live, and I really like my life. This may be a hard day for me; missing someone never gets easier. I know the pain from missing Ray will, but I'm grateful for the life I have.

Walking up the front steps of The Holloway Ranch, I hear laughter coming from inside. I sigh, giving myself just a moment before opening the door.

"Hey, everyone!" I call once I'm inside. I hear little feet running my way, and I feel my lips stretch into a smile. Hazel, my older brother Knox's two-year-old daughter and my favorite human in the world, comes running around the living room corner straight for me. "Hazey!" I yell excitedly and crouch to catch her. Her face is lit up like the fifteen Christmas trees Mom has in the house. God, I can't believe I get to be this little miracle's uncle.

"Muncle Aldie!" she screeches as she hits my chest. I fall backward, acting as if this tiny little girl has taken me out. To be completely honest, she has the power to. There isn't a member in our family who isn't wrapped around her finger. I see Knox out of the corner of my eye as we fall to the floor.

"Hey, little brother," he calls from where he's leaning against the wall. We're the same size technically, but I am five years younger.

"Knox, what are you feeding her?" I demand. "She's gotten too strong. Did you see how fast she took me down?" I ask him dramatically. Hazel giggles and smacks at my chest. "Ohh! Haze, please have mercy on me." I beg.

"Okay!" she agrees and slides off me to stand by my side, offering me a hand. "I help you!" she says, and she doesn't even know how much she already is. I take her little hand in mine and stand.

"Thank you so much for your help," I tell her. She doesn't feel the weight of my words. The last two years of having her in my life have been my most treasured. From the moment I looked into her sweet brown eyes at the hospital, I knew I'd protect her at all costs.

"You welcome. I wanna hold you," she says, reaching up at me. I bend and pick her up, propping her on my hip.

"How's your day been? Were you out on the mountain?" Knox asks as I walk toward him with Hazel.

"No, I was planning to be, but this morning Jack called, and I ended up at the resort teaching kids classes." I can't keep the annoyance out of my voice.

"Today?" he questions.

"Yep, I had just made it home when he called, and he sounded desperate," I tell him.

"And the rest of the day?" he probes.

"Fine," I say too quickly.

"Really?" I'm starting to feel like a well-done piece of steak with all the grilling.

"Honestly? It's been a weird day. The resort has a new hospitality manager, and she's,"—I pause, collecting myself— "she's something," I finish. I'm unsure how I feel about my last exchange with Ivy right now, so I'm not sure how to tell someone else. I also don't want to let it slide that I met her last night. I may be a lot of things, but I'm not a kiss-and-tell kind of man.

"She, huh? Sounds like you've had an interesting day," he says.

"That's one way of putting it," I tell him with a sigh. "She's kind of a brat," I blurt out, but I can feel myself smiling. "She ripped me a new one for accidentally running into her on the bunny hills today." It was a little more than running into her, but Knox doesn't need to know that. "She wouldn't even let me get a word in while she reamed me out." I'm getting a little worked up just talking about it again.

"Down, pease!" Hazel yells, diving forward. I kiss her sweet head and then set her feet on the hardwood floor so she can run to the next family member.

"She didn't mind talking to the owner like that?" he asks, surprised. Yeah, about that.

"I didn't exactly tell her who I was," I confess, and Knox's eyebrows raise slightly. Disapproving. "I know, but she was just so..." I trail off, not finding the right word.

"Huh. Sounds like she might have gotten under your skin a little. You're not usually one to let something like that get to you," he muses. Like I don't already know that.

"Yeah, well, there's something about this one. She's got this raspy voice that drives me fucking nuts," I tell him.

"Uh-huh. And I thought it was Rhett who was oblivious," he mumbles, putting a hand on my shoulder and squeezing. "That's attraction, bud," he whispers, and I don't roll my eyes, but that makes me want to. She's hot. Gorgeous. A little mean, but I don't mind that. Of course I'm attracted to her. She's also going to be working with me.

"Nope. That's not a thing. She's decidedly off-limits and not exactly my speed." Knox laughs at that.

"Sounds like she left quite the impression," he concludes, and I shrug.

"Maybe. Where is everyone?" I ask, changing the subject.

"Mom, Dad, and Lo are in the den, finishing the last Christmas tree out of the six Mom's put up this year. Winnie and Rhett are on their way. Winnie's stopping by the bakery to get some cranberry scones and cinnamon rolls." That's the best news I've heard all day. Best cinnamon rolls ever.

The door cracks open just then, and a giggle fills the space. Turning, I see wild curls slung over my brother's shoulder as he shuts the front door behind them. Snow shakes loose as he bends and sets three tote bags down then Winnie. She's laughing, but he grabs her face, smiling, and kisses her quiet. I smile at that. It's really good to see them.

"Hey, where's my kiss, Winnie?" Rhett shoots me a dirty look at that. I love pissing him off. I actually attribute him finally making his move with her to me pissing him off. Winnie smiles at me and winks. She's always down to play a game with me.

"Rhett, calm down. I haven't kissed Alder in..." She pauses as if she has to think about the fact that we have never kissed. Rhett's jaw may not survive how hard he's clenching it. A laugh bursts from me. "...ever!" Winnie finishes, and we're both laughing as Rhett takes a breath. "I love that you still get jealous even though I've agreed to marry you," she tells him, waving her hand that now holds a big shiny diamond on her slim ring finger.

"Ha ha. You guys are hilarious," he finally gets out.

"We really are," I agree. "How is engaged life? Are you making your big house a home?" I ask, knowing Winnie has already started all the renovations.

"It's turning out so beautiful, Alder! You'll have to come have dinner with us and see it all," she confirms.

"Absolutely, just say when." I let her know.

"Never," Rhett chimes in, and it makes me laugh again.

"Okay, tough guy. Need help carrying any of Winnie's baked goods?" I don't even mean for that to sound as suggestive as it does, but I'm cut another dirty look from my little brother.

"The cinnamon rolls! Come on, Rhett. Mind out of the gutter." Again, I'm fighting the urge to roll my eyes.

"Dinner will be ready in just a few minutes!" Mom's voice carries from the other room. Mary Holloway is one of the best people you'll ever have the pleasure of meeting. She and Dad are easily the blueprint for marriage and commitment. I walk around the corner and see everyone starting to gather in the kitchen. Dad is getting something from the oven, and when he turns around, I catch a glimpse at his apron. Tonight's is "This Guy Rubs His Own Meat."

"Dear god, who bought Dad that apron?" I ask, not sure if I even want to know.

"That would be me," Mom says. No. I definitely did not want to know. We all laugh though. I love that my parents are still in love with each other. Some kids grow up saying "eww, gross" every time their parents hold hands. That would have been exhausting in our house.

"Hey, Baby Lo." I hear Rhett greet our sister.

"Rhett, I'm twenty-seven. Baby Lo has run its course."

"Never!"

"No, it hasn't!"

"It never will."

The whole family chimes in on that, even Hazel. I chuckle.

"Sorry, sis. Baby Lo stays," I tell her, and she shakes her head but grins. She's a really good sport. Being eight years younger than Rhett, she got just about anything she wanted. With three older brothers who let her paint their nails and do their hair, she didn't want for much. Knox even let her put makeup on him when she was maybe four. That never happened again, but the fact that it happened at all is a small miracle. He's such a fucking grouch, or he was. Then he had Hazel, and now we see his soft side more.

"Dinner!" Dad gets our attention, and we all go to sit at the big table in the dining room. It's set with red napkins and gold candlesticks. It looks like Christmas exploded in here. There's a big window at the head of the table that normally looks out over the countryside. Now, there's a fifteen-foot tree you'll have to look around to see that view. Tom and Mary Holloway love the holidays. We all do. There's the tree lighting ceremony in town, and the high school always puts on a production of *A Christmas Carol*. This year two of the boys on the hockey team are in it, so we'll all be there in the front row to support.

Mom and Dad have always instilled a good sense of community in us kids. We support this town when we can and know we can count of them when we need it. I needed it in the past and they really came through for me. Losing someone can change you, and when I went through the darkest year of my life, there was no shortage of helping hands.

"Alright, everyone, dig in," Mom announces, and we start filling our plates.

"How are things at the bakery, Winnie?" Lo asks from across the table.

"Really good. I'm excited to have a booth at the Tree Lighting Festival. I have so many holiday recipes to try out and a spiced plum cider I'm going to have," she tells her animatedly.

"I've been meaning to ask you—" she starts in on asking her about ideas she has for the hotel, and I look over at Knox. He's helping Hazel cut up some of her food while Rhett makes faces at her, making her giggle. I smile. I may not have been looking forward to coming here this afternoon, but being here with them has been what I needed.

After our meal is finished and all the plates have been taken to the kitchen, my dad stops me on my way back from taking some trash out.

"Alder, how are you, son?" I could tell him that I'm fine, but he'd see right through it.

"Better now that I've gotten to spend time with all of you, but it's hard knowing Ray would have been here with us. I miss him and I don't know if the guilt I have will ever subside," I admit. I know the accident wasn't my fault, logically, but sometimes logic doesn't stand a chance against the ache that death leaves in your soul.

"I don't think it will ever be easy, but just know that we're all here for you. Always." His steadfast declaration isn't the first I've heard from him.

"Thanks, Dad. I'm doing okay," I let him know. "I do need to get going though. It's getting late, and I don't want to hit any black ice at night."

"Alright, be safe getting home. Love you, son."

"I love you too, Dad."

After all the goodbyes have been said, I'm taking home two cinnamon rolls and a picture that Hazel drew for me. A valued possession that I'll be putting on my fridge. Driving up the mountain at night is so quiet. I look down on the town I love, and, yes, I do love it, but I'm looking forward to being home in my cabin for the night. It will be nice to have some solitude and avoid everyone.

That thought is the last one I have before my life is derailed for the second time today by the same person. Flashing taillights off the side of the road catch my eye. The vehicle's owner is standing beside it, arms crossed over her chest, shielding her eyes from my headlights. She may not have been thrilled to see me this morning, but the redhead on the side of the road right now has absolutely been starring in my thoughts since I left her bed this morning. I slow down and pull off to the shoulder just past her. I hop out of my truck and walk toward her, fully expecting the fire from earlier in the day. She doesn't seem to have a problem with voicing her displeasure.

Getting closer to her, I still like a deer in her headlights. I was prepared to be met with more of the sass and spice from earlier. The last thing I expected were watery eyes and a red nose. She's sniffling. The instinct to wrap her in my arms comes over me, but I push it down, afraid she may claw my eyes out if I get too close. I settle instead on removing my wool-lined coat and sliding it over her shoulders. Slowly, so she can stop me if she wants. She doesn't.

"Hey, it's alright. Need some help?" I ask her, and she makes a noise that, if I had to name, would be a sarcastic snort.

"Now, why would a woman, who's new to town, doesn't yet know her way around, and is stranded on the side of the road, need any help?" *There's the fire.*

IVY

I'm not a cautious person. Confident. Assertive. Honest. Capable. I have many great qualities. Being careful isn't one of them. That's most likely the biggest factor contributing to the predicament I find myself in.

"Why would a woman in that situation be out on the roads she doesn't know at night in the first place, princess?" The man whose coat is keeping me warm shoots back at me.

"I'm a very capable woman, Mr. Holloway. I've been driving a car for let's see, at least a solid decade now, I can handle a ten-minute drive into town," I snipe, but then remember that my SUV is stuck in a snowdrift on the side of the road. Minor details.

His smug grin is gas on the flames. He waves a hand to my SUV and opens his mouth. Then shuts it. I wait for him to argue my point. I hope he's wrapped his wrists because I don't pull punches. A sigh that's visible out here in the cold air escapes him.

"I'm sure you are Ms. Rutherford," he addresses me as I have him. "Do you need me to call you a tow?" he asks.

"I've called one, thank you." I sound snobby, so I add. "I'm fine to wait here alone. You can get on with your night."

"I've got nowhere to be. I can wait with you," he offers.

"Not necessary," I retort, sliding his coat off and holding it out to him. He just stares at me, a tight smile pulling his mouth to the side shaking his head at the outstretched garment.

"There's that word again," he muses. "I thought we covered that the other night...and stopping to check on you was not my way of pissing you off, just so we're clear," he lets me know. I sigh, and I am pissed, so pissed that tears gather in my eyes again, making his outline smudge. But not at him. Not really. *Shit.* I hate that I'm an angry crier. I'd just gotten a social media notification of Noah's engagement being announced in the paper, and I needed to do something to take my mind off it. I knew he was engaged, and it's not a shock that it's in the paper, but it still hit me hard, and I decided I needed to get some more oranges for my sugared candy peel stash. A drive into town to the grocery store sounded perfect. Until I started sliding around.

Snow is starting to fall again, and I want to scream. It's enough already.

"I—" My voice cracks. Swallowing, I try again. "I just needed a few things from town. My app said the roads were clear," I defend myself through gritted teeth. He grips his coat that I'm still holding onto and takes it. Good. Leave me here to dwell in my own misery. I shut my eyes to ward off more tears, but the weight of the coat being placed back on my shoulders makes it really hard. I slowly open my watery eyes.

"Ah, I see. Those apps don't always give the whole truth.

They are *mostly* clear, but you still need to watch out for black ice." I cock my head at his words. "The sun was out today and thawed the snow, then when temps dropped this evening, it froze over again. It's like glass, really hard to see even when you're familiar with it—" he cuts himself off with an easy smile then finishes, "—or a very capable woman." I bite the inside of my cheek, not wanting him to know I find him funny. Charming. Not wanting him to know that I've thought about him at all after last night. I have one objective and role-playing the damsel in distress with a real-life action hero isn't it.

"I guess that's something I'll need to be more careful of," I relent.

"It could happen to anyone. Now, are you going to let me drive you back to the resort?" he asks me again.

"I think I should wait for the tow. The guy on the phone said it would be forty-five minutes,"—I check my phone for the hundredth time—"sixty-two minutes ago," I say with a groan, hanging my head and pressing my right thumb to my temple. Crunching snow draws my attention to where Alder is now walking away from me and back to his truck. Okay, well, that's not the reaction I expected. He roots around in the cab of his truck for a minute, not getting in. I look up at the swirling white flakes that are starting to come down faster.

"What's your number?" he asks from right beside me. What?

"My number? You want my phone number right now?" I ask, flattered, but time and place, hotshot. He chuckles, interrupting my train of thought. He's holding up a piece of paper and pen.

"I'm leaving the tow driver your information," he informs me. *Oh.* "I doubt they even come tonight, but just in case, I've let them know you left because the weather turned. If you want to spend another night with me, we can do that somewhere other than the side of the road. You need to let me give you a ride before we get stuck here," he insists again, and as much as I want to tell him that he can get lost, I know the only option is to accept the ride.

"Fine." I sigh and tell him my number. He writes it down before trapping it under the windshield wiper.

"Let's go," he says it in a way that sounds like I have a choice, but I know a command when I hear one. He's very self-assured. I'm annoyed that I like he isn't afraid to take charge.

"Lead the way." I extend an arm up the road from us.

Inside Alder's truck, I already feel myself starting to thaw. I wrap his coat around myself tighter, and as stealthily as I can, I breathe in its scent. Spicy, but not like cologne. Soap? It's clean and also warm and I snap my head up because he's going to catch me smelling his coat. I glance at him from the corner of my eye, but he's staring straight ahead.

"Do you mind if I turn on some music?" I ask, trying to avoid conversation. Not only am I in a bad mood, but I don't want to talk about our night together.

He shakes his head with a grin and hands me his phone. "Not at all. It's already hooked up to my phone. Feel free to play whatever you want." Hmm, I'm surprised at how easily he hands his phone to me. I'm not going to snoop through his messages or anything, but the pull to know something else about him is strong. I settle for digging into the playlist he has pulled up. Soft Rock Goes The Hardest. A surprised laugh bubbles out of me, and I clamp a hand over my mouth.

"Something amusing, princess?" he questions. There's that nickname again. I roll my eyes.

"No, no. I'm just looking through your music," I tell him, hitting play, and Boston fills the space between us, singing about a woman named Amanda.

"Good choice," he praises, and I let out an indelicate snort.

"It's on your heavy rotation," I state flatly.

"Exactly," I don't need to look at him to know he's smiling. I continue to scroll the playlist. Alder is a very '70s and '80s classic man. As a very '70s to now girl—I like that. *Not that I need any more reasons to like him.* He's given me plenty.

After a few songs, I watch him lean forward and turn the volume down slightly. We pass the main lodge and drive on to all the cabins and chalets. I'm really not in the mood to talk, so I hope he isn't looking for a dazzling conversationalist. My mood is as sour as the bag of candy in my room that I'm ready to devour.

"How are you liking Silverthorne?" His question makes me huff out a laugh.

"Considering I've been here less than twenty-four hours, and in that time, I was tackled to the ground and also had my car slide off the road? Not loving it," I answer him honestly.

"I think you're leaving out some key details about your first night here. But it does sound like you've had an interesting introduction...and I did not tackle you."

"Who said I was talking about you?" I quip then point at the chalet up on the right. "That's me."

"Been plowed into more than once in the last week, princess?" His question is dripping with innuendo. My eyes are going to get stuck in the back of my head if I have to hear him call me that one more time. He parks, and I lean over the center console. Two can play at suggestive. I take my hand and absently let my fingers play with the sleeve of his flannel button down. I watch my hand as I speak to him.

"If I had been—" I start, sliding off his coat. Letting it fall to the floorboard, I drop my voice low. "—I can tell you one event was far more enjoyable than the other." I slowly slide my eyes up to meet his icy gaze from under my lashes.

"Oh yeah?" He's smiling, sure of himself. I bite my lip to conceal my laugh. "Tell me more," he drawls and leans in.

"I would, but I don't kiss and tell." Then I swiftly open the door to his beat-up Bronco and slip into the flurries falling down. "Thanks for the ride, Lover Boy," I call over my shoulder and shut the door with a slam. I'm smiling, pleased with myself when I hear him yell my name. I school my face and spin around.

"I'm available for a ride any time you need or want one, princess." He winks and then drives off. Laughter bubbles out of me into the sparkling night. I tilt my head up and, not for the first time, feel like I'm living inside a snow globe—and Alder Holloway has just shaken it.

Once I'm inside, I take off my hat and jacket, both are damp, along with my hair since I stood outside for too long in the snow. My forgotten phone chimes and I find it in my discarded purse. Sixteen missed calls and seven texts. All from Sienna. The last text is time stamped seventeen minutes ago. Oops.

SIENNA

You're doing what now?

SIENNA

Is this a joke?

SIENNA

Stop being cryptic.

> SIENNA
>
> IVY! What's going on?!
>
> SIENNA
>
> You sent me a message saying you were leaving town for three months with no follow-up, and now you're not answering your phone.
>
> SIENNA
>
> You're already there?! WTF?

That one was from early this morning in response to me telling her I made it here.

> SIENNA
>
> I know you like to do things on your own, but we talked about you keeping me in the loop. I just want to know that you're safe.

Now I feel like a bitch. I think I just didn't want to deal with anyone else's drama over the situation when I've got plenty of my own. It wasn't my intention to worry her though. It's never my intention to hurt people, but man am I good at it. Sighing heavily, I hit her number. She deserves a phone call. She picks up halfway through the first ring.

"What's going on?" she asks in way of a greeting. I mentally prepare myself to make *her* feel better about all of this.

"Hi. I'm fine, Sienna. It's just been a long couple of days."

"I've been worried sick, Ivy. You haven't replied to any of my messages," she accuses.

"I know. I haven't been on my phone a lot." *Except for when I was checking Noah's engagement announcement.* "I didn't have much warning with all of this. I was told I was coming here about three hours before I was on a plane," I relay.

"And you couldn't have sent one message explaining? Not even from the plane?" she whines, and the sound grates on my already frayed nerves. She doesn't mean to, but Sienna will take any opportunity to make a situation about her. I'm guilty of the same. Tonight, I just don't want to deal with it.

"Sorry, Si. It's just been a lot to process," I explain.

"Yeah, that part I get. I've been dealing with your disappearance all day. I've had to talk to everyone in town asking about you, and all I can tell them is that you're in Silverthorne, Colorado, wherever that is, and I have no idea why," she tells me, exasperated. Like it's her whose life has been upended. I roll my eyes, not convinced anyone is missing me. They want to know the gossip, more like.

"It's in Colorado," I deadpan. "And I'm so sorry you had to deal with all of that. It must have been so difficult for you." My voice is sickly sweet.

"Oh, fuck off, and thank you. It was," she responds as though she's accepting a real apology. God, she's the most self-absorbed person I know. I laugh until she laughs with me and decide to tell her the condensed version of why I'm here. She was there for the wrecked boat and most of the nights that put me on my father's radar as irresponsible. I may not speak to her for a while so I fill her in as best I can.

"Right. Well, unfortunately, I don't have time to tell you all the details, but the short version is that I'll be here for the next three months running this resort that my father purchased. Then I'll be back home and ready to step into my role at Rutherford." I breathe in deeply and shut my eyes. What a mess I've created. Was I always this way? No. I know that I wasn't.

"Oh, so basically, a luxury resort winter vacation? That

sounds like a dream, Ivy. I'm not sure why you're being so dramatic about all of this." I snort at her cavalier attitude. Why indeed.

"Right, something like that. Listen, I need to go. I'll talk to you later." Maybe. Maybe I won't talk to her later. I haven't decided yet.

"Sure, sure. Bye, babes!" She hangs up, and I'm relieved. I'm not sure when we became friends. If you can even call it that. I just remember feeling broken, and Sienna knew how to have fun. I needed to have fun. After years upon years of feeling trapped, trying something else seemed like a good idea.

I unpack one of my suitcases of clothing and put it into my drawers. I need to start brainstorming. Tomorrow, I'll need to start making calls and sending emails. If I want this gift shop to open the week of Christmas, I'll have to get it up and running in less than two weeks. I grab my stashed bag of sour candy and change into my comfy pajamas. Lying down on my bed, my mind races with all the things I need to get done, and then, unbidden to me, it fades to Alder Holloway right before I drift to sleep.

IVY

Snow is silently falling outside my window when my alarm goes off. There's something gentle about it, it makes my limbs feel warm and weightless. Looking out the big window in my bedroom, I can see the sun just peeking up over the distant mountain tops. Always having been an early riser, I catch the first glimpse of the morning often. It's something that I thought would come in handy years ago. I flinch, shutting my eyes tight. Flinging the blankets off my body to sit up, I plant my feet on the floor. For years, I've tried to outrun or outsmart memories, but they always catch up to me. Whether at the bottom of a bottle or in a stranger's bed in the middle of the night, sharp and painful reminders that I'm not living the life I thought I would be seem to find me in these quiet moments.

I mentally do a rundown of my day after pushing the button on the coffee maker. Sending emails and making calls is what most of my day consists of, so I don't need to be too bundled up. Jeans and a T-shirt it is. I dress and pull a beanie over my hair. A shower last night would have been ideal, but I was too tired after my phone call with Sienna. I didn't even get around to calling my father. He didn't exactly get around to calling me either, I remind myself. It shouldn't sting after years of the same thing. It shouldn't.

I think back to a couple of mornings ago after being stranded on the side of the road, and the voicemail I woke up to.

"Hey, Ms. Rutherford. This is Silverthorne Towing. We got your note and wanted to let you know that your vehicle will be at The Edgemont in the morning. So sorry it took us so long to get up there last night. The snow really delayed us. We won't be billing you. This one is on us and don't hesitate to reach out if you ever need help again. Thank you. Goodbye."

And it was. Parked in front of the Edgemont when I went into the office, just as the message said. That's one thing I'll have to get used to. Small towns. People doing things out of the kindness of their hearts. I'm not familiar with that.

Walking out the front door of my cabin, I turn in the direction of the main lodge. I now know where my office is inside the building, and I'm grateful I don't have to worry about finding myself in one that doesn't belong to me with a colleague who I don't need to be spending any extra time with. That man conjures a visceral reaction from me. I'm on edge when he's near, and I snap at him before thinking better of it. He makes it hard to think straight at all. The problem with this is that I wouldn't even give my snapping a second thought if it were anyone but him. Most people would view me as a spoiled brat. They wouldn't be completely wrong to assume that. I am and have always been spoiled. I guess that's what happens when you grow up without a mother and with a father who didn't want a daughter.

The Edgemont is a beautiful sight this morning. The sun is starting to paint the rest of the world in a golden glow. It makes me feel closer to something. I'm not sure what yet. I spot my SUV as I take the steps and enter the warm cabin. My office is down the same hallway I was in yesterday. Walking in, I sit at my new desk and look out the window. The ski lift has started running, but no one is out there yet. The gondola starts up as I'm watching. I really want to ride that. Maybe tomorrow morning, I'll be able to ride it to the top of the mountain at sunrise.

I sink back into the leather chair behind the desk and sigh. I need two ways to bring in a crowd in the next three months. Something to show an increase in revenue and prove that I have good ideas and can be trusted. The gift shop is the first. I'll start making calls to vendors and local boutiques today. I want it filled with artisanal items. I'll also need to scout a place to start renovations or maybe a new cabin altogether.

Before I know it, it's lunchtime. You have to be better about eating. I scold myself. I'm not going to be doing anything on my list if I faint again. I pull out my jar of citrus peels and pop a couple into my mouth. There are only a few left in here. I really do need to make it into town so I can make some more. I've always loved these. I can't really remember, but I think I made them with a nanny one Christmas.

"Hey, Ivy!" Jack calls from my doorway.

I smile. "Hey, Jack. How are you today?"

"It's a beautiful day out there and things are running smoothly, so I can't complain." He smiles at me. "I was heading over to the restaurant to get some lunch. Are you hungry?" The invitation is surprising, but not unwelcome.

"Starving."

"Would you like to come with?" he offers.

"I'd love to," I say, closing my laptop.

"Perfect." He leans onto the door frame. His chestnut-brown hair slides onto his forehead, and his chocolate eyes assess me, making me feel unexpectedly warm. I grab my corduroy jacket and stand.

"Thanks for the invite, I was going to have to go in search of something soon," I say, and he laughs.

"I noticed you hadn't left your office all day and figured that was the case. Are you getting some work done?"

"I am. I have a couple of ideas that I'm excited to bring up in our next management meeting," I answer, a little shocked at the excitement in my voice. Jack grins back at me.

He steps in front of me to open the door, "I'm excited to hear all about it."

"Thank you," I say as I pass by him into the restaurant. "It smells amazing in here."

"Yeah, that's partially the chef we have, he's amazing and for some reason, he likes working here when he could work anywhere he wants. It's also the baked goods. We get those from the town bakery, Thistle and Sage."

"That may be a place I need to visit." Today, actually. I need to run into town anyway. I'll leave after our lunch, so I can make it back before dark. I don't need a repeat of last week's events. Even though I have thought about mine and Alder's verbal sparring match more than once today. I need to get a grip on my wandering thoughts. It's a recipe for disaster.

Two hours later I'm loading up the few groceries I bought in downtown Silverthorne. There are Christmas trees and lights in every direction. I'm not big on the holidays. Mostly because Sullivan Rutherford isn't. He prefers to spend holidays alone or working. But I find myself smiling at the town's holiday charm. Walking the sidewalk, I notice the various window displays in all the shops. They range from snowmen skiing to Big Foot snowboarding.

I see the sign for Thistle and Sage, and cross the empty street. Opening the door with a chime, I'm immediately enveloped by the smell of coffee and freshly baked bread.

"Hi, welcome in!" a woman calls from the corner of the shop. I would have missed her if it wasn't for her beautiful curly hair. When she stands, I see that she's covered in flour. The petite brunette smiles kindly at me and then moves to step behind the pastry case. She trips on—well, nothing, and I instinctively reach out toward her, wanting to protect this small woman. She's at least a good six inches shorter than my five foot nine. Thankfully, she catches herself on the counter.

"What can I get for you?" she asks, a little out of breath. I smile, her caramel-colored eyes drawing me in.

"Hi, well, I just came from The Edgemont." I point with my hand in what I hope is the direction of the mountain and resort. "I had lunch there today and was told that the pastries and breads came from here."

"They do! I make all the pastries, breads, and desserts. My boyfriend's— no, my fiancé's, that's new." She giggles before continuing. "Sorry, my *fiancé's* brother works there, so he comes in to pick up orders for the restaurant. He should be by today actually. Soon, come to think of it. Were they out of something?" she rambles, and it's—*endearing*.

"You're the owner then? I had one of your cinnamon rolls and just wanted to see what else you had here."

"Yes, I'm Winnie Parker." She wipes her flour-coated hand on her apron and reaches over the counter to me, and I take it in mine.

"Ivy Rutherford. Nice to meet you."

"You as well." She beams. "Are you visiting then?"

"I am—er well kind of." I struggle to explain the situation.

"Would you like a latte while you look around? We have a seasonal caramel pecan right now. Or a spicy mocha?"

"The caramel pecan sounds amazing. Thank you."

"You got it," she replies and gets started on it. I glance around the shop. It's so cute. The industrial meets with the natural wood perfectly, and all the holiday decorations make me feel like I'm on a movie set. The door chimes, and in walks a man who can only be described as one of the most handsome men I have ever had the pleasure of seeing.

"Hey, honeybee," he says with a smile.

"Hey, Coach," she calls back with a grin. Winnie steps out from behind the counter again, and no sooner does she clear the edge of it that this man sweeps her up and is kissing her like he's been starved for her. My mouth may be hanging open while I just stare at them. I should look away, but I can't bring myself to do that. This couple is H.O.T. hot. He sets her down, breaking their kiss and pushes a curl from her heart-shaped face.

"How was your day?" he asks her, and she looks dazed as she answers, and damn, I don't blame her.

"Good. I got my list made for the lighting ceremony, and I'm just making some final updates to my recipes," she tells him. I decide I've been staring long enough and turn to look out the window to give them some privacy when Winnie says my name.

"Ivy, this is the fiancé. Rhett, this is Ivy. She's staying up at The Edgemont," she explains and then goes to grab the steamed milk to pour into my latte.

"Hi, Ivy. It's nice to meet you. Are you enjoying your stay? The lodge is always a little magical at this time of year." I have to remind myself not to get lost in his eyes, seeing as Winnie probably wouldn't be okay with me ogling her fiancé.

"It's nice to meet you too. Honestly, this is only my third day here, and yesterday wasn't the best day I've ever had," I confide. "It's really beautiful here though," I add, and oh my gosh, am I blushing? How embarrassing.

"Here's your latte," Winnie says, and I walk over to grab it from her.

"Did you say he had a brother?" I whisper conspiratorially, and we both giggle.

"Right? God, he's beautiful." She outright eye fucks him while he checks his phone and sighs. "He does though. Two." She winks.

"Yeah? Single?" I ask, playfully.

"Both." She laughs and looks out the window. "Oh, here comes one now," she tells me quietly. Another chime, and then I hear a voice that I can't seem to escape.

"Winnie Parker, you're the most beautiful woman I've ever seen. Please forget my brother and marry me instead," he declares and Winnie dissolves into a fit of laughter. I turn to look at where he's speaking from. Alder's arms are crossed over his heart, and he's covered in a small dusting of snow. It's snowing again? He looks good. Too good. I'm surprised I didn't see the similarities before. It's obvious these men are brothers.

His smile falters slightly when he sees me.

"Ivy?" he asks, confused.

"Hi, Alder," I reply.

"I didn't expect to see you here. I'm picking up the bakery order for the resort," he explains.

I nod at him "Yeah, I hear you have an in with the owner you're trying to tempt into an affair," I say, hitching a thumb back at Winnie. "Though in the five minutes I've been here, it's been made fairly clear that she's already spoken for. At least that's what I gathered from the smokin' hot kiss they shared in front of me a couple of minutes ago." I grin, and he grins back at me. Damn, there's that fucking dimple.

"Oh *that*? She's just trying to make me jealous." Then he winks at her. "It's working by the way," he adds, and Rhett growls at him. *Growls.* I can't help it, I start laughing. Winnie joins me. I take a sip of my latte.

"Holy shit. This is amazing." I turn toward her. "Could I get a cinnamon roll and two of those molasses cookies for the road," I ask.

"Of course." She's still chuckling when she answers. "So how do you two know each other?"

"I didn't get a chance to tell you earlier, but I'm the new hospitality manager at The Edgemont, so we'll be working together," I answer.

"I also gave her a ride home last night after her car slid off the road," Alder cuts in.

"He also ran me over in the snow yesterday morning, so maybe don't try to sound like such a hero?" I'm looking at him now as I say this. I reach for my wallet, but he stops me. His hand on mine, causing that familiar shot of heat to run through me.

"Allow me to start making amends then." He doesn't break eye contact with me as he sets his card down on the counter in front of me, assuming to pay for my baked goods and coffee.

"Okay, Casanova. It's on the house tonight," Winnie says with an eye roll and I laugh. He smiles, and Rhett laughs from behind us.

"We're going to AJ's Tuesday night for drinks, and there will be live music. It should be a good time. Do you want to come, Ivy?" Rhett asks me. Alder is looking at me like he knows my answer will be no before I say it. And it would have been if he wasn't looking at me like that.

I turn to Rhett before speaking "I'd love to. Thank you so much for the invite." Then I look at Winnie "Thank you for the coffee and treats, Winnie. It was so nice to meet you," I tell her honestly. I don't have a lot of girlfriends...or friends really.

"Anytime, Ivy. Please come back and visit me. I'm glad I'll be seeing you around." She smiles.

"I will absolutely be back for more coffee. I'll see you all Tuesday night then." I walk to the door and turn around so my back is pressed against it. When I turn, Alder and I end up face-to face. I gasp.

"I thought I'd walk you to your car," he says.

"I think I can manage." My voice betrays me, I don't sound very sure.

"All the same. I'll feel better if I know you make it there

without sliding into a ditch." He winks and now I'm pissed off backing out the door with him following me.

"First of all, I was in an SUV that slid into a ditch, I'm told there was very hard-to-detect black ice on the road. Secondly, I would have been fine without you stopping." I poke him with the hand that's carrying my coffee as I end my little rant. He chuckles and then sighs.

"Be that as it may, Ivy. You couldn't have made me leave you there alone. I'm finding it hard to leave you alone at all." It sounds almost like a warning in his deep voice.

"I think I could have made you do whatever I wanted," I say in a low voice as we make it to my SUV. Why am I flirting? He grins.

"That,"—he pauses opening my door when I click the unlock on my fob—"is probably true," he agrees, and I snort, surprised. I was expecting an argument.

"Goodnight, Alder. Thank you for the pastries and coffee, or at least the offer to pay for them."

"Anytime. Goodnight, Ivy. I'll see you at work." He shuts my door with a mischievous look, and I watch him jog back over to Thistle and Sage. I shake my head. The electricity ebbs in my body again when he isn't near. *This is going to be a thing.*

ALDER

"So what was that all about?" Winnie asks once I'm back inside the bakery.

"What was what about?" I answer with another question.

"You know what. I don't remember you mentioning that the new manager you met was a long legged, incredibly gorgeous redhead. Did he mention that to you, Rhett?" She turns to my brother as she poses the question.

"I don't remember hearing about her at all actually," he tells her, slipping his arms around her waist and kissing her hair-covered temple. Seeing them find their way to each other is... I'm really happy for them.

"That's because there was nothing to say," I tell her and head to the back to grab the crates of bread and other delicious food items.

Following behind me, I hear her ask, "Was? So, is there something to tell *now*?"

"No. I don't know. I don't really think she likes me much," I stammer out, not wanting to share that I met Ivy on her first night in town. That information feels private somehow. I don't remember thinking anything about my sex life was too private to share before now.

"Impossible. Everyone loves you," she says offhandedly. Like it's a given. Obvious. It's nice to hear, but it's also far from the truth. I can think of a whole family that holds me in the lowest regard. A small pang runs through me at that thought.

"What's not to love?" I ask, effectively hiding the awful feelings that seem to creep in a bit easier at this time of year. A laugh sounds in my head. A deep booming laugh that I still hear in my sleep sometimes before it turns to screaming. "Is this everything? I need to get back home and get my gear ready for in the morning."

"Yeah, that's all for now," Winnie confirms. "We'll see you Tuesday night." She hefts a bag to the top of the load I'm carrying. "These are for you," she tells me.

"Thank you, Win." I lean down and kiss her cheek. Winnie has always been family to me. I've kissed her cheek since she was thirteen. She's always looked out for me; it doesn't matter that she's younger. Winnie exudes big-sister energy, and I've only ever thought of her that way. Thank God because I think Rhett really would murder me if I meant any of the flirty comments I made to her. He stands in the doorway now, and the vibe he's giving isn't all too far from that at the moment.

"Goodnight, little brother." I flash him a grin.

"Good night, brother." His words sound friendly, but I can hear the *get lost* hidden underneath them. I chuckle.

"See you guys in a couple of days at AJ's. Rhett, make sure you have a song prepared. You already know what mine will be," I say, pushing the door open and walking to my Bronco parked on the side street. The snow has stopped for the moment, and we aren't supposed to get a decent one for another couple of days. I've always watched the weather, needing to know when the best day for boarding would be, but it's been something I do a lot more now. Is that a getting older thing? Or maybe a truths-of-the-trade type of thing?

I've seen a lot of people get stuck out in the weather on a hike or even a drive. Mom and Dad always taught us to be safe, but I may be on another level than my siblings now. The training for my certifications is ingrained in me now. I'm thankful for that though. It keeps me alert. I'm told being hypervigilant after an accident that results in loss is a trauma response. It may be, but it helps me sleep at night.

I start up my truck after stowing the bags in the passenger seat, looking out into the night. The whole town is lit up with Christmas lights. A perfect postcard. I see families walking in and out of the shops and restaurants. I'm happy with my life. I like where I am and what I do. It's not lost on me that I'm thirty-six and haven't had a serious relationship in...I don't actually remember.

I'm not jealous of my brother and Winnie. I'm more than happy that Winnie will legally be my sister. I just feel something deep inside me sometimes. Something that feels an awful lot like loneliness. Loneliness—even when I'm surrounded by everyone I love. The same feeling when I wake up next to a woman who will be gone before the week is over. I don't help myself out in that regard. I try not to make it a habit to sleep with anyone who lives in town, and I never take anyone to my place.

I put my truck in drive and start up the mountain. As I make the drive home my thoughts drift to a different December. It feels like a lifetime ago. Back when dreams didn't wake me up in the middle of the night. Sometimes my fists are clenched so tight that I can still feel the rope in them. The burn as it slips. I clench my jaw against the pain that memory brings. I spent two weeks in the hospital. I look at my hands, ones that required skin grafts. I couldn't hold anything in them for a month. I take my hand off the wheel and examine it. They look fine, completely normal even, the doctors and nurses were an amazing team. The only physical sign left of the accident is my hands sensitivity to temperature.

I shake my head and focus on the road. The sun was out again today, so it would be wise to take my own advice and stay alert. The winding road to the top of the mountain is comforting and familiar. The Edgemont comes into view, and I feel my shoulders start to relax. I pass the main lodge, it's lights still on, and I notice there are holiday wreaths on the front doors as well as a large tree standing in the main lobby. We don't usually go all out up here for Christmas. I never cared to put in the effort and the previous co-owner wasn't on site very often.

I make the connection as I pass her cabin, also lit up with a wreath and a tree in view through the window. I slow, feeling like I may be intruding, but my curiosity wins out tonight. I catch a fleeting glimpse. She has her hair piled up on her head, and I can almost make out the column of her delicate neck. Okay, Alder. Keep it moving. I do and arrive back to my place exactly two minutes later. I like that she's just down the road. Decorating her cabin and staying warm. I don't want to analyze that too deeply.

I may not like to have reminders everywhere at my place, but I'm glad she does. I'm not sure why I care either way when

I don't know her, and the few interactions we've had haven't exactly been friend-worthy. Our first encounter was decidedly not friendly. It was more...and the second—well I will take a small amount of the blame for that one. Running into her was an honest mistake. She'll have to figure out a way to get past it if we're going to be working together. If we're going to be spending time together outside of work as well. Of course my brother and meddling soon-to-be sister-in-law would invite her out with us to AJ's.

It's not me who's hell bent on not spending time together between us, though, is it? I am starting to feel a little bit of remorse for still not mentioning that I don't just *work* at the lodge, I'm an owner. Along with her father I've surmised. As soon as I heard her last name it clicked for me. She's my new business partner's daughter. A quick google search confirmed it. It's not a problem for me, but how do you bring that up without her feeling like I've kept something from her? That feels like a problem.

Stepping into my A-frame cabin, tucked into the forest, I feel myself sag. I'm taking a run down Kettle Peak in the morning. It was Ray's favorite. His name isn't quite as searing as it used to be, but it's still painful to think about. Time does that. It doesn't heal all wounds like advertised, but it does give you perspective. And the opportunity for therapy. I snort into the empty room. Both have been crucial to my recovery.

After I gather all my gear, I'm in bed by nine o'clock. Just the way I like it. I lean over to turn my lamp out and the abandoned leather-bound journal catches my eye. I haven't written anything for what feels like ages. I pick it up and read over my last few entries. Mostly small poems, some are just lines that got stuck in my head. I haven't felt like writing much the last couple of months.

After Ray's accident, I saw a therapist. It took some encouragement from my family, but it wasn't hard for me to see that I needed some extra help to navigate life after loss. One of the tools that Dr. Sable and I agreed would be helpful was journaling. I've always enjoyed words and poetry, but it wasn't until after I experienced this specific kind of pain that I decided this could be an outlet for my grief.

Tonight is different, though; tonight I'm feeling inspired. A pair of green eyes and an arched auburn brow are at the forefront of my mind, and I may not be able to shake them loose unless I get them out somehow. I grab my pen, and inked words start flowing over the page. One after another, after another.

It's still dark when my alarm sounds in the morning. I stayed up later than anticipated, having had inspiration to write for the first time in a while. I stare at my ceiling for a moment before flipping my covers back and getting out of my bed. Standing, I stretch my limbs. Thirty-six isn't old, but I'm starting to feel all the things I've put my body through over the years. I dress quickly, in a hurry to get out to Kettle Peak.

I drive over to the ski lift on the north side of the resort. No one's ever out this early; it's quiet and peaceful. I love this time of day. The sun is starting to come over the ridge as I make it to my destination. I run through my checklist of things in my backpack. I have my emergency kit, hydration pack, dried food, an extra flare, and my SAT phone along with my radio in case I'm needed for an emergency. Most boarders who are planning on a few runs down the mountain would view my preparedness as overkill. I would assume we've had wildly different experiences.

After Ray, I got my pilot's license and received my FAA Medical Certificate. I am now an EMS helicopter pilot, and with all the courses and classes I've taken, I'm also Alpine Search and Rescue certified. I usually have to lead a rescue once a year. Luckily, it's been mostly minor situations, and I haven't lost anyone. For years after losing Ray, I didn't want to get back on a board or go near this mountain. Learning how to do something I've loved since I was a child in a way that makes me feel in control is the only reason I'm here today.

Slipping my pack over my jacket, I grab my board and helmet, take one last sip of my coffee from my thermos, and then it's off to the races. The mountain is calm this morning. The sun is making all the fresh snow glitter like the inside of a snow globe. It reminds me of the one I gave Hazel last year. She loved that thing, made me shake it over and over, and then giggled and clapped her chubby hands when I did.

Being a father wasn't something I considered until Knox brought her into our family. I want Hazel to have cousins. I know Rhett and Winnie will be having kids, probably as soon as they're married next year even though my mom would prefer that they just start now. That makes me chuckle. Most mothers appreciate their children following society's acceptable order of how to do life. Engagement, marriage, babies, etc. Mary Holloway would be fine with me having babies with anyone as long as she got to love them. I, on the other hand, do not feel that way.

I haven't found anyone who I would want to have kids with. I saw how wrecked Knox was when he found out Hazel's mother was pregnant. They weren't on good terms when she finally told him and that was months after she knew. He felt blindsided. He couldn't trust her after that. That's not something I want to go through if it can be helped. I want a true partner. That's something my younger brother got right. Winnie is his perfect match. Lately, I've been thinking that I wouldn't mind my life looking like that too. When I come home to my cabin alone, I feel relief, but also longing. It would be nice to be alone—with someone else.

The lift has arrived at the top of Kettle Peak, so I hop off. The crunch of the snow beneath my board is one of my favorite sounds. I make my way over to the top of the peak and start riding down. I'm tense today, but after a few minutes, I can feel my hips start to loosen up and my spine stretch. Snowboarding can be tough on you physically, but I'm much more in tune with my body the older I get. I'm much more in tune with my emotions as well.

That's how I know that the feelings I get when I'm around Ivy Rutherford are more than just casual. More than just friendly. I thought that first night could be a fluke or maybe it was just that she was new. Different. She's both of those things but a hell of a lot more. The way she weaves her words together in a way that feels like foreplay. Being brushed off like I'm dirt under her expensive boot may be the most arbitrary thing I've ever been turned on by in my life, but *I am.*

I look out over the sparkling mountainside, and where I usually see solace and respite—today, I see loneliness. I wish I had someone to share this with. My love for these mountains runs deep. Exploring them, appreciating this small piece of heaven on earth. I want to experience that with someone else. Someone who can hold their own. Someone who none too recently told me they were a capable woman. That thought has me cutting my morning alone short. I'm off today and have nothing scheduled, but I'm thinking about stopping by the lodge, and I'm hoping when I do, I catch a glimpse of the spitfire that I can't seem to get out of my head.

It's Tuesday evening. Time has gone by excruciatingly slowly and, somehow, today has come at warp speed. I'm regretting that I agreed to come tonight, and on top of that uneasiness, I'm running late. I don't know if you can say that when it's on purpose. Telling Winnie I would come in front of Alder just to prove a point was a dark cloud over my day today. His looking like he did at work earlier was also a point of contention for me. To be so deeply attracted to a man who I feel so much annoyance toward makes my temples ache. Although, I'm not sure it's really him that I'm annoyed with or if it's the way those damn butterflies let loose when he's around.

Why do I feel so strongly about him? I'm not sure, and I don't plan to think too seriously about it either. He's annoyingly good-natured and takes everything I throw at him in stride. I find that unsettling. This morning, when he tried to make polite conversation with me, I told him that he had hat hair from his beanie and he should fix it. He didn't. He looked like he stepped right out of a snowboarding magazine, and then, to no one's surprise, he just laughed off my comment and ran his hand through his shaggy hair. The action made me jealous. Wishing I was running my hand through his thick strands. I shake my head at the memory and refocus.

I'm here to make an appearance. I would rather be back in my cabin, drinking wine in my cozy slippers. The long day is wearing on me, and being out in the cold, even in a town as charming as Silverthorne, is not how I would choose to spend my night. Walking into AJ's is like walking into a movie scene. It's just as I remember, but it's also been transformed into everything I would have imagined a perfectly holiday-themed bar to be. The bar top is a slab of polished, live edge wood, and the bar stools are a thick black metal. Some tables are scattered around the small space that are a little hard to see with all the people packed in. There must be a big turnout since there's live music tonight. I make my way to the counter and spot Buck. He's chatting up a woman at the end of the bar. Wait, I think that's Marilyn from the hotel the other night. That makes me smile. I have a feeling he was a ladies' man when he was younger.

With eyes that sparkle with mischief, he greets me. "Hey there! What can I get you, hun?" He smiles, and his eyes almost disappear with the action. I grin back.

"Hi! Can I get a glass of white?" I ask, and his smile widens.

"Course you can!" he replies and grabs a wine glass from where it hangs over his head. "It's nice to see you again, how long are you here for? Will you be in town for the festival?" he asks, selecting a chilled bottle from the small fridge behind the bar.

"Um, I'm actually here for a bit. I just started working at The Edgemont," I tell him.

"No kidding! You've probably met Jack then. He's around here somewhere. He's one of the resort managers." I nod before replying.

"I do know him. He was actually one of the first people I met since I've been here. Apart from you and Marilyn." I nod my head in her direction.

"And Alder Holloway," he says, setting my glass in front of me. "He was here the night we met, too, if I remember correctly." He poses the last sentence like a question, even though I'm fairly certain nothing really gets by this man. "The snowstorm had him stuck in town, I think." I open my mouth to confirm but shut it when the hair on my neck alerts me to someone's presence. Then I take a breath in through my nose. Citrusy and warm. It makes my mouth water, and that annoys the hell out of me.

"You asking about me, Ivy?" he rumbles softly at my side. I roll my eyes then turn toward him. "You know you can ask me anything. You don't have to question our local bartender. I'll tell you anything you wanna know," he teases.

"No." The word comes out a little more forceful than I wanted it to, and I'm wishing I sounded less defensive. Even more so after seeing the smirk on his face.

"Hey, Alder. How ya doing tonight, son?" the man behind the bar asks him. He doesn't look away from me as he answers, still smiling.

"Good, Buck. Real good." He faces him then. "And you?"

"Oh, you know me, I can't complain. Getting things ready for my booth at the Christmas tree lighting ceremony this weekend."

"Beer and Chili. It hits every time, Buck." He winks at Buck and they both chuckle. I'm not sure what that means, but I smile.

"Good to know. I'll have some seasonal IPA's this year and mulled wine and ciders to try too," he says excitedly. "Be sure to stop by, Ivy." He winks one of his crinkly eyes at me and goes to his next patron. Leaving me alone with Alder. I take a sip of my wine and look around the room. It's loud and filled with chatter, but there isn't a band playing like I thought there would be.

"Do you want me to show you to our table?" Alder asks me. No.

"Sure," I say and grab my glass of wine from the bar top.

"Right this way, princess." I narrow my eyes at him, but he just starts walking through the crowd. I follow him while looking at all the lights in here. The green hanging lamps over the tables are composed of mosaic glass, and there are hanging twinkle lights above us to really sell the Christmas vibe. I glance at the people tucked into their tables and booths, talking amongst themselves and laughing. It's so freaking cute in here. There are red and green bows, wreaths, and fairy lights. I'm ogling a Christmas tree with all cream and gold trimmings when I smack into a wall, almost spilling my drink. Only it's not a wall; it's Alder who's stopped at our table.

"Hi, Ivy!" A sweet voice cuts through my embarrassment.

"Hey, Winnie," I greet her as she scoots closer to Rhett who shifts closer to another man. A very attractive man. He's gorgeous. I'm not sure how to describe his eyes. They're hazel, but they seem to be dancing. Bright. *Wild.* What are they feeding the men here? I muse to myself.

"Sit down!" she encourages me. I do, and Alder sits across

from me. "How are you?" she asks me. She has her curly hair down tonight, and Rhett is talking to the man who I don't know while absently playing with a lock of it. It frames her delicate face perfectly. It highlights her kind eyes and sweet smile.

"I'm good. It was a long day, but I got a lot done." I smile as I'm speaking to her, then follow up by asking her the same.

"How are things at your bakery? I'm not sure if I told you, but I've had dreams about that latte, and I loved visiting. I'll probably be a frequent flier," I joke.

She beams. "Thank you so much for saying that! I hope you'll be back as often as you can. I'm glad you decided to come out tonight." She smiles as she says it, and she's making me feel marginally better about my decision.

"I'm glad too," I tell her honestly. "So when does the live music start?" I ask.

Winnie looks at Alder and grins. "The first act starts in five minutes," she answers, and I look over and catch his eye roll. I'm feeling like I may be in the dark about something.

"Okay, what am I missing?" I ask, looking between them, but before I get an answer, a blonde woman in green scrubs hugs Winnie from behind, and they both squeal.

"Mare! You made it!" Winnie yells. "I thought you were stuck at the hospital tonight."

"Grant covered for me so I could come to see the show."

"Oh, it's Grant now? Not Mr. Steal Your Food?" she asks, and I look up at the scoff that comes from across the table. The man with the wild eyes is who the sound came from. He pushes his chair back and stands.

"I'm getting another pitcher," he says under his breath and leaves. Mare continues like she didn't hear him.

"That was months ago. We're past that now. He apologized for all that," she says, waving her hand in the air.

"No, I remember the phone call about the apology. I just don't remember the name update," Winnie tells her friend. "Speaking of names," she starts and motions toward me. "This is Ivy. Ivy, this is Marigold."

"Hi, Ivy. It's so nice to meet you. God, you're gorgeous." I laugh, this coming from the actual angel before me. Sapphire-blue eyes and blonde hair combined with her delicate nose and berry-pink lips. The woman is an oil painting. I'm not the biggest history buff, but the saying *the face that launch'd a thousand ships* comes to mind. Her smile turns just a little strained, and I fear I've been quiet too long, so I rush to fill the silence.

"Hi, Marigold. It's nice to meet you too."

"So how did you end up out with these guys?" she asks, and Winnie answers.

"She came into the bakery a couple of days ago, and we hit it off." My chest warms a little at the casual way she says it, and I'm fighting a blush. It's very unlike me. "And then I found out that she works with Alder at The Edgemont," she finishes.

"You mean you're stuck up on that mountain with him?" She nods at Alder, who I hadn't noticed leave our table. He's walking over to the small stage in the corner that I assumed was for the live entertainment tonight.

"Yeah. Uh, what's he doing?" I ask, and Rhett answers.

"You're in for a real treat tonight, Ivy. The official welcome to Silverthorne, if you will," he tells me, sitting back in his chair and curling his arm around the back of Winnie's.

"Truly," Winnie comments with a laugh. "This is The Holloway men's bread and butter."

Mare takes the vacant seat, and then the lights flicker,

signaling that the show is about to begin. Oh Lord, I don't think I'm ready for what's about to happen. The lights dim, and the crowd quiets. I look around, trying to get a good look at what's going on, then a lone light shines down above the stage. When Alder's profile comes into view, the crowd goes wild. Oh, god.

The first few notes of an '80s power ballad start, and he tips his head into the spotlight, bringing the mic to his lips. He starts singing in a low but building voice. In a smooth and practiced motion, he starts tapping his heel to the beat, which draws my eyes to his very tight rear end covered by very-fitted blue jeans. Oh my lord. The tips of my ears are hot. I tuck my hair behind my left ear and hear "I'm not like the other girls" in my head. Now my cheeks turn hot as well.

Alder is giving the crowd what they want. He's swaying his hips and scanning his eyes over all of us as he sings. He stops when he meets my eyes and sings a particularly sexual line, gotta love the '80s. He keeps his gaze trained on me. The dimple that I've thought about too many times since arriving in town is on full display. He knows he's hot, and he knows I think so. I get the feeling of eyes on me. More than those of the man up on the stage, and I avert mine to the side to find most of the faces in this bar turned to mine. The warmth in my ears and face has now spread to my neck.

Attention in any form can be dangerous, but attention from Alder Holloway may be catastrophic. I'm used to being watched. I've always liked attention. In therapy, we talked a lot about that. I guess it's something I didn't get from the right people in my life growing up. It's that Daddy-didn't-notice-me effect. I've sought it out in different ways, mostly self-destructive. Exhibit A: my marriage to someone thirteen years older than me at twenty. *Are you there, Daddy Issues? It's me, Ivy.* I begin to relax as the show goes on. I'm encouraged to let loose by all the cheering that's happening around the room. The people can't get enough. I count myself in that group.

Alder's song comes to an end and someone else gets up on the stage after. I'm smiling so big that my cheeks are starting to hurt. My sides burn with each wave of laughter. Marigold leans across the table to lay her hand on my arm, and Winnie is leaning into my side. I've had a great evening with these people who I barely know who have made such an effort to make me feel included. I'll think about this later and how it's a little sad that I haven't had this much fun with anyone else in a long time. For now, I let their laughter and casual affection keep my chest warm and the smile on my face.

I look at Alder then at the man he's laughing with. The man who keeps bringing us pitchers of beer. I've discovered his name is Colt through his conversation with everyone at the table with me, and he's Winnie's brother. He looks up and winks at me. Although I typically find men winking at me grounds for letting my bitch flag fly, when he does it, it's incredibly charming. So is the friendly smile he wears. I smile back at him. I hear a throat clear and slide my eyes back to Alder's icy-blue ones. I think this is the first time I've ever seen him annoyed. Or is that jealousy I see?

"So, Ivy. How long are you here for?" Colt asks.

"Too long for you, Colt," Alder answers him without breaking our eye contact. Colt makes a sound half-snort and half-laugh. "Are you ready to head out yet?" he asks me.

"I drove myself. So you don't need to worry about when I'm ready," I tell him.

"The roads may be slick again, and it would be easier for me to follow you now than have to find you on the side of the road later," he tells me with a smug smile. My cheeks heat. Lover Boy has some bite to him after all. Let's play then. I bite the corner of my bottom lip and give him a confused look.

"But what if I wasn't planning on going home at all?" I ask innocently. His smile falters just for a moment, but then a smirk takes its place.

"If you wanted me to take you to my place, then you could have just said that," he says. I think I may finally understand that saying "shooting daggers out of your eyes" because I feel like I want to throw something at him.

"Sorry, Lover Boy. I don't think you and I would be a good mix," I tell him.

"No?" he questions. "Hmm...that's not the impression I got the other night," he states as the main lights in the bar come back on, and being a redhead has never been more inconvenient. I know my blush is on full display. I played right into that.

I look around, and the whole table pretends to be looking anywhere but at us. Rhett and Winnie both take sips of their drinks, Rhett muttering something about *"this bar and jealousy"* under his breath. Great. That embarrassing bit of info would be my cue. I swallow.

"Thanks for inviting me tonight, I think I better head out," I say to Winnie. "I'll see you around." I grab my coat and slide out of my seat. A hand on my arm stops me, and I turn to see the adorable tiny brunette pulling me into a hug. My throat tightens.

"Please come by the bakery soon! I have some new coffee and treats I'd love for you to try, and we can hang out," she replies.

"Yes! And we're having a wine night on Friday! Say you'll

come," Mare chimes in. I nod and smile, not sure if my voice is shaky. Then I make a beeline for the door. I hear harsh whispers as I open the door and step out into the now-dark sidewalk. I take a deep breath. I don't think I've been embarrassed in a solid decade. I don't really *do* embarrassed. I don't do very many negative emotions actually. I walk toward my parked SUV and hit the fob to unlock it. I open the door and go to sit when I sense someone at my back.

I swing my elbow as hard as I can, and I make a direct hit to someone's jaw.

"Oh, fuck!" I hear my attacker's muffled voice. I grab the pepper spray attached to my key fob and click it open, ready to spray and knee this piece of shit in the balls.

"Back off, motherfu—Alder?"

ALDER

I feel the blow to my face and step back as far as I can to avoid another hit.

"Oh, fuck!" I hear myself say.

"Back off, motherfu—Alder?" Ivy asks.

"Yeah," I confirm. "It's just me.

"What the actual fuck? Why are you out here following me? What is wrong with you?" So many questions, not enough time to answer them all, and my jaw is starting to throb. She really went for it. As much as it hurts, I'm also really proud. Ivy Rutherford knows how to throw a punch and that's irritatingly sexy in this moment.

I push those thoughts aside so I can speak to her, "I just came out here to say I'm sorry." I look at her, rubbing my jaw. "For being an asshole inside, but I guess now for scaring you too," I tell her.

She grabs the side of my head, not gently, but she at least takes care to avoid my newly injured jaw.

"Let me see." She sighs, and I lean my head down into her

hand. "This is your fault—" she starts, and I almost start laughing, but I bite my tongue, not wanting her to stop touching me. "But I'm sorry you didn't think before creeping up behind me," she adds, and this time I can't help the small laugh that escapes. I clear my throat to try and cover it.

"I took it too far in there and realized it immediately, but that was still too late. I really am sorry," I say.

"Mmm," she hums. "It sounded more like your family and friends brought you to this conclusion," she teases.

"I'll admit I received an earful, which, if you knew Rhett better, you would find that interesting, but I came to the conclusion all on my own, Ivy. That's not how I operate, and I shouldn't have said what I did not knowing if you wanted anyone to know what's gone on between us," I get out in a rush. It's the truth, and I hope she sees that. *And by the way, since we're being honest, I'm kind of your boss. I think, but I still don't say.*

"Besides you spilling the tea to your friend group, I'm not looking forward to facing the wrath of every woman in Silverthorne after your little show earlier," she says with a gentle swipe to my jaw.

"You noticed?" I ask.

She gives me an eye roll. "Everyone in the bar noticed, Lover Boy."

"I wasn't after any other woman's attention, Ivy. Just yours," I tell her. She removes her hands from my face, crosses her arms over her chest, and steps back toward her SUV again. She leans against the side of it and looks down at the ground for a moment, then lifts her chin to look at me.

"You probably shouldn't be doing that," she says quietly.

"Doing what?" I ask her and take a step closer. Flurries are starting again, and she looks like an angel in the dim glow of the lights above us.

"Trying to get my attention, Alder. It's pointless. I'm not going to be here for very long, we're going to be working together, and, if I'm being honest, you're not really someone I would typically date," she says. Her words initially sting, but I recognize denial when I see it.

"It's just us out here, Ivy. I was there, and that isn't how it felt that first night. Are you telling me you didn't enjoy yourself?" If she lies, I'll know it. The sounds she was making are engraved in my brain for eternity, and there's no way in hell she was faking it. Any man with a pulse knows the real thing.

"That's not what I'm saying, and you know it," she says with narrowed eyes, and the annoyance in them makes me smile.

"I just wanted to make sure we were being honest with each other," I tell her, and she shakes her head.

"I'm not sure if you're being intentionally obtuse or if you're playing into the whole snowboarding persona—" she says, lifting a hand at me. I raise my brows at her. "But you're not hearing me. I'm not interested in starting something with you, action hero," she finishes. She hasn't looked at me while saying all this, so I step closer still, not quite touching her. She doesn't move or tense when I place my right arm against the car beside her shoulder. She doesn't shy away from my nearness. She seems to relax into where my forearm meets her body.

"If that's really how you feel, I'll stop," I tell her quietly. Reaching up with my free hand, I tuck some loose hair behind her ear and lightly cup her jaw. She closes her eyes, leaning into my hand slightly, and I turn her head to me. "But I'm going to need you to look at me when you say it. Tell me there isn't anything between us, and I'll back off. We can just be friends." Her eyes open, and then her mouth, but no words come. I stare at her parted lips and lean my head closer to hers until we're only a few inches apart. "Tell me to stop, Ivy. Tell me you don't want me to kiss you senseless and then put you in my truck," I coax.

Laughter and a door flying open have us both snapping our heads to AJ's entrance. Ivy moves out of my touch and opens the driver-side door wider. She shakes her head and smiles. A nervous laugh bubbles out of her, and I chuckle along with her.

"Goodnight, Lover Boy. I'll see you tomorrow," she says, and I shake my head.

"Not tomorrow. I'm on call for my other job, but if you want, I can stop by to say hi. If you get to missing me too badly or want to finish this." I wave between us and receive another eye roll from her tonight.

"There's nothing to finish, and I'm not going to start anything with you. I'll see you around." She slides into her seat and shuts the door, effectively cutting off my view of her. A shame. I really like looking at her. I knock on the roof of her car twice and call out a goodnight. I think about staying at AJ's for a bit longer, but I already know I won't be doing that as my feet find their way to my Bronco, and I start it up. She may not want me looking out for her, but I can't help myself. Call it selfish, maybe that's what it is, but I need to know that she's made it home and isn't stuck on the side of the road in the cold again.

I catch up to her once I start the climb up the mountain, she's driving slowly. Good. She isn't used to these roads yet, and I've seen more than my fair share of accidents on mountain roads. I give her plenty of space, trailing far behind. The snow is coming down a little heavier up here, but it's still safe to be out. I watch as she pulls into her parking spot beside her cabin, and she's getting out as I drive by. I wave, and she gives me one back. I smile, thinking about our almost kiss. She can tell me she doesn't want to date me all she wants, but her body language is telling me a different story.

Once I'm home, I tug off my boots and get ready for bed. I've got another early morning. I start my shift at six o'clock. and need to be alert for it. Some days, I don't receive any calls, and then there have been days where they seem to come in nonstop. I used to wish for slow days, but that only ever seemed to bring me bad luck. Now, I just resign myself to the fact that the day is going to be what it is, and I will be ready for whatever it brings.

I love my job. Helping people has helped me in a lot of ways. Healing from an unexpected loss isn't linear. I hear my therapist's voice in my head. I have more sunny days than dark ones, and I have a better system in place to help me through the dark days. I had always loved snowboarding, but I started teaching classes six years ago as an outlet. I don't pay myself for the classes like I do with the other instructors. It's really just another way I can make sure people know how to be safe on the mountain.

Climbing into bed, I tuck my arm behind my head and look out through the skylight in the ceiling. It's a clear night, so the stars are easy to see and stand out like diamonds against the dark night sky. They make me think of another gemstone. I close my eyes, thinking of green slanted eyes and a pouty smirk. I can still feel soft red hair between my fingers. The snow is falling softly. I can hear it tapping against the glass pane. I let the soft sound pull me to sleep. All my thoughts on the gorgeous redhead down the road who refuses to admit she wants me too. Somehow, I just need to get her to trust her instincts and this growing attraction between us. That first night wasn't a fluke, and I'm nothing if not relentless.

Days like today are one of the reasons I love my job. I woke up ready and slept better than I have in months. My verbal sparring matches with Ivy lately may have something to do with how worn out I was. The need to touch her and not being able to is starting to wear on me too. That woman drives me crazy without even trying.

I was able to help two people make it back to their families safely. We had a car slide off the road a couple of counties over. Luckily, no one was injured, and the airlift wouldn't have been necessary, but the paramedics who arrived first thought the woman might have had a concussion. Thankfully, she didn't, but they made the right call. A head injury isn't something to brush off.

I'm drinking a coffee from the doctors' lounge now, waiting to hear about our other rescue's prognosis. My shift ended half an hour ago, but I always like to hear how a patient is doing before I take off. Mare is with him now. I know he had a dislocated shoulder, but I worried that he also had some broken ribs. He was having a lot of pain while breathing which could have just been severe bruising; I guess we'll see. His family is in the waiting room and has been assured that his life isn't in danger.

He had been snowboarding on a trail he shouldn't have been and picked up too much speed. He slammed directly into a tree. Thank God he had the good sense to have a helmet on; he isn't facing a head injury because of it. As lucky as he is to only be facing minor injuries, his body is definitely going to feel the impact for a while.

"Mrs. Stephens." I see Mare call from the swinging double doors.

"Yes, that's me." A woman in her late forties slides the head of a sleepy little boy off her lap and stands. Mare walks over with a reassuring smile on her face. She's really good at that.

"Hi, Mrs. Stephens. I wanted to be the first to tell you that your husband is going to make a full recovery, though I would absolutely recommend no more snowboarding or skiing or snowmobiling this trip. He does need to spend the night tonight because we had to give him something for the pain in his ribs, but he'll be ready for discharge early tomorrow morning." Mrs. Stephens lets out something between a laugh and a sob and reaches her arms out to hug Mare, thanking her. She accepts the hug and pats Mrs. Stephens's back a few times. I'm thankful he'll make a full recovery. Too many times, people don't.

I throw my disposable cup into the trash and walk down the hall to the elevators. I could bother one of my siblings or my parents, but I think I'd rather be home for the rest of the evening. I have a class to teach at the resort, and I need some rest before I start my shift there in the morning. I'll also need some rest before I see Ivy again. I want my head to be clear when I tell her there's something between us. I don't want her denying it anymore.

IVY

I'm staring at my computer screen. It has my email pulled up, and I've hit "compose email" seven times, hit the "x" to close it just as many, and that brings me back to my staring. I'm supposed to be sending my father an update on the progress I've made and the plans I'll be implementing. I've spoken to two contractors and their crews, they'll be here tomorrow to start work on the gift shop. I started collecting items from local artisans and now have a plethora of products to showcase.

I'm going to be running an ad for the resort in Denver, hoping to bring in new customers and some of the residents around the area as well. I have a special on our social media account, so if it's mentioned, you'll get a promotional 15 percent off your stay with us. That alone has had the phone ringing all morning. Between Jack and I, we've managed to book out all the main cabins until New Year's. We only have two suites left, and then we'll be considered completely booked for the holiday season, while still able to handle more traffic from the people coming in just for the restaurant, gift shop, and to ski and snowboard.

I've managed all of this in my first week here, and yet, I have no idea how to tell my father and him not make me feel like I haven't done enough. I know my ideas are good, and they're obviously working. Jack told me this is the most action this place has seen in years. I just know that my success will be met with more expectations, most of which will be unattainable. That's Sullivan Rutherford though. He sets the goals just to move the post later. You'd think I would become accustomed to it. That after years of coming up just a little short in his eyes, I would be more accepting of my family dynamic. It still stings though. I hate that I care. That I've always cared when my whole life has been a one-way street. I give and he takes, and that's when he's feeling generous.

It's not hard to see how I ended up in bed with an older man who told me I was special to him. Noah isn't quite old enough to be my father or anything, but thirteen years feels like a lot when you're nineteen years old. He said all the right things that a broken teenager wanted to hear, and I preened at every well-positioned compliment.

"Ivy, you're such an old soul."

"You really know what you want from life, and I'm starting to think I do too."

"You're going to be snatched up before I've even had a chance to throw my hat in the ring."

"I just want to be here for you, Ivy."

"I care about you so much; I think I might be falling for you."

That all lasted from age nineteen into twenty until I told him that I missed my period. I wasn't planning on having a child so soon either, but because of what he had told me, I assumed it wouldn't be so bad. I was wrong. He was furious. He accused me of trapping him. First for his money and then because I was obsessed with him. That hurt. I didn't need or want his money, and I thought we cared about each other. I thought I might have been in love with him. I think back to the morning I found out.

Two pink lines.

I stared down at my bathroom counter, and two faint pink lines were looking back at me. What does two mean again? I already knew what it meant, but I grabbed the instructions again anyway. I'd read them seventeen times since I opened the box, but I needed to confirm what I believed was a positive pregnancy result. Pee needs to be in the stream for five seconds...wait three minutes...one means...two means...positive. Fuck. Okay. Okay, okay. Shit. Okay. Tears form in my eyes. Is this something I want? I wipe my face with the back of my hand, and it comes away wet. I press a hand to my stomach.

It's me and you, sweet babe.

I told him that I didn't need him. I could raise the baby on my own, but he found a way to gain something from the situation. My life and that of our child became a bargaining chip in my father's business.

He would marry me to avoid scandal, but my father would have to make him a partner in his company. I shut my eyes at the onslaught of memories that follow. The early months when things weren't so bad. I was happy, and Noah was content. The first time I smelled another woman in our home. The sudden trip to the hospital. The months of depression. The drinking. The facility, and then finally, our divorce. Thankfully, five years was all that was contracted.

My life became my own again a little over a year ago. Just a few weeks before, Noah humiliated me with a new woman on his arm. I was grateful to be apart from him, but the social circle in which we moved had a field day when the news broke. I had to find out with everyone else. I take a deep, steadying breath and start drafting a new email. I won't delete this one. I'll send it and comply with the terms of my father and my agreement. I need something that's mine, and when I'm the new COO of Rutherford Wine, I'll finally have that, and I'll be in a position to start phasing Noah out of my company.

I send my email and sit back in my chair. There. Sent. I still need something else. One more stream of revenue for this place, and I'll be on my way back home. Home. It may be a stretch of the word to say it's home, but it's where my life is. A life filled with things and people who don't seem to care about the real me at all. I'm really good at surrounding myself with people whose intentions I don't have to analyze. If I already know that they don't care, then I never have to worry if they do. Vibrations rumbling through my desk pull me from my very introspective thoughts. Thank God, no one should have to spend time in my brain alone. Even me.

I don't recognize the number, "Hello?" I answer.

"Hi, is this Ivy?" a sweet voice asks me.

"It is, can I ask who's calling?"

"Hey, Ivy. Um, it's Winnie," she tells me, and I briefly wonder how she got my number, but I chalk it up to being in a small town.

"Hey, Winnie. How's it going?" I haven't seen her since last Tuesday, but I was planning on stopping by Thistle and Sage soon.

"It's going well. I was wondering if you had plans for the weekend. I know Alder was completely out of line the other night, but I swear he's not normally like that, and I know he's sorry," she rushes out, and I don't really have plans. Well, unless you count finally getting around to reading my book and drinking a few glasses of wine, which I do count as plans, but...

"He did apologize, and I don't have any big plans, what's up?"

"The Christmas tree lighting ceremony is happening in town on Saturday, and I wanted you to come and hang out with us—" I bite my lip. I've told Alder I don't need to be spending extra time with him, and I have a feeling he'll be involved at least marginally. "If you want to. It's also the winter carnival, so there will be food and activities. They're actually bringing in an ice-skating rink this year. I'll probably avoid it, but it's fun to watch!" she says. I take a moment to contemplate her offer. It does sound fun, and I would like to visit downtown again.

"Sure, I'd love to come," I agree, and she lets out a small squeal. It's adorable and makes me giggle. Since when do I giggle?

"Perfect! I can't wait to see you. If you meet me at my house first, we can walk over together. That way, you won't have to worry about parking."

"That sounds great and thank you for inviting me."

"Of course. Open invitation. You have my number now," she tells me, and I'm taken aback by how genuine she sounds.

"Thank you. See you Saturday."

"See you then! Bye!" She hangs up, and I set my phone

back on my desk. I look out the big windows in my office and feel my lips turn up at the corners. I've never had a good group of friends. I've had people to go out with and people to invite to things, but I don't remember having real friends. I take in the snowy mountains and the sloped landscape. I look at the gondolas that I still haven't been on, and Silverthorne grows on me a little more.

Now, it's time to get back to work. I need to call the few local artists and embroidery shops that I have contact information for and see if they would be interested in designing and producing the clothing and merchandise for the gift shop. I have a to-do list a mile long, but I'm smiling. I'm really enjoying my work here. That's something I didn't think I'd ever say.

It's nearing lunchtime when Jack pops his head into my doorway.

"Hey, Ivy. I was getting ready to get some lunch. Would you like to join me?" he asks with a smile that makes me smile. The whole town is getting more yeses from me than I've given in the last year. I don't remember the last time I was so agreeable, but also, I can feel my blood sugar getting low and a headache trying to set in. It would be better for me to head that off.

"That would be great; I'm running on fumes in here," I tell him, standing and grabbing my purse.

"How are you settling in?" Jack asks as we walk the hallway of The Edgemont.

"Fine. Good actually. I spent some time with Winnie Parker the other night, and I'm going to the Christmas tree ceremony with her and some of her friends this weekend. People here are really nice," I say.

He's nodding and smiling at me. "They are. Silverthorne is

pretty much exactly what it seems. People like to help one another, and they really care. That's a very special thing, and it also means you'll have plenty of eyes on you and noses in your business," he tells me with a chuckle.

"I can imagine," I say, and that's really all I can do. I don't have experience with small towns or the people in them. "So, what are you doing when you're not here?" I ask him.

"Well, I ski, and I like to go snowshoeing, so I'm here on the mountain a lot," he says with a laugh, and it makes me smile. "But when I'm not here, I'm probably at home. I'm not someone who goes out or likes to be very social. I get enough, maybe too much, peopling working here," he jokes, and I laugh.

"I can understand that," I tell him, even though I actually don't understand that too well. I hate being alone. I'm working toward being happier with being alone. I think one of the reasons I started reading was to not be alone with my thoughts. I wasn't always a big reader, but shortly after I came home from the hospital all those years ago, it became clear I would need an escape from what my life would be for the next five years. Oh shit, didn't he ask me something?

"I'm sorry, what did you say?" He gives me a patient smile before repeating his question.

"How does Silverthorne compare to your life back in California?"

I blow out a breath. "I wouldn't say they have much in common at all really, so that would be a very short list," I say, and thinking about a list now makes me think of twinkling blue eyes. I push onward with my reply. "I grew up on a vineyard until I was in seventh grade and have lived in sunny Southern California since I started boarding school with very minimal visits home," I answer honestly.

"Did your parents visit you while you were away?" *Ouch.* I know that Jack can't know my history. That wouldn't be why he's asking, but this particular question speaks to deep-rooted pain.

"Not really." Is all I say, and luckily, Jack drops this line of questioning, instead sticking to hobbies and traveling. I'm surprised to find I'm having a nice time. Jack's very sweet and extremely handsome. It's actually a little astounding that I haven't met an unattractive man since I arrived. My irrational vampire theories are going to run wild later tonight when I'm alone with them and my other chaotic thoughts.

He walks with me back to my office after our lunch. I have a few more emails I need to send, and I need to grab my coat and phone that I left on my desk. The weather is nice today, and there's a flurry of activity around the resort.

"So, I know we don't know each other that well, but I was wondering if you'd like to do this again. Maybe next time it could be over dinner?" Jack asks as we reach the door to the lodge. It probably shouldn't come as such a shock. We get along, and we're both attractive single adults. The funny thing is I would have said yes, but now I can't. As soon as I picture going to dinner with someone, it's Alder Holloway who I see sitting across from me. Unfortunately. How frustrating that he hasn't been here all day, and yet he's still messing with my head.

"I'm flattered, Jack."

"Oh, no," he groans, but his words are good-natured. I give him a tight smile. "Let me guess, it has nothing to do with me." I laugh at that because even when I'm turning him down, he remains so incredibly likable.

"You would be right in assuming that the issue lies with me. I think you're great—"

"But..." Jack encourages. I glance up to see a faded green Bronco pass by. If that isn't comedic timing, I'm not sure what is.

"But I don't think it would be a good idea...because of the previously mentioned issues." I finish my sentence, still staring at the truck rumbling down the mountain road.

Jack turns, and too late, I realize my mistake. "Ah, I see," he concludes.

"I don't want you to get the wrong idea here. It's really not like that or like anything. I don't even like him most of the time," I rush out.

He raises his hand slightly and smiles a kind smile. "You don't have to explain anything to me, Ivy."

"Thank you. And I hope we can still get lunch and remain friends. I have really enjoyed getting to know you," I stress.

"Of course, after I dust myself off from that brutal rejection." He pauses and winks. "I'm enjoying getting to know you as well. I hope you'll let me know if anything changes though."

"I will," I agree, and then give his arm a friendly squeeze before heading inside. What a day it's been and a strange turn of events. Annoyingly, I have a certain helicopter pilot on my mind. As I grab my forgotten phone and check my notifications, I find myself wondering how his day was and wanting to ask him. Six texts, all from Sienna, and a missed call from...my father? I expected an email, not a phone call. He's probably pissed I didn't answer.

I debate on calling him back tomorrow but decide I should just get it over with. If I know him, and I undoubtedly do, this will be brief but probably painful. I sit down in my chair and pull up the email I've sent him, not wanting to be caught unprepared for any questions or concerns he might bring up. I tap his number on my screen and close my eyes.

"Ivy. Nice of you to call me back finally." *Finally* is twenty minutes after I missed his call, but sure, finally. I sigh.

"So sorry I missed your call. I've been busy, as I'm sure you've seen from my email," I tell him in a sickly-sweet voice.

"There's no need for that, Ivy. I just wanted to check in. How are you?" His question throws me momentarily. He doesn't ask how I am. He asks if I need anything, meaning money and things he could buy with his money, but never his time or attention. That's never been on the table.

"I-I'm fine. Things are moving fast here, I may not even be here the full three months you've given me," I propose. At that, I get a grunt.

"We'll see. I called to tell you something, but I can't remember what it was now. Which is why you should always answer when I call. I'll send you a message when I have time, but I'm busy the rest of the day. Next time, answer the call, Ivy." He hangs up before I can say goodbye. I stare at my phone. It's not the first time this has happened, but I keep wondering when it will sting just a little less. I toss the offending object into my purse and head home. The rest of my emails can wait until tomorrow. My stomach is uneasy after that phone call, so I'll have to trade out my glass of wine for a sparkling water and read my book tonight.

ALDER

Today has been...a day, and it's only eleven thirty. I'm in the middle of a private lesson with a family that seems like they would rather be anywhere but here. The father is trying to connect with his kids, and all they really want to do is take pictures of themselves in their very expensive gear and check their phones.

I couldn't care less about that, except it's my job to make sure, if they decide to go down anything more than a bunny hill, that they at least know how to stop safely. Or else it will also be me paying for it later when I have to lead a search party up the side of the mountain. That happens more frequently than you'd like to think. I love flying, but typically, when we have to get the helicopter involved for a rescue, it means someone is in a higher-risk situation. Going in on foot means that the conditions are still manageable without an airlift.

I look up to see the daughter of the group staring at me. Again. If it's not the mothers, it's their daughters. Sometimes it's both. I walk a very fine line between keeping guests happy and keeping them from slipping their numbers. I would be lying if I said that I didn't slip a few in my pocket. Ray and I were reckless with our jobs and never thought about the consequences. He always made our most boring days here fun. I miss that. I miss *him*.

"So how long have you been working here?" the teenage girl asks, looking up at me from under her lashes. I inwardly groan.

"Oh, I'd say since you were probably in diapers." This doesn't always deter them, but I take a gamble. It pays off. She wrinkles her nose. Her game is not quite as fun as before.

"Right," she says, walking back over to where her parents are arguing. "Daddy, I'm going back to the chalet. I'm bored, and it's cold," she tells him, trudging by, not waiting for a reply. She would have been waiting a while if she had. Her father continues to talk in circles with her mother. Their son sits on the snowboard he hasn't bothered to strap into. I'll try one more time to get him interested.

I head to the top of the hill and come down the steeper side, making sure to hit the two small jumps we have for the intermediate riders. I do a front hold on the first one and decide to do a Rodeo on the bigger one. I launch myself high and flip myself forward, twisting at the same time, landing goofy footed. It's clean. A practiced move I've done more times than I could count. The man and his wife cheer for me, and she even claps. I chuckle.

The son does take notice, though, and stows his phone in his mom's jacket pocket.

"Whoa, do you think you could teach me to do that?" he asks, excitedly.

"You're probably not quite there yet, but the best place to

start is getting on the board and getting comfortable," I say. He nods and goes to strap into his board. Movement up above in the lodge's big window catches my eye, and I peer up to see Ivy. She's standing by a Christmas tree. Looking as beautiful as she was when I saw her this morning. Her all-black spandex thing she was wearing with a puffy vest over it was so damn cute. It also gave me a great view of her long legs. I wave, expecting her to look away. She just stares and then barely lifts her hand before backing away.

Ivy Rutherford is an enigma to me. Half the time, I think she hates me, and half the time, she looks at me like she wouldn't mind climbing me like a tree. Both are becoming a problem for me because my body reacts the same either way. I like her fire. The way she handles herself. She asserts dominance, and damn if I'm not all in for that.

She's gorgeous and tempting, but I can tell there's so much more to her than what I see. I want to know her. *But damn*, she is prickly. Maybe I'll go see if she's running hot or cold after I finish up with my class.

An hour later, I'm walking down the warm, now holiday-scented hallway to my office. I think back to a few days ago when I found Ivy curled up on my couch and chuckle. She was so short with me when she woke up all flustered and embarrassed. Her office door is open, so I peek inside. I take just a moment to observe her. She's got her hair up on top of her head with a purple pen stuck through it, and she's chewing on the end of another one. She's looking at a notebook in her hand. The sight makes me smile; she looks so fucking cute.

"Do you buy those pens in bulk?" I ask into the quiet space. She jumps, knocking her chair back, and the look on her face tells me I should have knocked. I should have announced my presence. I should have thought about how she punched me in the face the other night outside the bar. I feel like shit. "Hey, I'm sorry. I didn't mean to scare you. Or, well, surprise you that much."

Her hand is on her heart, and she glares at me like she's about to shoot lasers out of them. I'm starting to believe she may be able to. "What. Is. Wrong. With. You?" she says slowly. Like she's barely containing a little demon inside her. It's so fucking cute, but that's not the point right now, I try to remind myself as I smash my lips together and cough.

"I am sorry," I tell her sincerely. She stands up straighter and puts her hands at her sides.

"Was there something you needed, Alder?" she asks, her voice regaining its steady tone and also the icy bite that's always lingering just under the surface.

"I was just checking in. I finished my classes for the day, and there is a couple arriving later today staying in the chalet on the west side of the property. I think it needs some snow cleared. Do you want me to get Terry over there to take care of it?" This is only the backup reason I stopped by, but she doesn't need to know that. She tilts her head, suspicious of me.

"That would be great," she tells me., "I should probably get a basket ready to send out too," she mumbles more to herself than to me.

"A basket?" I ask. "For what?"

"Yeah, I've started gathering some local items and putting

them together into welcome baskets. I'm starting with the bigger chalets, but eventually, I would love to have a scaled option for all guests," she says while busying herself with some papers on her desk until she finds what she's looking for. "Actually, I need to speak to Winnie about a couple of ideas I had for some pre-made mixes to have in the gift shop as well," she continues.

"Gift shop?" I sound like a fucking parrot repeating everything she says, but we don't have a gift shop.

"Yes, Alder. A gift shop." She says it slowly, like I'm a small child. And why am I just as happy when she's treating me like I'm dirt under her boot as I am when she's laughing at something stupid I said only to make her laugh? Ivy Rutherford is a mystery I am all too willing to investigate. Sign me up.

"When did we get this gift shop, princess?" The nickname she so aptly has earned makes her green eyes snap to mine, narrowed—stunning.

"We don't have one yet, Mr. Holloway," she huffs out, then walks around to the front of her desk, leaning back against it and crossing her arms over her chest, pushing her breasts together. It feels calculated, but she can't help it that she has really nice tits. I swallow. Now could be a good time to mention that I'll be the one finalizing these plans of hers, but she keeps talking. "I'm working on getting one up and running before the Christmas and New Year's rush. I've been talking with as many local businesses as I can, as well as two clothing shops to print merchandise for us. Edgemont sweaters, hats, beanies—" She points to my head. "Sweatpants, T-shirts... you get it. I feel like it's a missed opportunity here." She shrugs her narrow shoulders.

"And you think people will want to buy things that say The

Edgemont on them?" It's a little of a foreign concept to me. I've worked on the mountain since I was a teenager, and I love it here. I mean, I moved to my cabin from town, but for someone to want a souvenir? Interesting.

"They absolutely will. People, families especially, love having keepsakes," she tells me, and I think about that for a minute. How many sweatshirts does Lo have from all her trips? How many do I have from all our vacations growing up? A lot. I can't believe no one thought of it sooner. It's nice to see her care about this place. It's nice having her here in Silverthorne.

"That's a really good idea, actually," I tell her, but it must have been the wrong thing to say because she snorts and looks up at the ceiling.

"Actually?" *Oh.* I see the error of my ways. I could have complimented her more fully. "Yes, Mr. Holloway. I actually have good ideas. Even for a spoiled princess." She throws the words at me.

"I didn't mean to offend you, Miss Rutherford. I was trying to pay you a compliment," I explain.

"Yeah? Do you have much practice doing that? Because you're sorely missing the mark from where I stand," she volleys. Damn, she doesn't give a fucking inch.

"Do you ever give anyone the benefit of the doubt? You have a way of taking anything I say and twisting it into something to be mad at me for," I ask, a little incredulous.

"No," she says simply. I stare at her, and she stares back at me. What happened, or what she must have gone through to make her behave this way? I want to crack her open like one of my books and read all that's between her pages. Looking at her gemstone eyes, almost glowing with defiance, I want to reach inside her and drag all the things she's keeping hidden out into the afternoon sun.

I know she wants me to take the bait, if she didn't, she wouldn't bait me as often as she does, but I won't. Instead, I step closer to her. Leaving my spot against the door frame, I walk until I stand directly in front of her. Towering over her from where she's still leaning against her desk. She looks up at me, and I see her bristle.

She's ready for the fight. I won't give her one this time. "Then I guess all I can do is apologize." At my words, her face shifts from stone to confusion. Yeah, baby. Lay down that sword. "It wasn't my intention to offend you, but I can see how what I said may have been offensive. I'm sorry about that. I think your idea is a damn good one, and I'm on board to help." Her pouty lips part. I think in shock. I'm thankful, in this moment, that Mary Holloway made sure her boys knew how to apologize to a woman.

"I..." She stops, then starts again, "Thank you for apologizing," she rushes out and then stands to her full height, which is just shy of my six foot three. I look down to those heeled boots and back up to the mess of russet hair on top of her head and that purple fucking pen holding it in place. Her eyes flick between my mouth and my eyes. I feel myself lean closer. Her eyes leave mine and go wide at what she sees behind me. I go to look, but she grips my face in both her hands and, with a frantic look in her eyes, screams—please.

"I need you," she whispers. That is not helping the situation happening down south.

"Ivy—" I start, I don't want to tell her this can't happen because it can, and I want it to. Just not here in her office with the door open and someone walking down the hall. I can literally hear their voices. "You are so beautiful, and it's not that I don't want—" she cuts me off with a hand over my mouth, and her eyes roll so far back in her head I can see the full whites of them. *Never mind, I'm into this. It can happen here and now.*

"Oh my god, Lover Boy. Not now." Her voice is a harsh whisper that I wouldn't mind hearing in a different position. "I need your help." I am...confused. It must show. "Alder, I need your help. Please just go along with it." The *please* has my eyebrows hitting the ceiling. I nod. I will go to war for this woman. Please is not necessary.

"Ivy?" I hear an unfamiliar voice from the hall. Ivy releases her hands from my face, uncovering my mouth, but instead of backing away, she wraps them behind my back, pulling me closer, all while retaining eye contact. She gives me a *little-help-here* look, and I return her embrace. As casually as I can, considering I've never hugged her. She smiles. It's—*sweet?* I don't know how I feel about it. Then she turns us so we can see the doorway just in time for a man in a navy suit to step into view. She takes a breath and then greets him like she knows him. I don't like it.

"Noah? What on earth are you doing here?"

IVY

I'm pressed against Alder's side smiling so wide my cheeks will be sore if I keep this up. God, please don't let this end in disaster.

"Hey, Red," he greets me with that familiar nickname that makes my stomach turn sour. Turning his attention to Alder, he assesses him. There's no question that he's intimidated. His eyes flick back to meet mine, and I'm just sending up prayer after prayer that my smile hasn't turned manic. I try my best to soften my face. Alder gives me a small squeeze with the arm wrapped around my back. Right. I have given him nothing. No explanation.

I look up to see Alder wearing an easy smile. It looks so natural. Like I'm in his arms all the time. That thought is stopped in its tracks when Noah clears his throat and speaks again.

"I, uh. I didn't know you would be here until we landed," he says. *We? No.* Coming into view now is her. *Margo.* I feel light-headed, but I also haven't eaten, and I was getting ready to check my blood sugar when Alder came into my office and scared the shit out of me. I clear my throat. I don't know what to say or if I can respond. My vision is starting to feel a little fuzzy on the edges, and if I faint right now, I don't know if I can bear to come to, with my ex-husband, his new fiancée and woman I despise, along with Alder standing over me. My skin feels clammy, and I fidget. "I know this isn't exactly ideal. When I heard your father acquired a ski lodge, I never would have thought you would be here. You hate the snow and..." he continues to speak, but all I can hear is rushing in my ears. *Please no.*

I'm jostled slightly by Alder moving to reach behind me. I hear glass clinking and then smell oranges.

"Do you want one?" Alder asks me casually, holding out one of my candied orange peels. He pops one into his mouth, and I nod. He grabs two from the container and offers them to me. I pop them into my mouth and chew. He pulls me to him and leans me back into my desk, letting me use it to keep steady. "Why would it be a problem that Ivy is here?" Alder addresses Noah. "I'm Alder, by the way." He steps toward him with his hand extended.

"Noah James," he says his name like it holds weight. He will always be in his father's shadow. Try as he might to step out of it. "It's not a problem for me that Ivy is here; it's just that I know the divorce was hard on her, and I don't want to open any old wounds." Well. That has my vision clearing, only now it's tinted in a violent shade of red. That mother fucker thinks it's *him* that I was upset about. I'm not sure why I would expect anything less. It's Noah we're talking about here. I believe

Carly Simon wrote a song about him. I open my mouth to correct him, but Alder responds before I can.

"Ohh... the ex-husband. Is he your son? Or nephew, maybe? I know it's hard when family gets involved." His words are polite, but they hit their mark perfectly. Noah is only forty-three, but the premature balding spot at the top of his head tells a different story. I choke on air. On words that I haven't yet said. I cough, trying to hide the hysterical laughter that threatens to bubble over. "That could be awkward, but I can assure you that we will do everything in our power to make sure you and your family's stay with us is pleasant," he finishes. I stay silent for a moment longer. Noah is fuming.

I try to de-escalate the situation. "Um, Noah *is* my ex-husband," I tell Alder, and his eyebrows shoot up before he can stop them.

"Oh, sorry. I read that all wrong," he tells Noah. My ex's face is turning red as he fights to control his expression.

"Not at all," he says to Alder, then asks him, "And how is it you know Ivy so well?" Alder doesn't look the least bit flustered and is ready with a reply, but I choose this moment to spring my half-hitched plan on him.

"Alder is my boyfriend," I blurt. To his credit, Alder shuts his mouth quickly and just smiles. Noah is less than convinced.

"Your boyfriend?" he asks, surprised, pressing me for more information.

"Mmhmm," I hum. I'm winging it so hard I may take flight. Really playing at the angle of less being more right now.

"Yep," Alder confirms. "Meeting her really knocked me on my ass." He sends me a wink, and I giggle. I am going to owe him so big for this. I'm a little nervous about what he'll ask for. I might also be excited. Alder, in a word, is exciting.

"Right," Noah replies. "Well, I just wanted to give you the courtesy of hearing it from me that Margo and I will be here through the new year," he says, pulling the small, petite blonde woman close to him. Through the new year? That's at least three weeks.

"Three weeks?" I question, not even attempting to hide the outrage in my voice. He never so much as took a weekend off the five years we were married. That hurts. Not because I loved him or because I wanted to spend more time with him...well, that's not really true. I wanted our marriage to work at first. I tried. I wanted it to mean something after the way it happened. He was trapped, and so was I. I guess I just thought that we may be able to find some common ground. Possibly find a friendship. For all my efforts, all I got were weeks without speaking and nights alone in his big house that was as hollow as me.

"Margo wanted to celebrate our engagement with a trip. She's very fond of winter and all things holiday," he says, chuckling like he wasn't an absent and emotionally abusive asshole when we were together. She looks completely uninterested in this whole interaction.

"Well, whatever Margo wants, she should get," I bite out. I need to be away from here. No, I need him away from here. The raging sea inside is so close to spilling over, and I'm afraid I may physically be sick or physically attack the man in front of me. Alder presses closer to my side, and Noah sighs.

"Ivy, I hoped we could move past this. Our families are always going to be tied together, and I do hope you can move on." His words are as cold as him. I think knowing he never cared about me isn't the worst part. It's knowing that he wouldn't have cared for our child—had I been able to carry him to term. My loss that I mourned while he fucked the woman standing beside him, the French, *would-be* nanny we chose together. *Fuck.* I blink rapidly. My heart rate is increasing, and the orange peels weren't nearly enough to bring my blood sugar up to normal. I'm going to crash. Alder tightens his grip on me.

"I'm sure you'll have a lovely stay celebrating your engagement. Let us know if you need anything, but I'm absolutely certain you won't be needing anything from Ivy." He almost threatens. "The chalet should be ready, and if you need help with bags or directions, Jack should be at the front desk," Alder tells Noah, dismissing him. "We'll see you around the resort, Noah." He smiles that casual, unaffected smile, and it helps me remember I should try and smile as well.

"Have a nice stay," I say weakly.

"Thank you," he replies, holding an arm out to let Margot go first, then they walk back down the hall and out of view. My shoulders sag, and the dizziness is in full effect. I feel arms band behind my back and my knees, and the sudden lightness tells me I'm being lifted. My eyes fly open to see the landscape outside tilt sideways. I'm cradled for only a moment before I feel myself softly lowered into a chair.

"What do you need, Ivy?" Alder asks me. Concern is marring his words, and I feel fatigue start to claim me.

"I need something...to drink. Something with sugar," I say weakly. Drinking something fixes the issue quicker. Staying on top of my glucose level is best, but here we are. I hear him leave. His soft footfalls against the wooden floor. I tip my head back against the chair. This feeling is like a punch to the gut. Being helpless is a fear I still fight to master. I have variations of it in the form of nightmares from time to time. Sometimes I'm screaming, but no one can hear me. Other times, I'm in a room, and there's a door but no handle. I shiver, pushing the memories back down. I'm contemplating how I can be better at keeping track of my sugars when I feel his presence.

"Here," he says. He moves to reach behind my neck, presumably to tilt my head up, but absolutely not.

"I've got it," I tell him, sitting up and seeing what he's brought me. It's a can of cherry cola. He can't possibly know this, but cherry cola is my favorite. I will never tell him. He cracks the tab and hands it to me to take a sip. I take two big gulps and set the can on my desk. He stands there, arms crossed, but not in a *Lucy, you got some 'splainin' to do* way. It's more intense. Watchful. He's studying me. My body and movements.

After a long moment, he speaks. "Does this happen to you often?" he asks.

"Not really," I tell him. It has happened. What definition of *often* are we working with here?

"Take another drink," he advises. I glare. It's weak, but I manage. He chuckles.

"Come on, Stormcloud. You need to take another drink." This time, he sounds more suggestive. I'm open to suggestions. I pick up the can and take another long drink.

I swallow audibly. "I'm fine. Or I will be," I tell him, hoping I sound more grounded. He shakes his head.

"I didn't doubt it," he quips, and I think he means it. There's no sarcasm there that I can detect. "Hypoglycemia?" he asks.

I nod with my answer. "Yes. I've been handling it for a few years now. I'm typically better about checking my levels, but someone,"—I look at him pointedly—"I don't want to name names or anything, made a surprise trip to my office, nearly scaring me to death before I could," I tell him as sweetly as I can. He grins.

"Was that before or after the surprise ex-husband showed up?" he inquires, thoughtfully. *Oh. Yes...that.* I take another drink of the soda and set it down, running my finger up and down the side of the sweating can.

"Noah, my ex-husband that I haven't felt the need to discuss or bring up because you barely know me—" I'm cut off by Alder's deep voice.

"Ivy," he says my name in a way that makes me want to be her. Whoever the Ivy is he's speaking to, he holds in reverence. I think I would like to be her. "You do not have to explain anything about your past to me. Nothing that you don't want to anyway," he tells me, eyes boring into my own.

"I appreciate that, Alder. Really. You have been, so much kinder to me than I had any right to expect, and I know you mean what you're saying. So, that makes what I'm about to ask you to do a little more complicated." As I'm speaking, his head tilts in confusion. Something I've noticed he does when he's trying to understand something. It's endearing. "Noah and Margot," I choke her name out, "will be here for three weeks, and that is extremely distressing to me on a few levels. Not only was I married to him way too young, but also..." I shut my eyes against the vulnerable feelings this stirs up. "I was pregnant when we got married, and Margot was the nanny he and I decided on hiring before I..." I clear my throat and reinforce the wall I built a long time ago. "I lost the baby," I finish. He places his hand over mine and squeezes it.

"That motherfucker. Say the word, Ivy. Say it, and he's gone," he assures me. I snort.

"Are you going to tell me that you know a guy?" I ask. When an expression I can't quite pin down crosses his face, I continue my little confession. "So, when he came here today with her. I think I kind of lost my mind for a minute. I completely understand if you're not up for it, but I need you to do me a favor over the next few weeks." I swallow. I don't ask people for things.

Asking Alder for anything under better circumstances would have been enough to make me want to scream into the void, but now? After I've been so cold. It makes my skin itch. "If you're willing," I tack on, trying to sound like I don't need him. I hate *needing*. I get along fine on my own and have for as long as I can remember.

"What do you need, Ivy?" The way he asks it. I feel the armor I wear go transparent. He's seeing into me. Asking on a deeper level. It scares me that, on an introspective level—I haven't a clue. I don't know what I need anymore. What I should want. I shake myself, and my defenses settle back into place. Instead of thinking too long about the depths of depravity that is my wants and needs.

"I need you to keep up the charade I've placed you in for the next few weeks. I'll try to keep my interactions to a minimum, but just in case," I say.

"So..." he says, leaning down as he places his hands on either side of my chair's armrests. His sudden closeness has my breath coming a little faster. Then he looks up at me through the dirty-blond hair that's fallen over his brows. Hair I want to slide both my hands into and pull at the roots until his mouth falls open, and oh, that mouth... "You want me to what? Be your boyfriend? Is that what you're telling me, princess?" he asks me this, and internally, the sultry little vixen in me nods so furiously she's making herself dizzy. I flick her nose before I respond.

"*Fake* boyfriend. Yes," I answer as calmly as I can. I know my cheeks are flushed, but I'm praying he chalks that up to my low blood sugar spell. "Can you do that?" I ask him. Why did I do this? I'm not a teenager trying to make a boy jealous. I shake my head. "You know what, never mind. This was a horrendous idea. One of my worst, and that's saying something," I backpedal.

"I'll do it." I meet those icy blues. God how does he manage that earnest look of his? "Under one condition," he states. There's the catch. Men. I'm not sure why I'm surprised. They all want something. What does Alder want?

"So there are conditions?" I ask. "What is it you require from me then, Lover Boy? It better not be anything too nasty. I may not be into it." He doesn't need to know any of the things I am into.

He chuckles and drops his head, removing his cage on me as he stands to his full height. Which has to be at least six foot three. He was still a head taller than me in my heels today. "I think we both know I have a little bit of an idea of what you're into," he teases. I'm a tomato. "Let me teach you to snowboard," he says. Huh?

"You want to teach me how to snowboard? In return for helping me with my dilemma?" I question, standing from my seat. "What's in it for you?" I ask. Surely there's more to it than this.

"I get to spend more time with you." He smirks. "One on one." He steps into my space and lifts his hand to my hair, pulling my purple pen from it, letting it spill over my shoulders. The weight of it hitting my back sends shivers down my arms. "I've wanted to do that since I saw you today," he whispers, and I'm not sure whether he's aware he said it out loud or not. Then he tucks a piece of my hair behind my ear. "Deal?" His breath hits my face. It smells faintly of my candied oranges.

"Deal," I confirm. Fate sealed.

Ivy

Noah showing up with Margot to spend the holidays in the exact town I've been banished to wasn't on my bingo card this year. Honestly, neither was he proposing to her. Or crashing that boat. It was only in the harbor, and it's not like I sunk it or anything. And then there was the man in Spain who thought I said I knew how to work on his fishing boat. To be fair to Arnesto, I had said that, but only because I wanted to go out on a boat. That was a wild excursion.

After today, we can also add asking a man I barely know to be my fake boyfriend and then unloading my past trauma onto him. Come to think of it, a lot of shit that's happened this year wasn't on there, but here we are. Fucking bingo!

My saving grace is Alder. The way he stepped in to help. He's more observant than I'd given him credit for. I guess you would have to be when you're in his line of work. I chuckle, sinking deeper into my claw foot tub, thinking about his jab at Noah's appearance. *"Was he your nephew or son?"* Alder would have no way of knowing how insecure Noah is about his looks. He isn't *not* handsome, but I guess knowing him on a level deeper than...surface has changed how I see him over the years.

He was actually very handsome when we were younger. Dark, thick hair and lashes to match. I was nineteen, freshly out of my first year of college, and looking to piss off my father. He was thirty-two and infatuated with me. Neither of us ever planned for it to go any further than the summer. I think I could have forgiven him for the way he treated me in our marriage because it was never meant to be anything more. I could have forgiven him, but forgiveness isn't on the table anymore. Not after how he treated my loss.

I take a long sip of my club soda, and then place it on the small wooden stool I pulled over beside me. I need to get out of the water and get some sleep. Having my ex-husband here for the next couple of weeks will make life hard. Pretending Alder and I are together will be harder. As attractive as I find him, I'm uninterested in spending time with anyone seriously these days. I have one goal and one goal only. Get back to California.

Standing, I reach for my towel and wrap it around myself before stepping onto the bathmat. I grab my glass of water and make my way into my bedroom. When I check my phone, there are three missed calls and eight text messages. I'm sure most of the texts are from Sienna, so I toss it back onto the bed and get into my pajamas. Tonight's set have little Christmas trees and red bows on them. I curl up in my bed and reach for my book. The same book I've been meaning to read for the last three weeks but haven't found the time, and now that I do, I don't feel like reading. One of the worst feelings in the world is wanting to read and not wanting to read anything.

I decide to check my phone again and open my messages. It turns out six texts are from Sienna, a text and two calls are from my father, and one is from an unknown number. I glance at the one from my father.

SULLIVAN

Noah will be staying at the resort. Be professional.

I snort at that. Thanks for the heads up, asshole. The last text is the one I focus on, though, one that has me reluctantly smiling. Five words that have my heart pounding a little faster. One nickname that has butterflies erupting in my belly.

UNKNOWN NUMBER

Be ready at 7, princess.

IVY

How did you get my number?

I giggle and add his details to my contacts before tossing my phone on the bed beside me. I reach for my book, but it vibrates almost instantly, so I scramble for it in the blankets and open his message. Then I take a breath, trying to settle the butterflies erupting inside me. Calm down, Ivy. He's just a man. I remind myself, not fully believing that, but deny, deny, deny is my go-to.

LOVER BOY

I would tell you but...

IVY

Then you'd have to kill me?

LOVER BOY

Whoa, whoa, whoa. Easy, Stormcloud. That's so dark. No. Then I'd have to kiss you. Yikes. Have you been watching true crime at night?

I laugh out loud; alone in my bed. *Stormcloud.* Why do I like that so much?

IVY

Maybe. It's relaxing. So…how did you get my number?

LOVER BOY

You don't remember? I got it from you. The night I wrote the note for the tow truck.

LOVER BOY

Relaxing? Ivy, we can do better than that.

IVY

You remembered my number?

I choose not to ask what other ways he thinks I could be relaxing. I may like his answer too much. That seems to be the theme with him. He lets it go, but I snort at his response.

LOVER BOY

I have a photographic memory.

IVY

Liar.

LOVER BOY

It's true, at least it is for things I care to remember. It isn't just reserved for phone numbers either. I spent a night with a redhead a few weeks ago, and this may be more information than you care to know—but I don't think I could forget a moment of that night even if I tried.

My cheeks heat with a blush. Thankful no one is around to see it; I sink deeper into my bed.

IVY

Lucky you.

LOVER BOY

You have no idea.

I have *some* idea.

IVY

Now what am I supposed to be ready for at 7 a.m.?

LOVER BOY

Our first lesson.

IVY

Already?

LOVER BOY

I wouldn't joke about your education.

IVY

LOVER BOY

Tomorrow's going to be fun. Get some sleep, princess.

IVY

I don't remember saying I was available.

LOVER BOY

You are. I confirmed it with Jack.

Ladies and gentlemen, Alder Holloway—a man with a plan.

IVY

Fine.

LOVER BOY

Night, Ivy. Sweet dreams.

That *sweet dreams* is where our conversation and my racing thoughts end. I'm asleep in minutes. Haunted by tempting dimples and sapphire eyes that go along with his sarcasm I'm beginning to crave.

Looking out the window from my kitchen, I see that the snow has stopped again. It's six forty-five in the morning, and I'm drinking coffee in my purple ski suit. The suit seemed appropriate for today. I want to make sure I stay warm, and I also want plenty of layers between me and Alder. The more, the better actually. I don't know why, but every time he touches me, it feels like I've stuck a fork in an electrical outlet. It's not the worst feeling I've ever experienced, in fact, I'm beginning to look forward to it, but I do recognize it's probably bad for my health.

I take a sip from my mug and sink back into the cozy couch. I haven't had much time to think about our little arrangement. Now that I am, I think I must have looked like an absolute lunatic. Asking someone, a grown man, a grown man like Alder, to be my fake boyfriend. And he said yes. What does that say about him? Maybe that we shouldn't be doing this, and especially with each other.

Knocking at the door startles me, and I almost spill the drink I'm clinging to tighter than I realized. Am I nervous? I don't get nervous over men. I stand and walk my cup to the sink, taking one last long drink before dumping it and answering the door. When I open it, I'm treated to a sight not safe for a friendly snowboarding lesson. Alder Holloway is wearing a slutty crop top with a flannel over it and ski pants. Holy shit. That's a visual I'll be revisiting.

"Good morning," his deep voice rumbles out.

"Good morning," I greet him, and mine is still thick with sleep.

"Ready to go?"

I nod. "As ready as I'll ever be," I say on a sigh. Grabbing my bag and phone I step out into the dark morning—then immediately slip on the porch. Alder grabs my elbow, steadying me but also sending sparks skittering up my arm.

"Careful, there's some ice out here this morning," he tells me gently, still holding my arm in his large hand. I stand up a little straighter and pull my arm back as politely as I can, willing away the heat that a touch from him evokes in me.

"Thank you. I'll be sure to keep an eye out," I tell him, looking down to watch where I'm stepping. When I get to his truck, he opens the door for me and makes sure I'm seated before shutting it. He rounds the front of the Bronco and gets in, rubbing his hands together to warm them.

"So, where are we going this morning?" I ask him.

"We're heading to a favorite spot of mine this morning. It's great for beginners and has one of the best views in Silverthorne. It's called Lovers Leap," he answers with a grin.

"Lovers Leap, huh? Fitting for you, Lover Boy."

He smirks and lets out a snort. "It has a great lore. Would you like to hear it?" I can tell he wants to tell me this story.

"How long is the drive?" I ask.

"About thirty-five minutes."

"Sure, why not? What else have I got to do?"

"Well, don't sound so excited about it," he teases.

I clear my throat and then slip into my best Southern-belle accent. "Oh, Alder! Please tell me the story of Lovers Leap! I simply can't stand to wait another minute!" I exclaim, and he laughs loudly. I want to be inside that sound.

"I reckon I better get on with it then. I wouldn't want to make a lady wait," he says back in a lazy cowboy's drawl. I giggle. *Again, with the giggling?* I cover my mouth and then wait for the story. He starts to speak, and within the first sentence, I'm completely enraptured.

"This is the legend of Sampson and Nira. There was once a man and a woman who were so deeply in love that it's said the gods and all their angels were jealous of it. The fates conspired against them, doing everything they could to keep them apart. Nira's family forbade her from seeing Sampson, telling her that he wasn't to be trusted. His family was not to be trusted. They snuck out night after night to be with each other. Their love affair was documented only through the carvings they left in a nearby cave. Sampson was ready to leave his family and run away with Nira, so they set a plan into motion. Nira would go to their meeting place early in the day and wait for Sampson. He was supposed to meet her in the afternoon, and they were going to leave their town and find a new place where they could be together. Only the gods refused to let this slide. They sent a snowstorm after the lovers met that evening. The storm was strong, but they were able to wait it out in the cave. The next day, both families came for them, and they were going to force the young couple apart, so they decided they would take their fate into their own hands rather than be forced to live apart. They jumped. Hand in hand off the ridge. When they found their bodies at the bottom of the cliff, they were still holding onto one another, and that's where the name of the ridge comes from."

"Lovers Leap," I whisper.

"Lovers Leap," he confirms.

"How tragically romantic. It makes me wonder why anyone decided they wanted to fall in love when most of the greatest love stories also end in the greatest tragedies."

"Do you think falling in love is a choice?" he muses. "It would seem to me that even if it was a choice, anyone who's ever felt so deeply for someone else would still make the choice to be in love." He's staring out the front windshield.

"Yes, well. Most people are idiots," I tell him, and he tosses his head back with a laugh.

"Jaded," he accuses, his laugh still coloring his voice. He's not wrong. "If you don't mind me asking, what exactly happened back in California that brought you to Silverthorne?"

"I do mind, but honestly, it's more than I want to get into at..." I check my phone. "Seven thirty-five a.m., and I've only had one cup of coffee." I smirk and he reaches behind us into the backseat to pull out a thermos.

"Here. You can have some of mine. Your life story is not required," he teases me. The thing is, I never want to share my past, what happened in that marriage, but with Alder, I find myself wanting to share more with him than I should. There's something about him that puts me at ease. I feel safe, and that thought alone makes me nervous.

We come to a stop, and I look around. The sun is starting to lighten the snow around us. "Alright, we're here. Are you ready for your first lesson, princess?" he asks, and I nod.

"Well, I guess I have to be." I open the truck door and hop out.

"Before we get started, I want to show you something," he tells me and puts his hand on the small of my back, gently nudging me forward. After about thirty feet, I open my mouth to ask, "*Are we there yet?*" like a bratty teenager when I'm stunned silent.

The view that I'm beholding is one I've never thought I would see in real life or even believed was real. The sunlight is streaking the mountains in the most beautiful, brilliant gold I've ever seen. It looks like a painting. Like an award-winning photograph that someone spent their life getting just right.

"It's stunning," I rasp.

"It is," he agrees. I don't take my eyes off the view, knowing that it won't look like this for long, but I still snipe at him.

"You better not be looking at me, action hero." He chuckles.

"And if I was?" he challenges.

"I would roll my eyes, but I don't want to miss this," I tell him, watching the sun rapidly rise now. I can feel it on my face, and the snow looks like it contains thousands of specs of glitter. I smile. "Thank you for bringing me here."

"Anytime. Have you eaten this morning?" I hear him ask from somewhere behind me. I glance back and see him bending over in the snow, looking through a backpack.

"Uh, no. Just the coffee," I admit.

"Here." He pulls out a power bar and tosses it to me. It hits me in the chest even after my attempt to catch it, and I'm thankful he didn't see that. Not that I care all that much what he thinks of me, but shit, I guess I do. This whole day will probably be one that puts all my insecurities on display. *Why did I agree to this again?* Oh, yes, because he is pretending to be my boyfriend while my ex-husband galivants around the resort with his new fiancée. The turns my life has taken. I unwrap the protein bar and take a bite.

"You know, this isn't the worst one of these I've ever tasted. Most remind me of sweet, gritty cardboard." I tell him, holding up the bar, and he looks at me smiling.

"I order these specifically for that reason. That and they have twenty grams of protein. That will get you through the lesson until you can get a decent meal in you," he tells me.

"Thanks, Dad." I mutter, and he laughs.

"You got it, pumpkin," he croons sweetly, then I'm laughing with him.

"Oh my gosh, stop. Let's get this lesson started. What do I need to do?" I ask with my hands on my hips. I have been on a snowboard exactly one time, and it wasn't exactly for me, but I have to say...my instructor was nowhere near as interesting as Alder.

"We'll start slow. I just want you to get a feel for the board. Come here," he orders me. I wish I could say that I didn't like him ordering me around.

"Can I touch you?" he asks with his hands extended toward my legs.

"Yes," I say, entirely too fast. He smirks but says nothing about it. He just grips my calf and slides my foot into one of the bindings on the snowboard. He clicks it into place and asks me to stand on it. Once I'm locked in, he has me do a couple of squats while holding onto my hands.

"Okay, now I want you to treat the board like a skateboard and skate around for a minute," he says.

"Mmhmm. And what makes you think I know how to do that?" I question, and he grins.

"Have you ever seen someone on one? Hold on." He runs back to his truck and grabs his own board, attaches one foot, and skates over to me. Propelling his front foot on the board forward while kind of scootering his back foot.

"Okay, so like a scooter?" I ask.

"How many times in your life have you been on a scooter, and do you have photos?" he quips, and I shove at his chest, almost tripping over the board I forgot I was strapped into. "Now you try," he urges, and I do. I skate in a straight line.

"Good," he comments, and I roll my eyes. "Now, I want you to get comfortable with getting up in case you fall down. Sit back," he instructs, and I do until my ass hits the snow. He skates over and bends down to strap in my other foot.

"Okay, so first, I want you to reach forward and grab the board between your legs with one hand, and with the other, you're going to push off the ground." I do as he says, and my body pops upright. "That's great. Give me a couple more of those." I lay back into the snow a couple more times and rise to standing. "Okay, now we'll practice from our stomachs. I want you to lay back and then grip the board with either hand and pull it with you while you roll onto your belly," he informs me. Okay. I do, and it takes more effort than I thought it would. Now I'm face down in the snow.

"Now what?" I ask him, a bit muffled and out of breath. Just a little embarrassing. I'm not exactly the picture of health. I'm slim-ish, but I owe that mostly to genetics and mental health walks. I don't lift weights, and I don't skip dessert. "Alder?" I call when he hasn't given any further instructions.

He clears his throat, but his voice still sounds a little hoarse when he answers me. "Yeah, princess. I'm here," he assures me, and I hear him skate around until he's right in front of me. "I have to tell you, though, you, in this position, is a little distracting," he admits, and I flush scarlet. I think the snow under my face may start melting. Remembering that first night in town, I can see why this might jog loose a memory.

"Well, could you please focus? It's cold," I snap at him.

"Alright, on your knees, Ivy," he commands quietly.

My eyes go wide. "What?" I ask, not sure if I heard him correctly.

"You need to slide up onto your knees so you can stand," he tells me. *Oh.* "What did you think I meant, princess? Was there something else on your mind?" I want to smash his perfect dimpled smile into the snow.

"If I was, it's because you put the thought there on purpose," I blurt.

"Ah, so it's my fault. I'm the reason you can't help but objectify me? Victim blaming is not nice, Ivy," he taunts.

"I'm not nice," I state, and he cocks his head to the side.

"I would have to disagree with you, but I don't have time to argue today. We have a lot to get through before the mountain is covered with people, so up you go," he says while grabbing my shoulders and lifting me like I'm nothing. I'm not all about being dainty and petite, but damn, there's something about being made to feel delicate that gets me going. There's a lot about Alder that gets me going. This is going to be a long morning.

After a few more hours of going over the basics, I successfully made it down a bunny hill by myself—with Alder. He didn't have to help me up once though. Unlike the three times before. It hasn't been an overabundance of touching, just enough to keep my blood at a simmer and my cheeks perpetually flushed.

"Okay, I think I have one more run in me," I say.

"Hell yeah, you do," Alder encourages me. "I think she's getting a real taste for this," he comments, and I turn my head so he can't see the smile I'm fighting. "I don't mean to brag, but damn, I am such a good teacher," he boasts, shaking his head like not even he can believe how good he is.

"Oh my god, you are insufferable," I moan, making my way back up the hill. Actually, Alder is the most not-insufferable man I think I've ever met, but his ego doesn't need that boost— and I don't mean that in a *it's already so big* way. He doesn't need his ego stroked because he's extremely self-assured. It's annoyingly sexy.

"Keep telling yourself that, Stormcloud," he tuts, sliding by me, so I'm now following him up. Once I reach the top, I find him waiting for me.

"I'll follow you. Lead the way," he instructs. I nod, determined.

"Sure," I agree and start down the hill. I'm really doing it. A smile breaks over my face, and I feel like I'm flying. I'm picking up more speed than I have before, but along with the speed, my confidence is growing as well. Until I get my body too far forward and the nose digs into the snow a bit too much, sending me forward until I narrowly miss face-planting, but throwing myself backward was a severe overcorrection. I hit the ground with a small thud and slide on my back a few feet. Alder's at my side in seconds.

"Ivy? *Shit.* Are you okay?" His concern is evident. At this, I smile and then replay the fall in my head. A surprised laugh escapes me at the image I've conjured. A loud laugh. Completely uninhibited. I'm laughing in earnest when I feel his body flop on the ground next to mine. I have tears running down my face, and my goggles are starting to fog up, so I slide them up onto my head.

"You were really moving there for a minute," Alder says from beside me. I turn my head to look at him and find his eyes fixed on me. "Are you sure you aren't hurt?" he asks.

"My pride took the biggest hit there. My body may be sore, but I'll make it, hotshot," I say, unable to keep the smile from my face. This is fun. Maybe the most real fun I've had in years. He laughs with me. Not at me. It sends warm fuzzies from the top of my head to my toes. "You're supposed to tell me it wasn't that bad," I chide.

"I'm not a liar, Ivy." He smiles, and then it falters for only a moment before he speaks again. "This is going to be a really great story for the grandchildren one day." He sighs like he's imagining it.

"Grandchildren?" I almost yell. "Who said anything about kids? You're my *fake* boyfriend, Alder. You'd at least have to be my fake fiancé before I was ready for that," I tease.

"Who said I was talking about our grandchildren, Ms. Rutherford?" He tsks at me, and I roll my eyes. "You've given yourself away again. You are so into me." He flashes me a self-satisfied grin.

"Keep dreaming, Search and Rescue," I mutter.

"You couldn't stop me if you tried," he says with a wink.

I turn my head from him again and think about that for a minute. I wouldn't stop him.

Ivy

It's Saturday and just over a week until Christmas. I'm walking downtown Silverthorne, and it feels like I've been transported into a Hallmark movie. One of the many that starts with a failing bed and breakfast owned by the sweetest woman in town's family and ends with the big shot CEO from New York swooping in to save it and her from a life without love. I may have seen that one actually. The twinkle lights over the street and the Christmas trees on every corner have a smile curling my lips without permission.

It smells like citrus and spices. A memory pulls at the corner of my brain, but I bat it away. It's better I don't let it linger. I look to the center of the town square and see the big tree. It has to be at least twenty-five-foot tall. It's adorned simply but beautifully. Mix-matched red and gold ornaments are paired with velvet bows. I'm assuming it's not lit yet because this is a tree-lighting ceremony. I've never been to a community event. Holiday parties and galas, yes. But there's no trace of personal touches at those kinds of things.

It's stuffy suits and gorgeous gowns. Too much champagne and entitled men. Unhappy wives and husbands who don't care. I've been that unhappy wife, drinking too much champagne in a gorgeous gown. They're not memories I like to relive. Noah had to be at one every weekend in December. Which meant, for five years, so did I. That's roughly twenty-five evenings that I cried myself to sleep, hoping that in the morning, I would figure out a way to leave. I shiver, and it has nothing to do with the chilly early December night.

"Are you cold, princess?" *Alder*. His teasing gets under my skin. After our snowboarding lesson, I've warmed a little more toward him. If I'm being honest, I feel a little too warm when I'm around him. I turn to glare at him, but I come up short when I see a little girl in his arms. She's laying her head against his shoulder, and her tiny fists are wrapped around a tiny to-go coffee cup. It's one of the cutest things I've ever seen. She is adorable. Wait. He has a kid? No, he definitely would have mentioned that. I smile at the little girl.

"No. I'm fine," I tell Alder then speak to the child in his arms. "Hi," I say as gently as I can. For some unknown reason I want her to like me. She smiles, and I see a familiar dimple. So she is his.

"Hi," she greets me with a little wave, almost dropping her tiny cup. Alder rights it easily. I melt.

"Ivy, this is Hazel. Hazey, this is Ivy. She works with me," he introduces us.

"It's nice to meet you, Hazel. What a lovely name," I tell her, and the small grin grows. Alder snuggles her closer and kisses her head, making eye contact before speaking to her.

"Let's get you back to your daddy before he has an aneurysm. Okay, Hazey baby?"

"Okay, Muncle Aldie!" She lights up and slaps a tiny hand on each side of his scruffy face, tiny cup forgotten. Muncle Aldie? So he's her uncle. And looks to be a good one. That's… not something I want to find attractive. But I do. I really do. I look at his face. He's chuckling when he leans in to rub his face into her neck and make growling noises. My throat goes tight.

Turning his head to me he asks, "You coming, Stormcloud?"

"Yeah." My voice is thick with emotion I'm trying to hide. I clear my throat before continuing, "Lead the way." I wave my arm. He gives me a funny look but walks down the sidewalk in the direction of Thistle and Sage, tickling Hazel's side every so often. I'm giggling right along with her by the time we make it to the entrance. I'm getting the feeling that it's hard to resist Muncle Aldie.

As soon as we clear the door and hear the bell chime, a stern voice has my head turning.

"Alder, you said five minutes. It's been twenty." The man with the authoritative voice is sitting at a table with Rhett but stands when we come in. Oh my. Tall, dark, and handsome personified. What gene pool lottery did this family win?

"Hazey wanted to get a better look at the tree after we got her some delicious, citrusy wassail, and how am I supposed to keep being the favorite uncle if I don't do everything she wants me to?" Alder asks, and I snort. Then smooth my face when everyone turns to look at me. I want the ground to swallow me whole. My face flames, and Alder's sporting an absolutely winning grin. *Damn it*. I'm saved by a woman with a kind voice and graying hair coming over to take Hazel from Alder.

"Hi, baby girl. Let's get you a treat to go with your drink," she whispers conspiratorially. Then sends me a wink. "Hello, I'm Mary, Alder's mom. It's lovely to meet you," she tells me.

"Hello, it's nice to meet you as well. I'm Ivy," I tell her, and I mean it. I'm *happy* to meet her.

"Mom, the last thing she needs is more sugar. Rhett let her eat half of his cinnamon roll earlier." He cuts a look to his brother, and Rhett doesn't look the least bit chastised.

"She wanted some. I'm not above fighting dirty," he says, like it's an obvious answer. I am enthralled by this very unique family dynamic. Well, new to me. Foreign, actually.

"Knox, I raised four children, and you've all grown up to be decent humans, didn't you?" she asks pointedly.

"Yes, ma'am," he replies.

"Well then, I think a little treat on a special occasion will be alright. Don't you?" she asks him again in a sweet voice that makes me straighten my back slightly.

"Yes, ma'am," he answers again. I smile because I already really like Mary.

"And Alder? Rhett?" She eyes them both. "Check with your brother every now and then when spoiling your niece."

"Yes, ma'am," they say in unison. I am thoroughly enjoying this.

"I have some orange cranberry scones and cinnamon bread," Winnie calls from the swinging door she's backing through.

"Rhett..." Knox says with some warning in his voice. Weird. Then Rhett launches for Winnie just in time to catch one of the trays and steady her.

"Easy, darlin'. I got it."

"Thank you," she says sweetly, blushing. "I appreciate you heading off any potential clumsiness."

I look at Alder and find him smiling at them. I don't think this evening is going to be good for my plan to stay in control of the feelings bubbling up in me.

It's been two hours, and I have sampled four chili recipes, all A+, five ciders, also all A+, and I've had too many baked goods to feel healthy. I'm settling in to watch the tree light up. I broke off from the Holloway crew half an hour ago. I needed a little space and alone time. I laughed so hard my stomach hurt when Winnie's Uncle Buck told the story of Colt jumping off their shed roof with a sheet, thinking it would act as a parachute. I've laughed a lot tonight and smiled even more.

Now, when I'm alone again, I'm reminded of how devoid of love and humor my childhood was. I was alone in a house full of people. Nannies and house staff that cared for me, but not about me. No one will be telling stories of little Ivy. I scoff. How pathetic. Sad. I detest being sad. I think that's why I've turned to things in the past that helped me not be so sad. Buying things, going on trips, sleeping with strangers. It's shallow and vapid, but it worked—for a while.

After Noah, I felt like I had so much life to catch up on. It's funny when people ask me about my loss. They assume it's Noah that I grieve. They don't know about the deeper wounds. I never truly loved my husband, and maybe that's a horrible thing to say, but I am an honest bitch. I didn't want to be Mrs. Noah James, though, ever. I did want to be a mom, and I did want stability for my child. The air is sucked from my lungs, and I feel like I've been punched in the gut. Blinding pain consumes me as I try to will myself to breathe.

"Ivy?" Oh god. Please no. Anyone but him. "Hey...it's alright. I need you to breathe, princess." His hands are on my shoulders, and he's smiling softly, small lines etching his forehead are the only sign of worry. I hate that he's being so nice to me. He takes my hand in his and places it over his broad chest. I can feel the steady thumping there. "Feel that?" he asks me quietly, turning his head to look down the street. "Now look over there," he instructs, and I turn my head, still fighting with my burning lungs. The tree is slowly starting to brighten with each strand of lights coming to life. "Let's count with them," he suggests. "One. Two." He looks back at me. "Come on, Ivy. I know you can do this. Three. Four." He moves his hand from my shoulder up to my cheek, swiping at the wetness leaving tracks on my face.

"F-f-f-ive," I croak, looking back at him. He grins. Wide enough to pop that dimple.

"That's so good, Ivy." His voice is like a balm that speaks directly to unhealed wounds. My breath catches on an inhale. My chest warms at his words. "Six," he says, looking at me expectantly.

"Sev-seven," I finish, and when I look to the side again, the tree is lit up, and it's beautiful—and I'm breathing.

"How'd you...do that?" I ask Alder, my voice raspier than normal.

"Had a lot of practice," he answers simply.

"You're full of surprises, huh? A doting uncle, a helicopter pilot, snowboarding extraordinaire, and a therapist? What else?

Do you headline at the local strip club?" I ask, and he tosses his head back with laughter that makes my bones rattle.

When his laughter settles, and my smile isn't forced, he asks in a low voice, "If I did, would you be paying for a private room?" My hand is still on his warm chest, covered by his larger one. I'm unwilling to pull it away yet.

"No," I answer thoughtfully, then can't help but tease, "I don't think I'd have to pay to see it." My voice is soft and husky. I'm thinking of Alder losing items of clothing and moving hips that I know hold power. I've seen him use them on and off his snowboard. *Okay, Ivy. Calm down.*

"You're making me sound easy, princess." He sounds hurt.

"No, not easy—just willing," I taunt. He smiles, blue eyes sparkling, brushing off the comment with ease. He's so secure in himself. It makes me a little weak in the knees. He doesn't mind when I bite. And now I'm picturing biting him. *Get a hold of yourself, Ivy.* I shake my head, and he sighs.

"Unfortunately, I have to shatter your fantasies of me dancing on a stage that you're shaking your head to get rid of. I left those days behind me a long time ago." Now it's my turn to laugh. Surprised, belly laughter. It sputters out of me, and I bring a hand to my mouth. "You find something funny about that?" he asks me, mock offense front and center.

"Not at all," I reply once I settle. I'm trying really hard not to think about this man in front of me shirtless. "So no moon-lighting. Got it," I confirm.

"Don't get too disappointed. I do snowboard shirtless for charity every year, and I'll make sure to put it on that calendar in your office." He winks. That wink does things to me. So does thinking about his shirtless, muscular torso on a snowboard.

"Snowboarding shirtless...for charity?" I wonder out loud,

still trying to shake the image of bare skin and pecs I never got the chance to lick. "That sounds like a crowd-pleaser. Maybe we could do an event like that at The Edgemont," I muse. I do still need one more thing to bring in some revenue.

"You wanna snowboard shirtless with me, Ivy?" he asks suggestively. I roll my eyes, but on the inside, I give myself whiplash with my quick nods.

"I'm thinking more of a black-tie affair. At the lodge," I tell him. They were never my thing, but they do bring in a lot of money, and I'm thinking a portion of it will go to a good cause as well.

"That's definitely not a no," he quips back.

"I guess it's not."

"Are you feeling better?" he asks, and I guess we're going to talk about that.

"I am. I'm embarrassed you saw me like that," I admit.

"I can think of five things off the top of my head that you've done since I've known you that are way more embarrassing. This? Doesn't even make it on that list." He says it so matter-of-factly that I can't help but believe him. He means it, and that hits me somewhere in my chest. Not quite in the heart, but in the vicinity.

"Ah, another list enters the chat," I tease. "Well, thank you. For helping me."

"Anytime," he states simply and nods. "Are you staying for the caroling?"

"Are you singing?" I ask back, and he smiles.

"I never plan on it, but Mary Holloway always finds a way to get us all singing by 'Oh Holy Night.'" He tells me.

"As much as I don't want to miss that. I'm feeling pretty

tired after...everything. I think I'd better get home for the night," I say.

"Are you okay to drive yourself?" His question should piss me off, but it doesn't. I saw how he responded to me earlier. I see now the genuine concern on his face. He truly cares about my well-being. I don't know if I've ever felt that before.

"I'll be fine. You snapped me back fairly quickly. I've recovered. Promise," I tell him honestly. I'm used to brushing off my panic attacks. Telling the people around me that I'm fine when I'm not. They don't ask because they care. They just want to feel justified in having asked. Like the asking alone is what makes you a good person. Alder isn't like that, and I'm not sure how to handle his natural kindness. His empathy.

"If you're sure," he says. It's a question but isn't.

"I am. Thank you. And please tell your family that I had a wonderful time with them tonight. It's been a while since I was surrounded by a big, happy family." Or forever. "You're very lucky to have them."

"I am," He agrees, no buts.

"I'll see you tomorrow at work," I murmur, backing up. We have that large group coming in and the private lesson at eleven," I say, needing to get back on track. Back to my plan. Back to only seeing him as a colleague.

"I'll be there." He nods, and I turn to walk to my SUV. I get two steps, and he calls my name. When I turn, he's got his hands in his coat pockets and a glint in his eye, but his face isn't giving anything away.

"I'm just down the road," he tells me, then swallows. "If you need anything." My blood heats at his words. I need not to feel flustered. I need to be in control.

"That's good to know, Alder. I don't think I'll be requiring any of your moonlighting services tonight, Lover Boy." I pray that I sound nonchalant, and he smirks at me, at the nickname I've given him. He's never afraid to go toe to toe. Something I'm finding is a kink of mine.

"Maybe tomorrow night then," he shoots back at me after I've turned away from him. I laugh loud enough for him to hear me, but in my head, I hear myself reply, *maybe*.

ALDER

It's four days until Christmas and four since the tree lighting. I have a list of things to accomplish, and at the top is to finish gift shopping and wrap the ones I already have. Thankfully, I have a few things already ordered for Hazel and Mom. We have a predicted two feet of snow on the way, so tonight may be the only option for leaving my house until Christmas day. I was already planning on this shopping trip when Knox called and asked if I could watch Hazel for him and then take her to Mom and Dad's, so now, it's date night with my favorite girl. I'm pulling on my boots when there's a knock on my door. I'm not expecting anyone, but that doesn't always stop any member of the Holloway family from coming over unannounced.

I lace my boots up, and as I'm walking from the couch to the front door, I catch a flash of purple in the window, and my heartbeat picks up. Is this a Pavlov situation? Because that's going to be really annoying. I open the door, and there on my front porch, looking like she's been conjured from my dreams, is Ivy Rutherford.

"Hi," she greets me. A small smile on her lips. "Sorry to just stop by." Looking me up and down, her cheeks are tinged pink, she asks, "Are you going somewhere?"

"I am," I tell her. If she wants to know, she'll have to ask.

"Okay, I'll be quick then. I'm sure you're busy. I am too. Busy. I have a lot to get done. Which is why I'm here." Her small ramble makes me unhealthily happy.

"Go on," I encourage. Her eyes are starting to smolder. She's wising up to my game. Play with me, princess.

"I'm hosting an event on New Year's Eve at The Edgemont," she says forcefully, like I might question her on it. "I'm hosting an event," she starts again. "It's a silent auction, and there will be live music and dancing." She rushes the information out. Like if she were to slow down, I might interrupt her. I wouldn't. I like listening to her. And I've been thinking about hosting an event at The Lodge for some time.

"That sounds like a great idea," I say. "Do you need my help with something?" I'm not an event planner, but I've organized town events before. I can also put you in touch with the town's event committee if you want and see if they would be interested in co-hosting. Cross marketing. That sort of thing." Her face changes from one of a soldier ready for battle to a softer look of confusion as I offer to help. She should know by now that I like helping her.

She takes a big breath in through her nose before speaking. "That would be great actually. Thank you." I can tell by the reluctant thank you that she doesn't like saying it and definitely doesn't give them out often.

"Of course. Anything else?" I don't mean for it to sound as short as it does.

Clearing her throat, she answers, "No, no, that's all. I was just going to see if you thought I could promote it at AJ's in town, but I'm sure I'll get it figured out. I'll let you get going." She peeks over my shoulder into my home, and I suddenly feel like a dick. I should have invited her inside. Instead, I've made her stand outside in the cold when I knew it was already hard for her to come here and ask something of me. She turns to leave, and I open my mouth to apologize for not inviting her in, but she's already turning, and words are being asked.

"Where are you going?" she calls out, and I can't help but bite my lip. I think she cares about my answer.

"Worried about me going on a date, Stormcloud?" That earns me an Olympic gold medal eye roll.

"No, Alder. I'm not worried about you doing anything," she tells me, bristling. "I was just curious. You look..."

"Good?" I supply. She looks up to the sky, tilting her whole head.

"Nice." Is her begrudging reply. I'll fucking take it.

"Thank you, Miss Rutherford. You look nice too," I compliment her. Which is mostly a lie. She looks like I want to bury my hands in her hair and bruise her mouth with mine.

"Thank you...so, where are you going if it's not a date?" She smiles, asking me again. I hope she's jealous. I want her to be jealous.

"It is a date." I can't help but tease her. I like getting her all worked up. I want to let her take it out on me. Her smile turns to ice. Frozen in place, but I can practically feel her teeth grinding. "With my niece," I add, putting her out of her misery. "Knox is working on a case and has to be gone for the night, so I'm taking Hazel with me and dropping her off at my parents' tonight." I lean against the door frame and smile widely at her.

She bites her bottom lip at the corner, trying to hide her smile. I see it though. I see her. "I see. Well, I hope you have a good time then. Bye, Alder." She turns to leave again, but something in me just isn't ready to say goodbye to her yet.

"Do you want to come with us?" I call, and she whips her head around, eyes wide, questioning. "That way, I don't have to worry about you getting out in the next few days trying to get any last-minute shopping done. The weather that they're predicting coming in isn't something you want to be caught out in." I try to say this in a teasing way, but I mean it. It happens more frequently than anyone knows. You're heading down the road in the morning, and the next thing you know, you're caught in a whiteout with no sense of direction.

"I can—"

"—take care of yourself," I cut in. "I know, princess, and I believe it. The point remains the same. You haven't experienced it, and I have. It's not something to leave to chance. So, what do you say? Wanna spend the day with me and Hazel? I'll take you to the grocery store so you can get more oranges," I offer. She looks surprised at that.

"I do need more oranges," she says. "Fine, I'll go. I wouldn't want to get caught out in a blizzard." She sighs. "Just let me stop by my cabin and get my bag."

"I'll drive you. We can stop on the way." I grab my keys and coat from the hook by the entrance and walk out the door, twisting the lock on the handle before closing it. She walks to my old Bronco. It's a faded green. I'm sure it used to be a shiny forest. The color now looks like Ivy's eyes, and I don't think I'll ever be able to think of that color as anything but hers ever again.

Ivy opens the passenger door and hops in, slamming it behind her. I wanted to get it for her, but I also didn't want to fight with her about how capable she is of doing it herself. I like the way she looks in my space though. More than I should. I rub the back of my neck, trying to change the direction of my thoughts.

The only problem is all my thoughts eventually circle back to the redhead, with a penchant for purple, sitting in my faded-green Bronco. I wonder if she's even been in a vehicle this old. I'm sure she's used to new and shiny and sleek. I did a little research on the Rutherford name after I found out who she was. She comes from plenty of money. Her father is a big name in Northern California. I'm not sure why she's here instead of back there running one of his other businesses, but I'm definitely not complaining.

We drive in companionable silence for the couple of minutes it takes to get to her cabin. I'd like to ask her things; I want to get to know her. I mean, that's allowed, right? If I'm going to be her pretend boyfriend at some point, I should probably know something about her life. I slow to a stop when her driveway comes into view. She gets out and jogs up to the front door with the big green wreath that has cream and red bows on it. She disappears into the small cabin for only a moment, and then she's back out. I've passed this cabin more times than I can count, but seeing it today brings a smile to my face—knowing she's there. Here. On my mountain at my lodge.

I take an extra-long moment to appreciate her. She's wearing a purple corduroy coat with a wool collar, tan pants, and a sweater that's also tan but lighter. Her boots are like the ones I got Florence for her birthday a couple of months ago. They won't be keeping the snow out. My baby sister balked when I brought that up to her, insisting they were worn for aesthetics. Whatever that means. I lean across the bench seat and swing the passenger door open for her. It feels like a win, and I have to hide my grin when she gets in without commenting on it.

"Where to first?" Ivy asks, stirring me from my victory.

"We'll head into town to pick up Hazey from Knox's office. I thought I would take her by Winnie's bakery to get her a hot chocolate before we head to the shops. Does that work for you?"

"Yeah." I look over to her smiling at me. It looks sweet. I like that look. I want her to look at me like that more often. "What's that face for?" I grin into my question.

"Nothing," she says, sobering slightly. "You're just like some kind of super uncle, aren't you?" She shrugs it off, but I can tell she's a little surprised by my love for my family. That thought leads me to believe she doesn't feel the same way about her family.

"You don't have any nieces or nephews then?"

"Nope. I'm an only child, and my dad was one also, so no cousins either." She runs her shiny green fingernails up and down the sides of her legs. A nervous habit, maybe. I can tell that talking about her family sets her on edge. She's fidgety, and I don't know her well, but fidgeting isn't a word I'd use to describe Ivy. Most of the time, I get the impression she's sure of herself because she's had to be. I respect her for that, but I also wish she knew that leaning on others isn't the sign of weakness she makes it out to be.

"Only child, huh? What that must be like. With my two

brothers and a baby sister, you haven't met her yet, there was always someone around while I was growing up," I tell her in hopes she'll keep being open.

"I wouldn't know about any of that. There was no noise in the house I grew up in." I don't miss the way she says house and not home.

"That sounds a little lonely." She surprises me with a little breathy laugh.

"It wasn't all that bad. Don't feel sorry for me." She snorts. "I had everything I ever wanted. You've obviously sensed that about me," she says, holding her hand out between us. Her comment throws me a little.

"What is it that I've sensed about you?" I'm curious to know what she's thinking.

"Oh, come on. Don't act like you don't think I'm a spoiled brat and like you haven't thought it from the very first time we interacted. I know what you must have thought. If I'm being honest, I also know that I wasn't having the best day or week or month or year." She mumbles the last bit, but I hear her perfectly.

"I admit to thinking your attitude was a little high and mighty. High maintenance—"

"I am high maintenance," she cuts in. "I'm not ashamed to say that."

"You don't need to be. There's nothing wrong with demanding to be treated in a way you want to be treated," I say, and I wish I could see her while I'm talking to her. Ivy's hard to read even when you can see her face. I'm completely in the dark here.

"I don't think so, Mr. Holloway," she hedges, "but you know, someone at school keeps calling me *princess*." I laugh.

Loudly. Her smart mouth is so sexy. Out of the brief exchanges I've had with Ivy, I know she has this quick and dry sense of humor, and even though it's new, it feels like my exact brand. I want her to tease me. I want her to be mean to me. As long as she'll keep talking to me.

"I'm not going to pretend like I don't think you're a brat, Ivy." She doesn't respond, so I continue, "You are, but that's not why I started calling you that." We've reached downtown, so I slow down and take the last few turns to Knox's office. She sighs.

"I'm assuming you're going to tell me, even though I bet I can guess. Maybe because I was a bitch on the bunny hill that day. I know that. You know that. I get it. I don't often make a good impression. I wouldn't say I always make the best first impression but chewing you out because you were trying to make sure a small child didn't get hurt or sick...I've made better impressions, believe it or not." God, I think I love it when she's rambling, even if she refuses to bring up our actual first meeting. Her rambling gives me an inside track to her brain, and I want to be there more than anything.

"You weren't a bitch, Ivy, and to be even more fair, I tackled you to the ground." I laugh, and she joins me. We get quiet, and I park on the street in front of the office. I don't need to tell her why, but I want to. I don't want her to think anything other than good things when she hears me call her that. "The reason I called you *princess*," I say into the silence, heart beating out of my chest, "is because from the moment you stepped into AJ's and sat down next to me, you could have ordered me to do anything, Ivy. I was yours to command. Sit. Stand. Lie Down. I would have done it. In a heartbeat."

IVY

"*I was yours to command.*"

I replay that little, *huge,* comment over and over again in my mind as Alder chats with Knox, and they get the car seat settled into the backseat. I wave at Hazel, who's in her dad's arms. He's holding her up on his hip, instructing Alder what to do and what to absolutely not do while Hazel is in his care.

"You don't take your eyes off her for a second," Knox threatens Alder.

"Like that's possible. Look at her," he replies, smiling and reaching for his niece. She babbles something, but I catch Muncle Aldie in there somewhere. I grin. They have such a fun sibling relationship. I wonder what my life would have been like if I would have had a sibling of my own. We probably would have hated each other or competed for Daddy's attention. That neither of us would have gotten.

With Hazel strapped safely into her car seat, we are driving out to the Holloway family home. Shopping was more fun than

I thought it would be. Spending time with Alder has also proven to be more fun than expected. Seeing him with his niece is turning my hard and sharp edges into a pile of ooey gooey feelings. I flip my visor down to check my face, hoping I won't find evidence of the mall pretzel I devoured in thirty seconds. In the mirror, I see Hazel in her seat. She's kicking her little feet and looking at her second hot chocolate, the one that Knox said was not allowed.

My heart squeezes looking at her. She really is such a lovely little girl. I can see why the Holloway family fights over her affections. The emotion that stirs up is painful, but at the same time, knowing how cared for Hazel is loosens something in my chest. I don't need a therapist to tell me I have daddy issues. I've had a therapist tell me that, but I didn't need to spend the thousands of dollars I have to know that's where the heart of all my issues stems from. Poor Ivy, a rich girl who grew up in a big house with any material thing or comfort she could ever dream up. How very on-brand...but money doesn't equate to love.

In fact, I've found the opposite to be true 100 percent in my life. My father doesn't love me, and my mother left me with him before I was eating solid foods. So it's a double whammy in the issues department.

I wouldn't have made a good mother anyway.

A derisive snort escapes me, and Hazel's chocolate-brown eyes meet mine. I smile and she smiles shyly back to me. Impulsively, I stick my tongue out to the side and widen my eyes at her, and she giggles the sweetest giggle that makes one bubble out of me.

Alder turns his head toward me with a wide smile curving his perfect lips. "What's so funny, girls?"

"Funny face, Muncle Aldie!" Hazel squeals to her uncle.

"Ivy made a funny face at you?" he asks her.

"Yes!" she says, giggling again, then turning back to her hot chocolate as if it's the most prized possession she's ever owned. We turn onto a side road about fifteen minutes from downtown. This must be where we're dropping Hazel off. I blush when Alder looks over at me. Man, I'm really going overboard for this kid. I'm generally not a *make-funny-faces* kind of girl.

"All of us have done it," he tells me. His voice is full of warmth.

"Done what?" I pretend to be oblivious in asking, but he just chuckles.

"Let your hair down, princess. No one's judging you here." I hear his words, but I don't think he understands that I've been judged my whole life. Whether I am or am not a bitch, I'll be called one. If I'm overly friendly or smile too much, then I'm brainless. Expectations and other people's ideals have been projected onto me since I was Hazel's age. That doesn't change overnight. A big, beautiful house comes into view, and Alder parks us right out front.

"Hair is down, Lover Boy. Do you need your eyes checked?" I tease, and he grins at me, that dimple in full effect before opening his door, the cold night air swirls inside the truck now.

"I see you just fine, Ivy." Is his response before shutting his door and opening Hazel's to retrieve her from the backseat. I'm left wondering if he's seen a little behind the thin veil I have left with him, then I roll my eyes at myself. It's doubtful Alder hasn't glimpsed anything I haven't wanted him to. Wouldn't it be nice for someone to really see me, all the ugly parts, and still want to spend their time with me? Just because they want to because they like what they see.

"Come on, Hazey baby, let's get you inside. It's getting colder, and you know what?" he asks her excitedly.

"What, what?" she asks him.

"Nana made cookies and has all your stuffies for your sleep-over!" he reveals, and she claps her little hands.

"*Out! Out!*" she commands him while he unbuckles her from her seat. I'm startled from mindlessly watching Alder be even more annoyingly endearing by a knock on my window. It makes me jump, and I turn to see Alder's mother covering her mouth, and I'm sure laughter, with her hand.

"Sorry, I didn't mean to scare you," she says, holding up both hands. I turn the handle, manually rolling down the window.

"Hi, sorry. I'm not usually this jumpy," I tell her.

"No, no. This one's on me, sweetie. I just wanted to come out and ask if you had plans for the holiday." Oh. I really don't want to tell her the truth, that my plans are to drink mimosas and be alone.

I smile at her and say, "I'm not sure yet."

"Will you be in town?" she presses as Alder carries Hazel inside, wrapped up in a blanket.

"Buh-bye!" she calls out to me.

"Bye, Hazey!" I call back, her nickname coming out so easily.

"Well, if you are in town and have no other plans, we would love for you to spend it here with us," she says as she taps her hands on the window frame and turns to walk back inside.

"Thank you for inviting me," I tell her, my voice sounding just a little choked. She gives me a smile over her shoulder and waves. I don't think I've ever been invited over to someone's home for a holiday. Emotion clogs my throat for the second time this evening. It's...nice. To be included in someone's plans. It's not something I'm used to, and although the concept isn't that difficult to wrap my head around...it is hard for me to accept it's being extended to me.

I crank my window back up and watch as flakes start to drift around above. Taking a quick peek back at the house to make sure Alder hasn't come back out yet, I slip out of the Bronco and admire the tree all lit up in the big window of the Holloway's home. I turn around, looking out over the rolling hills leading to the base of the mountains and take a deep breath in. It's cold and hurts my lungs a little. It's not like I've never seen snow before but starting at age ten, I spent most of my time at the boarding school in sunny Southern California.

I chance another glance back to the house, and when I don't see anyone again, I tentatively tip my head back and stick out my tongue. I catch a couple of the small flakes on it and start laughing. This is something I've seen done on TV more times than I can count. It's so childish. I do it again, this time spinning in a circle. On my second revolution, I catch movement near the railing of the stairs and come to a stuttering stop.

"Having fun?" Alder calls from his spot on the porch, amused.

"Yeah," I say. I'm kind of interested in hearing what he's thinking. The way he's looking at me is very unfamiliar. Not *bad*, but not something I'm used to, that's for sure.

"You're beautiful," he tells me, and I feel heat creep up my neck.

"You're charming," I say with an eye roll.

He smiles. "Flattery will get you everywhere, Stormcloud." I hope he can't see my blush under the cover of the night sky.

Wishful thinking. The next words out of his mouth confirm as much.

"The blush you're sporting is going to give me the wrong idea, Ivy." His eyes sparkle like sapphires in the glow coming from the house. It's unfair really. He's so beautiful. And as much as I wish he could be, he's just not for me.

"I'm not blushing," I deny. It's a lie, but I need him to understand. "But if I was, that's exactly what it would be, just so you know," I say slowly, wanting him to hear me. Things may get a little confusing over the next couple of weeks. "The wrong idea," I finish my sentence.

"Is that right?" he drawls. "Well, I guess it's a good thing you aren't blushing then." He walks to my side—the passenger side, not mine—I remind myself. Nothing here is mine, especially anything having to do with Alder. He opens the door, and I walk over to get back in. As I'm brushing past him to get to my seat, he lifts a hand and runs it through my hair. I fight the impulse not to lean into his warm, callused palm. I slowly pull my head back, neither of us saying a word. I slip into my seat, and he shuts me in. I'm trying not to think too long about how good it feels to have him touching me.

The drive to the grocery store is quiet in an unexpectedly soft way. More often than not, I'm finding time spent with Alder is a balm to my perpetual flight or fight response. There are no more questions about my family history or life before coming to Silverthorne, which is appreciated. Being vulnerable isn't something I've mastered, and I'm out of my depth here. I'm actually getting a little annoyed that on more than one occasion now, he's mentioned that he sees me or thinks he has me figured out. There's not much more to me than what you see on the surface anymore. Life, and the people I've allowed to be in mine have helped see to that.

I don't remember a time in my life when I tried to be something or someone I wanted to be, and I wasn't immediately told I couldn't be it. My dreams and aspirations were always presented to me as unrealistic. By five years old, most of my little girl dreams were dashed. I wasn't talented enough to be a painter. I wasn't coordinated enough to be a dancer. I had long limbs even then. I've never been clumsy, but I don't think I've ever had rhythm either. My father is a brutally honest man. Receiving criticism growing up was expected but still hurtful. He may have never physically hit me, but his words felt a lot like weapons when they hit their mark. I think that's how I ended up with Noah. He's not an old man by any means, but I think I was searching for approval in people and places I had no business searching. Noah's attention was a welcome change to the indifference I felt from my father.

"I don't want to rush you too much, but I think they're wrong about the storm moving in tomorrow. I think it's going to be here tonight." I'm snapped out of my self-pitying thoughts by Alder's deep timbre. I look around and notice we've parked. Right in front of the grocery store.

"Sorry. Yeah, I can be fast. You don't have to come in with me if you don't want to. I'll be quick," I tell him, possibly needing a few minutes to compose myself. It's not often I let my thoughts drift, yet it seems to happen a lot with him. I file that information away to pull out to analyze later when I'm alone.

"I need to get a few things myself; I don't mind coming in with you," he says, turning off the truck and making his way around the front of it. I let out a sigh and then open my door.

He's standing by it, waiting for me and asks, "What's on your list?"

"I need some fruit and cheese. Oranges and chocolate. I may also need some frozen meals," I ramble off my mental list to him.

"Frozen meals? Like lasagna?"

"Yeah. Possibly some popcorn chicken. A bag of frozen fries. How long do you think we'll be stuck? Maybe I'll get a couple of bags of fries. And some bacon. I think I need more coffee beans." I really am rambling now.

"Ivy, I know it's none of my business..." That sentence never goes anywhere good. "But you have low blood sugar. Hypoglycemia." Oh, so now he's going to try and be invested in my health. I internally and externally roll my eyes.

"You know that I do because I told you that I did." That was probably the bitchiest response I could have spewed, but he just smirks. His hair slips over his eyes just a little, and I'm dying to smooth it back with my fingers. *No, I'm not.*

"Do you think you should be getting some things that would help you maintain a little more even blood sugar level?" His question sounds a lot like my doctor the first time I ended up back at the hospital, and I appreciate it about as much as I did then.

"I have been living with this on my own for the last five years, and I don't know if you've noticed, but I am still alive." I put just enough sarcasm into the statement to sound annoyed and pissed off.

"Noted, Ivy."

"And what are you? A doctor? Me thinks he's watched too many Grey's Anatomy episodes." He stops in the aisle and turns to look at me. I've successfully riled him up, and it's much less satisfying than I thought it would be.

"Or maybe...and I'm just spitballing here. His sister has low iron, so he is observant of people's diets and how they can improve their quality of life." He winks and then continues to walk ahead of me. I don't feel as bad now. He's too good-natured. It's jarring and unfamiliar. I open my mouth to tell him that I'm not his sister, and those aren't exactly the same thing, but he starts talking again. "Oh, and also, I am EMS certified," he throws over his shoulder, walking to grab a cart. That pulls me up a little short, my doctor argument now seems a little flimsy.

We walk beside each other in the small grocery store, and I shouldn't find it as attractive as I do when he pulls out these little pocket-size reusable bags from his coat pocket for me to put my produce in. There's something so exotically domestic about sharing a shopping cart and reusable bags. The easy rhythm we fall into is altogether the closest I've felt to another person in a long time and also the most annoying thing that's happened in just as long. I like how I feel when I'm with Alder. I also don't want to feel the way I do about him. It's been a long time since I've had to deal with conflicting emotions.

I glance his way and am hit all over again by his profile. He's handsome in a way that women notice him as we walk by. That's not something you see in real life often. Southern California definitely has its charms and its fair share of beautiful men. But Alder is rugged in a way that makes me want to crawl into his lap and snuggle in for the long winter. Those are the thoughts that I need to lock away. I don't need any more thoughts about him. I need to keep my head down and focus on my objective. I'll be gone before all this snow melts, and that's exactly how I need it to be.

"All done, princess?" he asks. Even after explaining that nickname, I'm definitely not sold on it. That could be a good thing though. Something else about him that annoys me.

"I'm done, Search and Rescue," I tell him, shaking my head. He reaches into his pocket, and I hear metal clinking, then he extends his hand to me and offers me his keys.

"Wanna go start the truck, and I'll get the groceries?" The way my body and mind have just reacted to the most innocent sentence should be studied. I know that I should fight him on this. I should pay for my own groceries, but I feel my stomach tighten and my legs squeeze together. Why is that attractive? I take his keys with a sure and make my way out to his green Bronco. There's already a layer of snow covering it. It's thin, but I'm starting to get nervous that we won't make it back up the mountain.

The truck is started and warming up, and Alder appears at the back, opening the hatch. I unbuckle to help him load up, but he stops me. "I can get this loaded. Just keep doing what you're doing." He tells me, and it confuses me because I'm not doing anything.

"And that would be?" I ask, confused.

"Sitting in the front seat of my Bronco, looking so pretty it hurts."

ALDER

I t's Christmas. Since our shopping trip, Ivy has been— elusive. I haven't seen her except for the very small glimpses I've caught of her around the lodge. She's avoiding me. At first, I just assumed we were missing each other in passing, but after this past week, I can take a hint. She's kept her office door closed, and yesterday, I actually made eye contact with her through the main cabin's window, and she physically ducked out of view. Just a flash of her hair and then nothing. I want her to come to dinner tonight. I also don't want to push her into something she isn't ready for. She's already so skittish. Skittish in the way you'd also describe a wild animal that's been cornered.

I'm just out of the shower when I hear a knock on my door and rush to answer. I tug my towel tighter around my waist and narrowly miss my hip on the kitchen island. Running my hand through my wet hair, I open the door. I see Ivy's SUV driving down the road, back toward her cabin, and then look down to see a meticulously wrapped set of gifts.

I pick them up and see the names written in cursive on each one. There's one that says Mary and three that say Hazel. There's even a present for Winnie. I smile. They're beautiful, and it, honest to God, warms my heart to see her think of my family. Does this woman really believe she can drop these off and not make an appearance at dinner? My mother will never let that slide.

I'm dressed and out my front door in record time. I stash the gifts Ivy brought in the back of my truck, and then I'm off to my family's Christmas. I just have to pick up something or someone, on the way. I chuckle, thinking about how she thought she was getting away with that stunt. As if I would let her spend Christmas alone, with her ex-husband and his new fiancée on the property.

I pull up to her cabin, and I see the curtain move in the front room. When I knock on the door, I expect her to ignore me, but to my surprise, she opens it immediately.

"What are you doing here, Alder?" I can see her attitude is visibly and firmly in place by the tilt of her hips.

I sigh. "I think you know, Ivy."

"It was really sweet for your mom to invite me to your family Christmas, but very unnecessary. I'll be just fine here," she tells me.

"Do I need to remind you how fun unnecessary things can be?" I ask, and her cheeks pink slightly. "I have no doubt you'll be fine, but how will it look if I show up without you at Christmas or if Noah sees you here without me?" I hedge. "I just really want to make sure I look like the boyfriend you deserve," I say with my hand pressed over my heart. She crosses her arms over her chest and leans into her doorway. Popping her hip out. A hip I've seen bare, one I want to sink my fingers into again. Ivy's voice cuts through my thoughts.

"What's that look?" she asks.

I tell her the truth. "I'll give you one guess, and it has to do with how we met."

Her slightly pink cheeks turn rosy, and I smile. She's so incredibly beautiful.

"Now, are you ready to go? My family will be expecting us," I say sweetly. She bites her lip. "It won't be so bad. You'll get a good home-cooked meal, my family will probably dote on you, and Hazel will probably want you to hold her the whole time, or at least when she doesn't want me holding her." I wink. "What's the worst that could happen?" I thought I would have to beg on her front porch for longer, but she surprises me, yet again, when she speaks.

"Fine. I don't have anything to bring though. Shouldn't I bring something?" she asks nervously, and it's adorable.

"No, my mom will have everything we need. The only other person who will bring anything is Winnie, and that's because she refuses not to bring baked goods everywhere she goes."

"Let me grab my coat then."

"Perfect. I'll wait here for you. Just in case you get the urge to run," I tell her, blocking the doorway with a smile.

"If I remember correctly, and I usually do, you were the one with the urge to run off the next morning." I hear her call from the other room. I'm surprised she brought it up. Since our night together, it seems she wants to avoid talking about it at all costs. Ivy walks back into the room, and I feel my heart rate tick up. She's drop-dead gorgeous. Her long hair is tucked into her full-length tan coat. It matches the cream pants and sweater she's wearing underneath. She likes wearing the same shade a lot.

When she walks outside, I grip her elbow gently, halting her steps. I slide both my hands up her arms to her neck, and her breath hitches. I lean in, and her eyes widen for a moment before closing. Does she think I'm going to kiss her? Would she let me? I reach under her collar and pull the hair out from inside her coat. Her eyes pop back open, and I can see it in them. She wants me to kiss her, but she's going to have to learn to start asking for the things she wants rather than expecting me to read her mind.

I pull my hands back and smile at her slight pout. I've felt those pouty lips on mine, on my skin. I want to feel them again. "If you want something, Ivy, just ask me," I say, working to keep my voice even.

"Nope." She shakes her head, sending a curtain of dark-red hair over her shoulder. "I'm good. I don't want anything." She stonewalls me. *So fucking stubborn.*

"Alright. Well, if you change your mind. I'm open to any and all requests," I state, then lead the way to my still-running truck and open her door so she can get inside where it's warm. It will smell like her by the time I get in the driver's seat. Her scent had only just faded from our shopping trip. I want it to always smell like her. I want a lot of things that I probably shouldn't when it comes to her. Things she may not be ready to give. For now, I'll take what she'll give me and deal with the fallout later.

Ivy

Christmas at the Holloway house is—everything you've ever seen on TV and more. From the moment I walked in the door, I felt welcome. Mary told me how wonderful it is that I was able to join them today. Tom nodded his agreement and placed a firm but gentle hand on my shoulder in greeting. Winnie hugged me with more force than I would have expected from such a small person. Colt winked at me, and that made Alder shoot him a dirty look. I liked that a little more than I should. Then, when I was flushed from attention and my heart was filling to the brim, Hazel squealed my name and lifted her tiny arms in the air for me to pick her up, and the organ in my chest burst, unable to contain the affection.

And that was just the first five minutes I was here. Alder carried in the few presents I bought and sat them by the large tree in the living area. I was promptly swept into the kitchen by Florence, or Baby Lo, as far as anyone in their family is concerned. She sat me on a barstool at the island, made two mimosas, and handed me one before joining me. Mr. Holloway walks by on his way to the deck with tongs and a meat thermometer. He clicks the tongs, and I smile when I notice he's wearing an apron. A very funny but inappropriate apron. I slap a hand over my mouth to try and cover my giggle, but it's no use. I lose it, and a snort comes out. Oh my god, I just snorted.

"What's so funny, princess?" Alder asks from the arched entrance to the living room. A few heads whip back and forth between us at the use of the nickname he's given me. I blush, and if I had to guess, it's somewhere between tomato and strawberry red. I shake my head, refusing to say anything else.

"Share with the class," he encourages me, and I roll my eyes.

"That's a very interesting apron your dad has on." And the whole kitchen erupts with laughter. I smile, but I'm a bit confused. Mary walks over and leans against the island beside me.

"I'm sorry, dear. I think we forget sometimes that not everyone is in on the joke. One year, I think it may have been Father's Day, Alder bought Tom an apron, it said 'It's All Fun And Games Until Someone Burns Their Wiener,'" she says, and I choke on my laughter. "From then on, Mr. Holloway has received at least one a year, and each year, they get worse and worse, depending on who's giving them to him." She eyes Alder as she says this. "I hope you don't find it offensive," she adds, and I shake my head.

"No, not at all. It's just...the arrow pointing down...er... really caught...me off guard." I try to get out through my laughter. She throws her head back, and I can see exactly where Alder gets his laugh from. Mary has a phenomenal laugh. I'm laughing so hard that tears are starting to gather in my eyes. I glance over again and meet those familiar ice-blue ones. They're squinted, sexy crinkles in full effect, smiling back at me. I'm really glad I came. I'm really glad Alder came to get me.

As laughter dies down but doesn't stop, there's a flutter of activity in the kitchen. I almost feel bad for not helping, but then Florence nudges me with her elbow.

"I don't cook," she whispers conspiratorially.

"I don't either," I whisper back, and she laughs lightly.

"Perfect. I have a drinking buddy," she says, holding up her glass, and I tap mine against it. The sound is just a quiet clink, but I feel it deep down. Like the clink of our glasses slipped through the carefully constructed walls I keep up, hitting me in the chest, and now I don't know how I'll ever go back. I smile, hoping it's not watery, and take a small sip of my drink. Not only do I need to watch my sugar, I also haven't been drinking since the night I got to town, not wanting to use it as a crutch as I have in the past.

"Can you tell me where the bathroom is?" I ask.

"If you go out the way we came in here and then go to the left, it's the door at the very end of the hallway," she tells me, pointing to the entrance we came through.

"Thanks, I'll be right back," I say, slipping off the barstool. I walk out into the living room and see all the guys, with the exception of Knox who's making something in the kitchen. They're talking about Rhett's hockey season and playing with Hazel, who keeps holding up a play phone to each of their ears. The sight makes me chuckle, but it's a sound tinged with sadness. A little bit of grief creeps through. I make it to the third door down the hall, spotting a snowboarding poster out of the corner of my eye, and I stop in the doorway. This must have been Alder's room.

I smile and turn back to the living room. Laughter floats down the hallway as I step into the bedroom. Light filters in from the window, and I can see the outline of the mountains in the distance. I walk to the end of the bed. The thick wool blankets all look warm and inviting. The nightstand has a leather-bound book on it. A journal, perhaps? I pick it up and flip through the pages once before placing it back on the small table. I would love to snoop through it, but I can't be in here forever. I'm sure he hasn't lived here in years, but somehow, it still smells of him in here. There are so many personal touches. I think back to my bedroom in my father's house and can't think of one thing that reflected me in that room.

I walk over to a tall dresser and look at the framed photos sitting on top. There are a few of him and his brothers. I see Winnie and Colt mixed in as well. There's one of him and who I'm assuming is Florence, when she was a toddler brushing his hair. Then there's one I see pinned on a corkboard above a desk. It's of him with a guy I haven't met yet. Alder has his arm wrapped around the man's shoulders. Both their smiles so bright that I can feel mine widen in response.

"That's Ray," a voice from the doorway startles me. I spin and stifle a scream.

"God, Alder. If you keep doing that, I'm going to make you wear a bell," I tell him while covering my throat with my hands. He smiles at me, his hip propped against the door jamb.

"Kinky," he says with a raised brow then his face turns thoughtful. "I'm not opposed," he tells me. I scoff and lean back onto the desk, checking to make sure it will support me before giving it my full weight.

"No? Tell me more. What else are you not opposed to?" I question.

"If it has to do with you, I'm not ashamed to say it's a very short list," he quips, and I fight a blush. More lists.

"So, the guy in the picture. Ray." I gesture behind me. "I haven't seen him around. Does he live around here?" I ask, trying to change the subject. Alder's blue eyes twinkle, and he pushes off the wall to come stand beside me.

"He would love that you're asking about him," he tells me with a small chuckle. He pulls open the drawer at my thigh and pulls out a hardcover book. Oh, it's a photo album, I see when he flips it open. He leans against the desk beside me, our shoulders touching.

"This is Ray," he says. He points to a photo of two small boys. Maybe eight years old. "We were friends from the first day of kindergarten through age twenty-four. I've never had a better friend."

"Did you two lose touch or...?" I ask, hopeful.

"Unfortunately, no. He died twelve years ago this month." This is a much deeper conversation than I had anticipated.

"I'm sorry to hear that," I tell him honestly, placing my hand over his.

"Yeah, I had a pretty rough go of it for a while after," he shares with me and flips his hand over to twine our fingers together. "He's a big reason I do what I do," he whispers.

"I'm sorry you lost him," I murmur. I know how loss can affect you. My loss changed me completely. I wonder if Alder was altered like I was and if having the support of his family kept him from going dark like I had. The months I spent at the spa retreat still haunt me. I shudder.

"I am too. He was a great person and would have been a

great man. I miss him every day. I've been fortunate to have found ways to cope with his loss and honor his memory. Those are the only reasons I'm able to keep going. Well, that and I have my family. They don't give up on the people they love. I am lucky enough to be one of those people," he says with a wink.

"I doubt it's all that hard to love you, Alder," I whisper. We're close. Too close to one another now. With his hand in mine, I hadn't realized how close his handsome face had gotten to mine.

"Ivy, I should tell you..." I can feel his breath on my mouth, and if I lean into him just a few more inches, I could feel his lips...but I don't. I might've, but I don't get the chance. A knock on the wall has me flinching away from him so hard that I ram into the dresser and knock a trophy and some books off it.

"Shit!" I yell, rubbing my upper arm as I bend to pick up the items now on the ground.

"I just wanted to let you guys know that Mare is here, and dinner is about ready." Rhett smirks from outside the room. "I hope I didn't interrupt anything." His tone is teasing, and even though all the Holloway men are grown, it's giving little brother.

"Not at all. I'm just going to go to the bathroom and then I'll be right there," I say and walk past him and down the long hall. I don't take another breath until I'm locked inside. What the hell am I thinking? I shouldn't have let myself get into this position. It's really easy to get swept up in Alder. I think it's been happening little by little since my first night here. I also know it would be much smarter, for both of us, if we remember that this isn't real; it's an agreement, that's it. The hand-holding and the near touches should probably be reserved for when we're in front of Noah or Margot.

I wash my hands and splash a little water on my face. In the mirror, I can see my face is flushed, and it has nothing to do with the sweater I have on. I'm playing with fire now, but it feels really good to be here with him today, and it feels really good to have him looking at me like he does. Like maybe he cares about me, what happens to me. That's new, and I don't think I want to give it up. Not yet, at least.

I make it back to the kitchen and am promptly ushered to the dining room, where the table is set beautifully with a view of the Christmas tree that stands across the room in front of the window that seems to tower over us. Everything on the table is in just the right place. The red napkins and the gold candle sticks. It's stunning, truly. When I get a better look at the tree, I notice it has small frames hanging off the branches. Little wallet-size photos adorn the huge tree from top to bottom.

Memories of all their family holidays, milestones, and achievements hang from small green and red bows. It's perfect. I've been to plenty of pretty homes that are lavishly decorated, but it's these personal touches, the ways this family is embedded into every inch of this home, which stand out the most. They make this the most beautiful Christmas I've ever been to. Being with this family makes me nostalgic for something I've never had. I'm sure there's a word for that, but I can't think of it right now.

"Alright, everyone," Mr. Holloway calls over all the side conversations. "I would like to start by saying that I'm so grateful to have my whole family here for Christmas." He takes an extra moment to look at Rhett, and his son nods in agreement before looking at Winnie, who blushes adorably.

"Christmas is a time to reflect on the past year. All the good things that it's brought us and all the hard things we have overcome. My wish for everyone here is that you continue to overcome the challenges life sets before you, but you feel joy in the wonderful opportunities you've been given." He raises his wine glass, and we all reach for our own, lifting them. "To the bright futures of everyone in this room and the years that have come before that made us capable of them."

There's clinking around the table as we all tap our glasses to one another's. I'm trying not to tear up. What a beautiful sentiment. To honor our pasts and old wounds by rising to all that life brings. I look around the table at all the seemingly well-adjusted adults. I look at Hazel. She's going to be such a lovely person. She has too many people who love her for her not to be. I feel my chest warm thinking about that. Grateful she won't be resigned to a life as empty as mine was. After spending the day here and hearing Tom's speech, though, I think I still have time to change that and make the most of mine. I smile and look at Alder, who's sitting right beside me.

"Thank you," I say quietly, so only he can hear. He turns to me and smiles. Hi, dimples.

"For what?" he asks me.

"Coming after me this morning."

ALDER

The days after Christmas are beginning to run together. I've been on shift most of them, with only one of those days at the resort. That's why I'm working here today, trying to play catch-up. That and possibly because I haven't seen a certain redhead around as of late. Having Ivy at my family's home for Christmas was the highlight of my year. The way she looked like she had been spending holidays with us forever, not just this once. It made me start wishing for more with her. She's still refusing to acknowledge that our feelings are shared. Today may be the day I finally do something about that.

I walk into the lodge and see there's a circus happening inside. There are too many people in here, and they all seem to be going in different directions. I spot Ivy over by a man with a clipboard and glasses. She's wearing jeans that look molded to her and a cream oversize button-down. Her hair is up on her head again, but this time there's no purple pen. It's being held back with a gold clip thingy like the ones that I've seen

Florence and Winnie wear, with the spikes. There are a few pieces of hair in her face, and when she tucks some behind her ear, I track the movement, wanting to do it myself. She looks so beautiful.

She laughs at something he says and touches his elbow. Deep down, I know she has the right to touch anyone she wants, but I want that to be me. I make my way over to them, and when I reach her side, I pull her to me, kissing her cheek tenderly. She stiffens just a little before relaxing into me.

"Hey, you. What's going on?" I ask her, and she gives me a smirk. I must be obvious when I'm jealous. I don't think I've ever been jealous before, so this is uncharted territory. *Be cool, Alder.*

"I'm just discussing the champagne fountain I want installed for the gala," she informs me. I raise a brow at her.

"Champagne fountain, huh? Sounds fancy." I don't think we've ever had a fountain of anything here. I trust her though. She knows more about these kinds of events than I do.

"Yes, Ross was just telling me our options. Care to weigh in?" she taunts, her green eyes bright and daring.

"Oh no, princess. I'll leave that in your very capable hands." I wink and turn for my office, chuckling to myself when I reach the hall.

Once I'm seated at my desk, I check on all the things I haven't been able to in the last few days. Ivy has so many things in place, and they all look like they'll be beneficial for the resort. She's really good at this. I know she plans on leaving when she gets her father's approval. I just can't help but hope she'll want to stay. Not only because things are starting to really blow up around here but also because I wouldn't mind spending more time with her. In fact, it's all I've wanted to do lately.

I hear soft footfalls coming my way, and I glance up to see Noah walk past my door. Unsure if I should, I get up to follow him, and then I see Ivy fly by and stop. I don't like the idea of him being alone with her, but I'm also very aware of how she can hold her own in a confrontation. I'm torn between letting her handle her own situation and being there to let her know that I'm supporting her. I go with support.

I'm at her office door when I catch the tail end of Noah's sentence.

"You can't be serious about this, Red. He's just a snow-boarding instructor, for God's sake. Is this what you needed all those years ago? Something to play with on the side?" *Well, that's a fun way to be described.*

"As much as it should, your observation doesn't surprise me at all. You've always been so chronically skin-deep. To be clear, Alder's not *just* anything, but it doesn't matter what he does for work, Noah. He's a kind person. A good person. He cares about people. He helps people. He listens to me and encourages my opin-ions, then respects them. We were never like that, Noah. *You* were never like that, and that's why we aren't together anymore," she tells him, and I feel my chest swell with pride. I have no idea if she really means what she's saying about me. I can only hope she does.

"Don't pretend you were innocent in the demise of our relationship, Ivy. You went crazy. Literally. You barely spoke for months, and when you did, you wouldn't stop crying. I had no idea what to do with you. I couldn't take you anywhere in that state," he says. I feel my hands tighten into fists. *Piece of shit.*

"You weren't supposed to do anything with me!" she screeches, and I flinch. Not from the volume of her voice, but from the small crack I hear in it. My chest cracks wide open at the heartbreak there, and I can't even see her face. "I just needed you to be there with me! I needed you to understand why I was so broken inside! I needed you to care that we lost Silas!" she continues to scream, and I can't go any longer without holding her. I detach from the wall and round the corner, I don't stop moving until she's in my arms.

I turn her into me so her back is facing Noah, and I'm staring directly at him. Into his soulless, spineless eyes.

"Leave," I demand. "Now." He doesn't argue with me; he just shakes his head with a clenched jaw before turning and leaving the room. Ivy's shaking.

"Shhh...it's okay now. I'm here," I say, trying my best to comfort her. She grips the fabric of my jacket and pulls us closer. She lets go of the hold she has over her emotions. Her body racks with sobs, and I move us back to the wingback chair in the corner. I pull her onto my lap and cradle her as I sit down. Rubbing circles on her back, I let her get it all out. She needs this release. I smooth the loose hair from her face and massage the base of her neck while whispering reassurances to her.

Forty-five minutes later, when the shaking slows and her breathing begins to even, I stand with her in my arms and carry her into my office. I lay her down on the small couch I have in here. The same one I found her on a month ago before I knew much about her at all. Now, all I want to do is know her better. I want to care for her if she'll let me. I take my jacket and sling it over her sleeping form. I let the back of my hand slide across her soft cheek and then lean down to press a kiss to her fore-head. Ivy should have been cared for like this her whole life.

Someone should have been there to take care of her when she was sick. When she was sad.

I want her to know what life should be like, and I want it to be *me* who shows her.

A couple of hours later, I'm deep in some paperwork I've been neglecting when I see Ivy start to stir. She takes in her surroundings and then my jacket over her. I can't contain the grin that breaks loose when I see her bring the collar to her nose and take a deep inhale. I clear my throat so she's aware of my presence, and I don't startle her like I have a track record of doing.

"Hey, princess. How ya feeling?" I ask. She sits up and lets my jacket fall to her lap, where she twines her fingers together, looking embarrassed and confused.

"How did I get in here?" she croaks, asking me a question instead of answering mine.

"I carried you," I tell her. "How are you feeling? Do you need something to eat or drink?" I'm worried that her blood sugar is low. She shakes her head then tilts it to the side.

"Maybe. I'm feeling fuzzy, but I'm not sure if it's because I need to eat, I'm embarrassed to within an inch of my life, or if it's from all the crying I didn't even know I had in me." She's self-deprecating. "I'm sorry you had to deal with any of that. For me."

"Ivy," I say her name and then pause, collecting my thoughts so I don't say the wrong thing. "Please don't apologize for having a reaction to the way he chose to treat you," I plead. She snorts but nods. "You have no reason to be embarrassed at all."

"You know, when I was at your house for Christmas, I had this strange feeling that you really were a good guy. That you were raised right." She chuckles, and I grin at her. "I thought I could have been imagining it, that I could pretend it wasn't true, but it looks like I wasn't. You really are a great guy, Alder. Thank you." Everything she just said is complementary. It might be the first time she's said something to me that doesn't end in a jab. I need to tell her the truth about my job here at the lodge. I just don't know how to bring it up without it sounding like I've kept it from her intentionally.

"I'm not sure if everyone would agree, but I am glad you think so," I reply, and she rolls her eyes.

"I doubt you've ever met anyone who didn't fall head over heels for you, Lover Boy. That's just your lot in life," she mutters. I can think of a couple.

"I don't think Noah is going to be sending me any secret admirer letters anytime soon," I tease, and she snorts.

"I don't think Noah has ever written a letter in his life. The best you could expect is maybe an email."

"And they say romance is a forgotten language," I mock, and she laughs.

"It's nice to hear you laugh, Ivy." She's blushing.

"Yeah, I'm not really big on laughter," she says.

"That's something we're gonna have to change, Storm-cloud. I like the sound of it too much." My compliment earns me another blush, and I mentally pat myself on the back.

She places my jacket on the couch beside her. "We'll see," she hums, then stands up. "I better get back to it. I'm sorry if I worried you. I'm usually better at keeping my shit together," she tells me and crosses her arms over her chest. I walk around to the front of my desk and lean back onto my hands against it.

"I already told you once not to apologize, I hope I don't have to again." Her eyes spark at that. Ivy likes to put up a fight and, in most cases, I wouldn't be surprised to find she doesn't like authority, but I think Ivy Rutherford may like me telling her what to do. "Where are you off to?" I ask.

She clears her throat. "I need to get back out there and help get things settled for the gala. I've been missing for over two hours, and I'm sure there were a lot of questions that went unanswered." She pats her pockets as she talks. "I don't have my phone. Have you seen it?" she asks me. I shake my head.

"I haven't seen it. It must still be in your office."

"Right. Well, thank you again, Alder. I appreciate you stepping in before." She looks into my eyes, and I know she means it. What she doesn't know is I wouldn't have wanted to be anywhere else. There's a draw to her, one I'm helpless to ignore. I don't feel like fighting it anymore. She opens her mouth again, probably to say her final goodbye, but I stop her with my question.

"What are you doing for dinner?"

"What?" she asks, smiling but thrown by my question.

"Do you have any plans for dinner?" I ask again.

"I mean, I'll probably eat one of my frozen dinners while I read my neglected book," she says.

"I'm hearing you have some serious plans, but can I offer an alternative? Have dinner with me instead."

"Why?" she asks, and I grin.

"Because you should eat a decent meal, and while I'm not the best cook in my family, I have a few good dishes on the menu, and because I want to spend time with you," I answer honestly. She bites her lip and looks down at her old-timey-looking shoes. Shoes that I feel like a founding father would have worn. I like them on her.

"What are you going to make me?" I think about her penchant for citrus, and I find it extremely lucky I know how to make a dish with it.

"I was thinking orange chicken and rice." I shrug, and she nods thoughtfully.

"That could work for me. I like orange chicken," she admits. I thought she might.

"Is that a yes then?"

"It is, but it's just a meal, action hero," she informs me, and I nod.

"Of course...for now." She rolls her eyes.

"Do you want to ride with me when you're done here?"

"I may be a little late, and I want to change before," she explains.

"Sounds good." I smile, and she smiles back before walking out the door. I contain the urge to fist pump the air. She may not have said it was a date; she actually did say it was just a meal, but she also didn't say it wasn't a date. That's good enough for now.

ALDER

Ivy's coming over. To my house. I've never had a woman over to my place. Seeing as I'm a thirty-six-year-old man, that may be shocking for someone to hear, but I've never had someone I've ever been seriously interested in. Or let myself be seriously interested in. As soon as she agreed to dinner, I ran to the store in town to make sure I had all the ingredients for orange chicken. I have made it, but it's been a while, so I've called in reinforcements.

"Okay the rice is simmering, what next?" I say into my empty kitchen.

"Put all your spices in the pot with your orange juice, soy sauce, and vinegar," Knox tells me. I have him on video call, and the phone is propped against a bowl I turned upside down.

"Okay, then what?"

"Mix the cornstarch and water until it's a smooth paste."

"Got it."

"You'll add that to the sauce, whisk it until it's thicker, and then take it off the heat."

"Perfect. I can do that. What about the chicken?"

"You're going to dip the little pieces into the egg and then the flour mixture. Once they're coated, fry them in the oil for two or three minutes."

"Okay, I think I've got it now. Thanks, big brother," I say, and I mean it. He's a busy guy, and his taking the time to help me cook is appreciated.

"So this is something then," Knox surmises.

I sigh. "I don't know. I want it to be," I admit.

"Huh. Well. Hazey likes her." At this, I smile.

"High praise."

"The highest," he corrects.

"The highest," I agree. "Well, I better get this all cooked and cleaned up if I expect to impress her," I say.

"I saw the way she looked at you at Christmas. I don't think it will take much, little brother."

"You're getting soft in your old age, Knox."

"Bye, idiot," he says, to prove he isn't before hanging up, and I chuckle as I take the chicken out of the frying pan and onto a plate to drain. I taste the orange sauce, and honestly, it's really good. I crushed this. I have just enough time to do a quick clean-up of the countertops and the few scattered bowls. Ivy should be here soon, and I think I'm nervous. I need to tell her about my part in the resort tonight. I just hope she doesn't cut me off because of it. It's this train of thought that's interrupted by headlights flashing into the living room. I wait for her to knock before leaving the island, not wanting her to think I'm as eager as I actually am.

At her knock, I cross the room and open the door. Thoughts of trying to come off as casual forgotten.

"Hi," she rasps.

"Hi," I say, staring at her appearance. She's changed her clothes. Her earlier preppy jeans and button-down have been exchanged for a matching sweatshirt and sweatpants. Light green. Her shoes are the same little boots from the other night, and she has her sweats tucked into a pair of thick socks. She looks adorable. She looks cozy and warm and like I want to wrap my arms around her and pull her into me.

"It smells really good in there," she comments, and I realize I've just been standing in the open doorway staring at her.

"Come in," I say, and she walks by me into my home, and if I thought she looked like mine before—seeing her in my home, my space. Now, I don't want her to ever leave.

"So this is your place, action hero?" she asks with an arched brow.

I incline my head and give her a nod. "It is."

She looks around my cabin, taking in the space and art and pictures I have up on the wall. "It's very...you," she surmises, and I snort.

"I have no idea if that's a good thing."

"I like to keep you guessing. Ya know, keep the mystery alive." She winks, and the action sends warmth spreading from my chest out toward my limbs. It makes my hands tingly, adding to the already painful need to touch her.

I clear my throat. "Are you hungry?"

"Starving," she tells me, taking off her coat and throwing it over the back of my couch like she's done it a hundred times before. I like looking at her things mixed with mine. "And before you tell me that I should be making sure I'm eating enough or watching my sugar levels." She looks at me pointedly. "I checked my levels before I came over, and they're good.

I'm just hungry," she finishes, still looking at me, and my lips twitch at the sassy expression she wears.

"Thanks for the report, Ivy." I smile at her. "Do you want to eat at the island or the table?"

She looks thoughtfully at both the wooden barstools and the small dining table I have. "Let's go with the island." She decides, and I nod and hold a hand out.

"Alright. You can have a seat, and I'll get out some plates."

"Yes, Chef," she replies in a breathy voice, and it doesn't matter that I've never wanted to cook professionally. New kink acquired.

"Do you want anything to drink? I have beer or wine or... water. Yeah, that's pretty much it." Maybe I should have spent a little longer at the store this afternoon.

"Water is fine. I've been trying to drink more, and today I've had more coffee than I should have," she admits, and I grin while I grab two glasses from the cabinet by the sink and then the pitcher of water from the fridge.

"I think I'll join you in that endeavor," I tell her.

After getting our drinks, I plate the food before sitting down next to her at the island. I don't mean to stare at her, but I watch as she takes the first bite of her meal. The one I've cooked for her. I realize in this moment that I've never cooked for anyone but my family. That's not surprising when I really think about it. I haven't wanted anything long-term, and I don't bring women here. I guess it's just that Ivy has me thinking about it. She has me thinking about a lot of things lately.

"Oh my gah..." Ivy moans while chewing. "That's really good," she says.

"Thank you." *Thank you, Knox. I owe you.*

We eat in companionable silence for a while, Ivy enjoying her food and me enjoying watching *her* enjoy it.

"So, how often are you actually in a helicopter?" she asks me while I scrape our plates and rinse them.

"Hmm...it really depends. For my job? This year, I've been involved in fourteen aerial rescues."

"Are they all in the mountains?"

"No, most of them are, but some of them are water rescues in the rivers and lakes," I say, placing our plates in the dishwasher and turning to lean back against the kitchen counter. Her eyes move over my forearms, where I've rolled up my flannel, before they flick up to meet mine. I don't mind being objectified. Not by Ivy. I smile, letting her know that I know she's checking me out before speaking again. "A lot of searches are on foot. Mostly hikers who have gotten lost. Fortunately, I've never been on a call where I lost anyone, but there have definitely been some injuries," I tell her.

Her eyes spark at that. "You know, I just saw a documentary pop up that's all about hikers getting lost in national parks."

"I think I saw that, too, but it looked more like a serial killer angle than people just getting lost."

"Yes. That's the one," she confirms. "I think it's called..." she trails off, thinking.

"Mary Is Missing," I supply.

"Yes! That's the one!" she shouts excitedly. Her excitement catches me a little off guard, and a small laugh escapes me. I round the island and walk into my living room, grabbing the remote for the TV off the side table. A quick search has me pulling up the documentary.

"What are you doing?" she asks.

"What does it look like?"

"Well, it looks like you're turning on Mary Is Missing."

"Looks can be deceiving, but in this case, they are not. That is what I'm doing. You said you wanted to watch it, and I aim to please, princess," I tell her, sinking back into my plush couch. I hear her slide off the stool and softly pad toward me. She's close when she speaks again.

"You're just going to turn it on?"

"Mmhmm," I hum. "And you're going to watch it with me," I tell her.

"Just like that?"

"Yes, Ivy. Come sit down by me and watch this probably very disturbing docuseries about people going missing in national parks and the connection it could have to a serial killer," I command, then add, "Please." I don't give her a chance to turn me down before clicking the button on the remote. It starts to play, and I catch her looking up at the screen. Sighing, she walks around the couch and sits down on the far end like she's afraid I'm going to maul her. That's...a good call on her part.

After the second episode of the six-part docuseries, Ivy is now close enough for me to feel her body heat. We made popcorn after the first episode and because I didn't have any of the candy she likes, I got a crash course in sour candy to always have on hand.

"Sour belts. Lemon drops. Sour Patch Kids," she recites. I nod and grab a pen and paper to make a list. I look up to see her grinning at me.

"What?" I ask, grinning back at her.

"You. Making another list," she answers and then shocks me by yelling, "Hey!" And pointing at my hand. *Oh, that.*

"Is that my pen?"

"I don't know. It might be," I say with a shrug.

"Alder Holloway." She says my name like it's an admonishment, but I don't care how she says it as long as it's my name she's saying. I look her in the eyes. She's so carefree right now. Openly teasing me and comfortable. "Do you have a crush on me?" she whispers, flirting with me. I should attempt to play it cool. Maybe I would if it were anyone but her. It is Ivy, though, so I'm blurting out the truth without much thought.

"I do," I admit. "A big one. Huge even," I continue. "I've thought about you and our night together more times than I haven't in the last month." My confession throws her. I can tell by the widening of her eyes and the fact that her easy smile that I've fallen for tonight has disappeared. She opens her mouth, then shuts it, and I try to add some levity back into our evening. "Whoa, did I render Ivy Rutherford, Queen of Sass, speechless? Color me surprised." That earns me an eye roll.

"I'm not speechless, Search and Rescue. The problem is I have too many things to say. Most of which you already know, but maybe I should tell you again. I'm not here for very long. I'll be gone, and you'll forget all about your crush on me. There is no shortage of prospects who would kill for a chance with you. So please, don't waste your time on me."

"Any time spent on you could never be a waste, Stormcloud. I'll take what I can get. If it's making you orange chicken and watching a docuseries, then I'm game. If it's showing you how you deserve to be worshiped and devoured in my bed, then I'm more than willing to do that as well," I tell her, and I see her eyes shift from jade to a sparkling emerald at my words. She can deny it all she wants. She likes me and she likes being here. With me.

"Let's just stick to dinner and TV tonight, hotshot," she says quietly; her voice wavering slightly.

"I can do that," I say, smiling.

Two hours later, we're sprawled out on my couch. Ivy's head is on the side opposite mine, her legs tucked up with her shins brushing against the outside of my thigh. We've been talking throughout our show; she finds what I do during a search and rescue interesting, and I find everything she says and does interesting. She told me about her time in SoCal, which ended up being most of her life. Her childhood isn't painted in a very flattering light. Her mother left when she was a baby, and her father, my business partner, sounds like an absolute ass.

She hasn't experienced enough kindness in her life. Least of all at the hands of the men in her life.

"Ivy," I start. "I need to tell you something." I drop my head against the back of the couch and close my eyes. "I should have told you this a while ago, but it just never felt like the right time to bring it up without it sounding like I was trying to make it sound like a jab at you." I pause, and she remains quiet. I can't look at her. I need to get this out before it eats me alive. "I don't just teach snowboarding at The Edgemont—I kind of own it...er a part of it. I'm a partner in the business. With your father, it would seem." I get it out in a rush and then just sit quietly. Waiting for the storm that I'm sure is brewing inside her at my admission. "I-I'm sorry I didn't tell you. I promise I wasn't hiding—" My rant is cut off by a small snore. I turn my head and find Ivy asleep.

Soft nasal noises come from her. Well, shit. I guess I'll have to find another way to tell her. I grip the blanket that's resting at her waist and pull it up over her shoulder. I sit on the couch with her a while longer. Unwilling to let the night come to an end. When the TV asks if I want to continue watching, I decide I should head to bed. I turn the TV off and allow myself one more moment to just look at her in the moonlight. I've never felt this deep tug inside me before.

If I followed it, it would always lead me to her.

ALDER

’m practically bouncing as I walk into the lodge. My not date with Ivy went better than I could have hoped. I felt like we were really getting somewhere.

When I take in the full scope of my surroundings, I’m a little taken aback by how good it looks in here. The Edgemont has been transformed into a holiday magazine spread. The trees that have been here since Ivy’s first week are still up, but now, instead of the traditional red and green, it’s all golden. The bows and wreaths, the silverware laid out on the tables, the banisters leading up to the balcony that’s been set up with outdoor heaters and sparkling lights; it all looks amazing. I follow them all the way up to the top, and then I see her.

She’s so beautiful. Wearing a dark-green dress that looks so soft, I want to reach out and run my hands over it, just to see what it feels like on her body. A body that looks just like it was made for studying, worshiping. The plunging neckline of her dress highlights her delicate neck that I want to lick, that I want to bite. It's given me and everyone here a stunning view of her cleavage.

Her hair reminds me of an old Hollywood film. It's down, and one side is pulled back with a gold clip above her ear, where a small red earring hangs. Her green eyes sparkle like emeralds, and her lips—God, her lips. They're a deep shade of red that I want to stain my skin. I want that color all over me.

She starts down the stairs, and I remember that tonight she's with me. She's mine. If she wants me to play the part of the doting boyfriend, then that's what I'll do. Happily. I won't be letting her out of my sight. I don't think I'm capable. I lift my arm when she reaches the last step, and she tucks her slender hand into the crook of my elbow, giving my bicep a squeeze. She meets my eyes, and she already looks annoyed with me. Game on, baby.

"Is this arm of yours real, or is it actually carved from marble?" Her question makes me laugh. Then she teases me further, "Are you flexing for me, Lover Boy?" Her voice is taunting as she arches her eyebrow and gives me a flirty grin. So we're flirting then? This I can do. This I'm good at. I've got charm in spades. She slides her free hand up my chest, and the small action is in danger of having a bigger reaction.

She stops at the base of my neck and smoothes my tie, leaning into me, pressing her toned body flush against me, whispering low so only I can hear, "I really appreciate you helping me. And please don't misunderstand me when I say this." She meets my eyes again, hand still on my chest, the other tucked in between us. She's stealing up all the air just like a fire does to stay alive. "You're really pretty, Alder. A literal Adonis." She looks at my mouth, and I want to kiss those red lips until we're both a mess of crimson "But you're really not my type." She smiles sadly, like she isn't the one who's just rejected me. "You do look really nice in a suit though," she adds wistfully.

I'm unsure what thoughts have her deciding this. I can honestly say I've never had a woman tell me I'm not their type, but more importantly, I don't like that look on her face. I want to have fun with her tonight. I'm here to make this night easier for her. To be what she needs me to be, and if what she needs is to pretend because she thinks she doesn't feel anything close to what I'm starting to, then I won't push it...yet.

"You look nice too, princess," I tell her, although nice is such a gross understatement that I immediately want to correct myself, but I bite my tongue. I'm not ready to show my hand just yet. Especially not coming off the heels of her letting me down easy—compliment sandwich. She snorts, and instead of letting her volley back, I decide to ask what the expectations are tonight. "So how do you want me to behave tonight?" I ask, lifting the arm she isn't holding onto to move her hair from her shoulder.

It feels like silk in my fingers. "So soft..." I say before I can catch myself. She shivers, and I see goose bumps appear. So she isn't completely unaffected by me then. She may not think she wants to date me, but I have a feeling she would be willing to do other things with me. She swallows, and I track the movement. Looking back at her eyes, I have to stop myself from pulling her into a dark corner when I notice they're glassy and her cheeks are flushed.

"Like you're obsessed with me," she rasps.

Looking away from me, her eyes clear as she surveys the room before turning back to me and smiling sweetly. "So, how you would normally act around me," she throws at me with a smirk before a voice comes over the speakers announcing the silent auction is about to begin.

We walk over toward the entrance, and Ivy greets almost every guest walking in. She's good at this. I shouldn't be surprised. She's told me time and time again that she's capable. Before tonight, I would have believed that but in a way of her being capable of commanding an army, of bringing an army to their knees before her. This, though, this version of her, it's commanding in a different way. A more subtle one. It feels dangerous. It's charming and endearing. Another piece of the puzzle for me to file away for later when my thoughts are consumed by her. Just like they have been since the moment I met her.

"Thank you so much for coming out and supporting our event tonight. Please let me know if there's anything you need tonight, and enjoy your evening," she tells Mrs. Anderson, the town gossip, as Sue enters the main room in the lodge.

I bend slightly and whisper into her ear, "Sue will be talking about this event for weeks, possibly until next year." She smiles at my words.

"I know," she tells me. "She's on the town's event committee that you put me in touch with, and I was advised to make sure she would be in attendance." She's pleased with herself, and I like the way it looks on her. I want to see how she would look if she was pleased by me.

"Lucky for you then that you have me," I say, willing it to be true. She laughs at that.

"Oh yes, lucky me." She bats those long lashes at me. "What would I do without a big, strong man to help little old me?" she asks me in an exaggerated Southern drawl. That could be something I think about later as well. Why is everything this woman does so freaking sexy?

"You don't have to find out, sugar," I say back, doing my best cowboy impression. I even tip my fake hat to her. She laughs loudly, head tilted back, mouth wide open. With that laugh, any chance I had at pretending I'm not half in love with her is out the window. I'm screwed. A waiter walks by and offers us each a flute of champagne. I grab two glasses and hand her one.

"Thank you," she says quietly before taking a sip.

"Ivy, why am I not surprised to find you with a full glass in your hand? How many has that been tonight?" Ivy's face turns to stone. She slips back into her mask so seamlessly that you never would have believed she was just having a good time with me.

"Noah," she addresses him. "Where's Margot? Don't tell me she's already figured out that you aren't worth the zeros." Her tone is innocent, but it eats at him like she's just thrown acid his way.

Noah hums, then gives Ivy a sneer. "I see you're still the same bitch you've—"

"If you finish that sentence, I will not hesitate to ensure you won't be speaking to anyone for the foreseeable future," I cut in. I'm not typically a man to threaten someone. I don't like to ruffle feathers, and I can let a lot of things roll off my back, but this asshole will not disrespect Ivy ever again if I can help it. I lower my voice, "And I'm sure you're used to men making threats and not following through, but let me be clear: I'm a man of my word. You need to be gone by tomorrow, or I'll escort you from the property myself. The choice is yours, but the second option won't end well for you." His eyes widen at my words. I can see the fear behind them even as his face remains stoic. "Are we clear?" I ask, and he nods. "Good."

I feel Ivy's hand slip into mine and give it a reassuring squeeze. "Okay, action hero, I think that's enough," she says a little shakily as she tugs on my arm and pulls us from the entrance. I give Noah one last glance as we make our way back into the main room. Jack's voice comes over the speaker again, letting us know it's almost time to eat, and everyone makes their way to their tables. I spot Rhett over by the snack table with Hazel. He's sneaking her a cookie while Knox is on the phone over in the corner of the room. He's got another thing coming if he thinks he's coming for the best uncle title.

"I need to go over to the stage now, but thank you. I'll add white knight to your list of attributes," she teases.

"There's a list, huh? And I thought I was the only one making those."

She smiles at me. "I'll be back in a few," she tells me, releasing my arm and walking off in the direction of the stage. I take this opportunity to say hello to the Holloway clan. By the looks of it, the whole town has turned up.

"Hey guys, you all look great, but especially you, Hazey baby." She smiles at my compliment and holds up the edge of her dress, showing me the lace trim. "Oh, it's so beautiful. Did you pick it out?" I ask her.

She shakes her head at me, "Uh uh. Andy Lo did." I know one day, she'll stop calling us Muncle and Andy, and I already hate that day so much.

"I love it, baby girl." She beams at me.

"Thank you, Muncle Aldie," she says sweetly, then she shoves the cookie she's been holding behind Rhett's back into her mouth, and we both laugh.

"Baby brother, how's it going at the school?" I ask. When Rhett hurt his knee, I didn't know if making the transition to high school hockey coach would be an easy one, but he's surprised us all by being happier than I've ever seen him. Winnie is probably the magic ingredient there. Speaking of which. "And where's Win?"

"The team is great. They're working hard, and we're on a nice winning streak that I'm hoping will continue for the rest of the season. I'm feeling really good about it." And I can tell by his genuine excitement that he means it. "Winnie is around here somewhere. She just went to answer a call from Marigold."

"Is Marigold coming tonight, or is she working?" I ask. Being a surgeon is something I respect and admire. I've had to pass on a patient to a surgeon a handful of times, so I know the things they see day in and day out can be a bit intense. Mare takes it all in stride though. I know she's been there for Winnie in the past, and she's always ready to step in and help at all the town events.

"She's coming," he says with a huffed laugh.

"Are you upset with her about something?"

"No, I'm not upset with her. She's the one who's upset. I guess her car got a flat, and she didn't have a spare, so she had to get a ride with Colt." He grabs another treat from the table and hands it to Hazel. Knox is going to have a fit later.

"Ah, one day, I think we need to lock those two in a room until they can get along." As I finish that sentence, Winnie comes into view beside my brother.

"I fear that would be putting both of their lives at risk, and since I love them both, I can't sign off on it. No matter how crazy they both make me sometimes," she tells us. "Hi, Hazey baby. Is Muncle Rhett giving you too much sugar?" she croons to Hazel. God, I don't know if this girl has a shot at not being spoiled. We're all her puppets.

"Yes!" Hazel shouts.

"Hello." A loud, raspy voice floods the room. I look to the stage and see Ivy there, looking too beautiful for words. "Firstly, I would just like to say thank you to everyone who's made time in their busy holiday schedules to be here with us tonight. It means so much." She speaks so eloquently. "I would like to let everyone know that all the proceeds from tonight's silent auction will be going to our EMS workers' charity. They work incredibly hard and extremely long hours to ensure the safety of the public; their bravery is unmatched. Some even lead dangerous rescue missions by helicopter..." Her eyes briefly catch mine before continuing, "To bring loved ones back to safety. They are truly pillars of strength and serve a pivotal role in this community and every other around the country." When she finishes, everyone in the room claps and mumbles their agreement. Her words hit me right in the chest. I'm not sure if she knows what that means to me.

"I'll be back up here throughout the night, but for now, I would like to invite you all to have a seat at your tables so we can get dinner served. Please enjoy yourselves, and let me know if there's anything you need. Thank you," she finishes, and I let out a whistle. She gives me a look, but I can tell she likes it. Ivy Rutherford is an absolute conundrum. I know she wants attention, demands it, but the more I give her, the more she tells me I shouldn't.

"I'll see you guys in a bit. I'm going to head over to my table."

"Oh, yeah? With Ivy?" Rhett asks.

"Yes. With Ivy. And the rest of the staff," I tell him. As I'm walking over, I see Marigold and Colt walk in and give them a wave. Colt smiles big and waves back at me. Mare waves a hand halfheartedly but stalks off to the bar. I shake my head. One day.

IVY

Tonight has gone better than I ever dreamed. The people of Silverthorne have been incredibly gracious and generous. I've felt the spirit of their community from the day I arrived here, from graciously hosting me to my car sliding off the road, but tonight—tonight, this community has raised $250,000. All while embracing my idea and, in turn, making me feel like I matter here. I'm blown away.

Even though the evening is coming to a close, there are still a few people out on the dance floor. I've been a little envious of all the guests experiencing it, but I'm also so grateful to have hosted this evening and watching my vision become a reality. It's a little bittersweet to see this whole community come to support my cause because this event brings me one step closer to leaving.

"Thank you for coming," I say for the hundredth time. You would think I was getting tired of saying it by now, but I'm not. I truly am so incredibly grateful. This event is going to get me one step closer to my end goal of running something that's all mine. My calls with my father lately have been short. Brief and to the point. My father isn't a kind man, but he does keep his word. If he says that the company will be mine, I'm inclined to believe him.

I walk up the stairs and out onto the deserted balcony. I let out a sigh, and a smile tugs at my lips. Tonight went well. *Really well*, and I'm proud. The moon is casting light onto the snow, and it makes it look like it's glowing. I lean against the railing and take in the view. I've been in such constant motion for the last month that I haven't taken enough time to really enjoy the environment I'm in.

"You were amazing tonight, and your speech was really good. I know it touched a lot of people," a voice that I could and have conjured in my sleep says close to my ear. Too close to my ear. I meant what I told him at the beginning of the night. Alder is attractive. Gorgeous. And he's kind and endearingly goofy. But it would never work between us. Dating men like Alder feels like too much, or rather, might make *me* feel too much. Not only that, but he lives here. His whole life is here, and it's a beautiful life. But it's not mine. My life is in California, and as much as I wish I could run away from all the things I've left behind me there—I can't.

I would never trust myself to be the kind of woman he needs. He's too warm. I'm so cold I'd give him frostbite.

"Thank you, and thank you for being by my side tonight." And I mean it.

"Anytime. It looks like Noah and Margot left early. Are you planning on being here a while? I'll stay and help," he offers. *He's so sweet.*

"Yes, I'll be here for a while. I should probably oversee the cleanup process and make sure everyone gets paid. You don't have to stay though. You've helped me out enough for one evening." I give him my sweetest smile.

"I don't want to leave you here alone, Ivy. Not with that prick hanging around." God, he is so protective over me, a woman he barely knows. I can't imagine how he'll be when he has a wife and kids one day. That thought hits me like a freight train. *Kids.* Just another reason it would never work between us. He's going to make an amazing dad one day. I don't even know if I can have kids after my surgery. That thought takes me back to darker days.

"Mrs. James? Are you awake?" a man's voice asks.

"I think so." I hear myself croak in return.

"The surgery was successful, Mrs. James. I would like to express again how sorry I am for your loss," he offers.

"Ivy, please." Being called Mrs. James feels wrong.

"There were no complications, but while performing the surgery, we discovered that you have a blockage in your left fallopian tube; it's no small miracle you were able to conceive at all," he informs me.

"A blockage? What exactly does that mean?" Confusion is the prominent feeling mixed with only a bit of pain.

"It means that it's not impossible, but it does make getting pregnant again unlikely. Now, there are treatments and procedures." He continued speaking, but somewhere after the word "unlikely," it started sounding like he was speaking to me from underwater.

· · ·

A pain that I wouldn't wish on my worst enemy washes over me, and I suck in a breath.

"Ivy? Are you okay?" Alder steps closer to me, but I hold up my hand. I don't want to be comforted by him again. It feels too good, and I can't let myself get used to his support, his easygoing kindness that I'm beginning to depend on. He reaches into his pocket, pulls out a crinkly plastic bag, and hands it to me. It's peach rings. I look at him curiously.

"I know it's not candied orange peels, but I wanted to have something on hand if you needed it," he tells me simply. My throat begins to burn, starting from the base of my neck, and then traveling up to behind my eyes. He's too sweet for me. He's too kind. *He's too good.* But I want him right now. I want to consume him and see if he tastes as sweet as he acts or if he tastes like the faint coffee scent that I'm always getting a whiff of when he walks by. This is absolutely a mistake, and I don't really care about me, but it's really not fair to him.

I kiss him—hard. I let all the pent-up sexual frustration he causes me out and throw it into this kiss. He opens his mouth, and I lick the inside of his lower lip before sucking it into mine and nipping it. He groans, then pushes me back against the railing of the balcony we're on, kissing the ever-loving shit out of me. He matches me bite for bite, lick for suck. I'm panting and melting into him. I assumed it would be me devouring and spitting this man out when I was done, but I have a small fear I'm working hard to push down that's telling me this kiss. *This kiss* is going to ruin me.

"Alder."

"Yes, princess?"

"You're not my type, and I'm not what you want." I pant and grind into him until I can feel his hardness through his suit pants. He opens his mouth to protest but I silence him with a look. I want to lay it all out there. He needs to know the facts. "I'm here for maybe two more months, then I'm leaving. I'm not nice, and I'm not good for you." He rolls his baby blues, and his lips part, so I press my finger to his mouth, stilling his words. His eyes heat, and that heat stokes the fire I'm barely keeping at bay.

"If we do this." He inclines his head. Just inches from mine now. "It's casual," I tell him. "No one catches feelings, and no one gets blindsided when I leave. Can you handle that, Lover Boy?" My question hangs between us. It's heavy, and I'm ready to strip right here and now if he agrees to my terms.

"I can do this however you want, Ivy. But I need you to do something for me." He reaches up and slides his hand around my throat till it rests in the hair at the nape of my neck, cradling my head and causing delicious tension between my legs. I want him. More than I will ever admit.

"What do you need me to do?" I ask, breathless and not caring.

"If we do this, however casual you want, it's still exclusive. I won't share you. I won't have you and know you're with other men."

"Who else would I be with?" I ask him, confused.

"No one. You won't be with anyone if you're with me."

"Are you a little territorial, Lover Boy? Are you going to throw me over your shoulder and drag me back to your cave?"

"If that's what gets you going, I'll carry a club too." I let out a throaty chuckle at that. "I'll do this your way, but it's just *me* for you, Ivy. No one else." I think over his words. There's no one else here I'd want to be with romantically or sexually, but I also don't tell him that. I don't want him to get the wrong idea, and Alder is exactly the type to get the wrong idea.

"Fine," I grind out while also grinding myself harder into him. He takes my hand and kisses the pads of my fingers. No one has ever done that, and it's oddly erotic. Why aren't more men kissing women's fingers? My mind is a jumbled mess of horny and uncomfortably romantic thoughts that I want to explore with the man in front of me.

He's going to take me to bed, and I'm going to get what I want from him, and then tomorrow, it will all be out of my system. "So, my place or yours?" I ask, and he chuckles and leans in to kiss my swollen lips. It lacks some of the passion from before, and when I make a move to deepen it, he pulls back just enough to move his mouth to my ear.

"Not tonight, Ivy," he says, kissing my neck.

"Why not tonight?" I ask somewhere between a gasp and a pant.

"Tonight, you're going to give me this dance," he tells me, pulling me from the railing deeper into him. "Because I've wanted to dance with you in this dress all night. Then I'm going to take you home and kiss you goodnight. If you feel the same tomorrow, then we'll be having a different conversation," he promises as he spins me away and then back to him. The music that's playing over the outdoor speakers is soft, but Alder hums along with it. It's an older song. His favorite kind. I love, and I hate that I know this about him. That and the fact that he won't be taking me to bed tonight is irritating.

"So, when you say you'll do this my way, you actually meant that we'll be doing this your way?" I snipe, and he laughs as he pulls me across the balcony, perfectly leading us in a waltz.

"No, princess. We'll do this your way; we just won't be doing it tonight. Tomorrow, we have another snowboarding lesson. You showed a lot of potential in our last session." I roll my eyes at that and can't stop my laugh.

"No, I didn't. You are such a liar."

"I'm not lying. I was surprised it was your first time on a board." I laugh harder.

"It wasn't the first time actually. The first time I tried to stand up on a snowboard, I fell backward on my ass and thought I was going to break my ankles." It had been on a class trip to a ski resort in Northern California, and I found out Thomas "Tommy" Caldwell had cheated on me with Rebecca Sampson. It wasn't the best introduction to snowboarding.

"It sounds like maybe you just needed a more competent teacher," he says, holding me closer. I let him. I want to be even closer.

"It's a good thing I have you for now, then, isn't it?" I tease.

"I'm hoping a very good thing, Ivy," he whispers, and I hum in response. Letting Alder in, even a small amount, is something I'm not sure I'm ready for. I've already had a taste of him. I'm unsure if I'll be able to give up the rush that comes with being with him. His attention and affection alone are so consuming.

We dance for another song before walking out of the big lodge and toward my cabin. Alder is still humming, sometimes singing softly. Over the last month, I've come to love the sound of his voice. He's one of those people who's always singing or humming or making up a song about the most inane tasks. It used to wear on my nerves, but this week, I heard him singing about putting away the snowboarding equipment and found it incredibly charming. I don't even think he knows he's doing it.

I'm in danger here. I'm playing with fire, but something tells me the burns would be worth it to let his flames lick at me again.

After dropping off the checks with the caterer, we walk the short distance to my cabin. When we arrive at my door, I'm reluctant to let him go. This is not at all how I envisioned my time here or even how I thought my night would go. In one evening, I have swung from one end to the other on the pendulum that is my attraction to Alder Holloway. Telling him he's not my type to practically begging him to take me to bed, and now, preparing for a night alone. I've never had to go to bed alone if I didn't want to. Not since I got out of my marriage to Noah. Something about that unsettles me.

"I'll see you in the morning, Ivy," Alder says, interrupting my internal struggle. "We'll be out at Lovers Leap, so I want to get an early start. I'll be here at five, be ready." He pulls me into his warmth. I'm always so warm with him around. He really is sunshine personified.

"Five o'clock, huh? Will the snow not wait until seven?"

"It takes some time to get up there, and I want you to see the sunrise from the gondola." That surprises me, and I pull my head back slightly to look at him.

"Why do I need to see the sunrise from the gondola?" I want to. I've wanted to from the minute I saw them out my office window...but I'm not sure how he knows that.

He rolls his eyes at me, and now Alder rolling his eyes at me is so cute I can't stand it. "Everyone should see the sunrise clear the peaks out here at least once, and you've stared long-ingly out your window at them every day you've been here. I think it's time you get on one," he says matter-of-factly.

"Oh, I see," I say somberly, biting my lip, and he cocks his head in confusion. "You've been stalking me," I tell him as gravely as I can manage. "Why does this keep happening?" I feign frustration. "I meet a guy. He bangs my brains out *one time*, and then he's obsessed with me." That last bit gets me a laugh. A loud one. I grin. I've never wanted someone's laugh so badly. Craved it. His laugh knocks something loose in me. It sounds like home. It sounds like *mine*.

"If you think I'm going to deny how obsessed I am with you, you've got another thing coming."

I lean back into him and drop my voice. "I would like to be coming, but..."

"Ivy..." he cautions.

"What? This is me telling you what I want. I want you to come inside," I deadpan. He doesn't take the bait though.

"There's an innuendo in there somewhere, but I'm not taking the bait. Not tonight," he says softly, kissing the hair at my temple.

"When you're home alone in a few minutes, I hope you remember this moment," I tell him, inching up slightly to bite at his lower lip. He leans into my mouth and plants his lips on mine. His tongue swipes at my closed lips, and I open, letting him in to deepen our kiss. Damn, can this man kiss. I'm floating again, relishing the feel of his arms circling around me and the contrast between my cold nose and his warm mouth. I'm melting into him, absolutely pliant. He kisses me for a few seconds longer, then pulls back briefly before planting the sweetest, most intimate kiss to my lips.

I open my eyes to find his blue ones blazing. Clearing my throat as delicately as I can before speaking, I lower my already breathy voice. "I also want you to be thinking about me and what I'll be doing. Alone. Thinking about that first night we met. I hope it doesn't keep you up late," I tell him with a wink.

"We have an early morning." I step back and instantly feel the chill it brings. I miss his heat. I miss how his body makes me feel.

He smiles at me, that amused, playful expression that's ever-present. "Goodnight, princess. I'll see you in the morning," he tells me as I open my front door. He frowns then. "Ivy, please tell me you lock your doors." I smile.

"Why would I need to? I don't think anything bad ever happens around here in Silverthorne."

"Bad things happen everywhere. Lock your door. Please." The *please* gets me. It feels like my chest is being lit up from inside.

"Okay, action hero. I'll lock the door."

"Do you promise?"

"Yes, Alder." My voice is reflective of a scolded teen. "I promise."

"Thank you, and about tomorrow?" I look at him expectantly. "Wear that purple ski suit. I want to see you in it, and if you're good—I want to take it off you." He winks and turns to leave, giving me an excellent view of his ass in those suit pants. I don't think anyone's ass has ever looked so good in suit pants. I bite my lip and shut my door, ready to strip out of my dress and take a bath but remember my promise and that Alder cares for me and my safety. It invades my senses and leaves this giddy feeling centered in my chest.

Smiling, I lock the deadbolt into place.

ALDER

oday's snowboarding lesson was more fun than our last one. Ivy knew how to stand on the board today, and she even made it down a green trail with zero injuries and only a few falls. I got to see her experience the gondola for the first time. She looked downright giddy, watching the sun come up from inside it. It was also more fun because I got to touch her. Almost constantly, all day. Positioning her hips and her arms. Helping her get started, helping her up. Not once did she complain. In fact, it felt like she may have been playing up her incoordination a bit just to get me closer to her. She looks so fucking cute in the purple suit. When we got to my place, she changed and had a shower before borrowing some old sweats of mine and a cut-off tee.

You know these T-shirts really do it for me, Lover Boy. She told me, and she took it and the sweats into my bathroom, wearing nothing but a towel. Now she's lying on my couch, in my home, and I'm rubbing her sore legs. Her incredibly long and tempting legs.

"Mmm, that feels good." She moans for the fifth time since she requested I give her legs a massage. Saying I was willing would be an understatement. I've never been addicted to anything in my life, but touching Ivy may be the first.

"Are you doing this on purpose?"

"Doing what?" She feigns innocence.

"So you know exactly what you're doing," I confirm. "Do you remember what I told you last night, Ivy?" I knead her calves with my hands while I speak.

"I do. You said you didn't want to sleep with me and that it would be better if we were just friends," she tells me as she ticks them off on her fingers. "You said you found me unattractive and dimwitted." She ticks another perfectly manicured green fingernail. "I did find that offensive." Laughter breaks free from my chest.

"That's what you got from last night? It's a wonder you agreed to spend time with me today. I'm baffled you're here on my couch with your legs in my lap, moaning."

"Well..." she starts and then sighs. "If things had gone my way, I would be moaning for a different reason altogether." She pouts.

"Is that so?" When I look over at her, she nods sadly. I grab her around the waist and pull her onto me. She lets out a little gasp at the action, but it turns into a giggle.

"I love that sound," I whisper.

"You told me that before."

"That's because I meant it." Lifting her up by her hips, I position her legs so she's now straddling me. I let my hands rest at the tops of her thighs, my thumbs dipping lower. Her arms rest on my shoulders, and her breath hitches when I give her a squeeze. "I thought I made sure you didn't take any bad spills today, no hits to the head, but I'm worried because you're having trouble with your memory," I say, sliding my hands up her thighs to her waist. The tips of my fingers just brush her ribcage. "I told you that if you were good, good things would happen," I remind her.

She grinds herself down on me, and I'm already harder than I've ever been in my life. Just the feel of her on top of me has me about to come in my pants. I look up at the wicked grin she's wearing. She fucking knows it. She slides her forearms over my shoulders and leans onto her elbows. Bringing her face close to mine so we're cheek to cheek, she whispers into my ear, "What if I want to be bad tonight?"

"Fuck, Ivy," I murmur into her neck and close my eyes, trying to regain some control. I know she wants to be the one in charge, and if that's what she wants tonight, then that's what she'll get. I have no intention of doing anything she doesn't want me to. She slides back on my lap in an excruciatingly sexy way. She pulls my too-big shirt over her head, and her hair that's still damp falls down her back, giving me a perfect view of her tits. "You're so beautiful," I whisper and run my hands up the sides of her waist. I pull her forward, and she arches into me. I suck a peaked nipple into my mouth, and she moans against me. The sound is almost too much for me. "If you keep making noises like that, I'm going to take you on this couch."

"Then have me on the couch," she sasses.

"No, Ivy. I want you in my bed tonight. Where you belong. Do you understand?" When I take her in, she's nodding back at me.

"Words, princess."

"Yes, Alder. Take me to bed." She doesn't have to tell me

twice. I stand, lifting her with me, and walk us into my bedroom. Laying her gently on the edge of the bed, I finally bring my mouth to hers and kiss her until we're both panting. I slide my hand under the band of her borrowed sweatpants and find her drenched.

"Oh, Ivy. You're fucking weeping. Is this mess all for me?"

"Yes," she mutters, chasing my hand.

"How long has your pussy been this desperate for me?" I murmur against her lips while I drag my fingers through her slick heat. She writhes under me. My finger slips in, and then I bring it up to her clit, rubbing slow circles. She jerks. "Are you sensitive, princess?" She nods. "Words." I press her, giving her pussy a gentle pat.

She bucks into me. "Yes. I'm wet, and I'm sensitive. Keep touching me." She gets out between pants.

"I wouldn't dream of stopping," I tell her, rubbing her clit with my thumb and curling two fingers deep inside her. "Are you going to be good and come on my hand before you come on my tongue, Ivy?"

"Yes!" she screams, and I feel her start to spasm around me. "Don't stop, please," she begs.

"Never. I won't ever have enough of the feel of you and this mouth. I have so many ideas for this bratty mouth." She squeezes my fingers in response. "Would you like that, princess? Do you want my dick to fill you up again?"

"Alder!" she moans, and I am treated to the most beautiful sight I've ever seen in my life. Ivy doing anything is sexy as hell to me, but she's just come undone at my hand, and I feel like I could die right now, and having seen this would make life complete.

"That's good, princess. We're not done though." I can't stop kissing down her body. I kneel on the floor in front of her and stop when I'm hovering over her clit. I spread her with my fingers and watch her face when I lick her. "You taste so good, Ivy. The best thing I've ever tasted."

"You don't...you don't have to do that. I don't get off that way." I'm shocked by her admission.

"Ivy, if you've never come from someone's mouth on this pretty fucking pussy then I'm all too happy to be the first. I've been dying to taste you since that first night. It was on the list. Now lay back," I order, and she listens for once in her life. I lick and suck on her until she's moaning and screaming things that I'm not even sure make sense, but I don't stop until she starts chanting that she's going to come over and over, and even then, I lick her through it.

"Oh my god, Alder." She gasps, and I stand and take my pants off, letting my dick spring free. "Holy shit." Her eyes are wide as she takes me in. I'm not insecure about my body, but knowing she likes what she sees has me feeling ten feet tall. I grip myself and stroke from the base to the tip. "I didn't spend enough time taking you all in that first night," she comments.

"We have time now. As much as you want. Now, sit back on the bed. I'm going to give you another orgasm or two."

"I don't think I can have another one."

"Yes, you can, Ivy. And you will. I'm going to bury myself inside you and fuck you until you're screaming my name and coming on my dick." When I look down at her, she gives me a lazy nod.

"I want to be on top though," she replies, crawling to stand next to me. *Who the hell am I to ruin her fun?* She grabs my biceps and turns me, gently pushing me back and laying me down on the bed. Then she's climbing over me but not touching me.

"I need your hands on me. Right fucking now," I tell her, and she grins.

"Then beg for me, Lover Boy."

I don't even give it a second thought before I start, "Please, Ivy. Touch me. Ride me. Put me out of my misery here." And she does. She sits up over me and positions my dick at her entrance.

"Is this what you want, Alder? Do you want your dick inside me?"

"Please, princess," I beg.

"Because you asked so nicely." The words leave her as she sinks onto me. I groan, barely holding it together. Then she starts to move. "Grab my hips, Alder. Help me fuck you how you want me to." My hands are on her body in an instant, and she leans back onto my knees. The windows in my bedroom are casting her in moonlight. She looks like a fucking goddess. Like an angel sent to earth just for me alone. She looks like *mine*.

I lift her up and down and buck my hips up into her.

"Touch yourself, Ivy. I need you there with me, baby." She slides her hand between us, and I see her fingers work. "Fuckkk, that's good, princess." She's making sounds that drive me closer and closer to my end, and then I feel her come around me as she screams. I call her name as I come, and she collapses onto my chest. We're both slick with sweat, and I wrap my arms around her, kissing her hair. I grab her head and lift it to kiss her.

"Please tell me that was as good for you as it was for me."

She sits back a little, smooths my hair back off my forehead, and presses her lips together, giving me a tight smile. "We'll work on it," she says with a couple of taps to my chest. Howling laughter comes out of me. I shake us both with it. "It's fine, Alder. I'm not upset, and you can practice. I can give you tutorials." She keeps going until I flip her onto her back. I look into her jade eyes that sparkle with mischief. I'm falling for this woman. Hard.

ALDER

I stare at the email on my phone I just received from my P.I. My last run-in with Ivy's ex-husband and the bad feeling that I have about him visiting here convinced me to have my guy look into him. It turns out, he's really struggling financially or at least he's going to be very soon. The IRS doesn't give second chances when it comes to fraud. I respond with the go ahead for him to file the report. The bastard deserves everything that's coming to him.

After finding out the information I did on Noah, I decided to check into my business partner as well. Sullivan Rutherford runs a tight ship but bringing Noah on board his company was a glaring error on his part. One I'm planning to use as leverage to make sure The Edgemont belongs solely to me.

I look over at the woman who's still asleep in my bed, and my chest squeezes. Everything she had to go through at the hands of the men in her life. It's no wonder she doesn't trust easily or let anyone take care of her. I send my offer to Sullivan Rutherford. I know he'll accept, but I'd like to know his answer soon. I'd like to be able to present an alternative to Ivy leaving as soon as possible. I feel like maybe coming clean about my job title regarding the lodge will be softened by having a romantic gesture in my back pocket. Her leaving isn't going to work for me. Telling her everything now is probably what I should be doing, but I don't want to bring this up to her until I have a solution.

I leave my spot on the chair in the corner of my room and walk into the kitchen, turning on the coffee pot. I start slicing oranges. I'm set on making these orange peel candies that Ivy loves, even though I think she should be finding a better snack to keep on hand for low blood sugar. I cut the peels off, throw them in the boiling pot on the stove, and gather the rest of my ingredients. I looked up how to make them last night after Ivy fell asleep. She mentioned her stock was running low, and I want to make sure she doesn't run out. The peels need to simmer for ten minutes, so I decide to get some fresh air with my cup of coffee.

After turning off the stove, I walk out onto the deck and take in the winter scene before me. I think today may be a good day for another lesson. She's getting the hang of it, and next week, I would like to take her on a blue trail just to see how she does. I'm really happy that she seemed to enjoy our last lesson. These early mornings together are something I want to keep sharing with her.

I'm lost in thought when I feel slender arms circle my waist, followed by a warm, citrusy scent. "Morning, beautiful." She hums behind me at my greeting.

"If you were actually looking at me right now, you might change your mind," she grumbles into my back.

I turn and tuck her under my arm, bringing her in front of

me to see she's in an old T-shirt of mine. I like that; I really like the sight of her wrapped in me. I kiss her head and then her temple, her cheeks, her lips until I feel her smile. This is how I want every morning to be from now on. This is what's been missing. *She's* what's been missing.

"You're stunning, Ivy." She blushes at my compliment.

"It's actually not fair that you look so good this early in the morning, Search and Rescue." I chuckle at her use of nickname this morning and pull her into me.

"What's not fair is that I have to go to work today, away from you, when all I want to do is spend the day with you in my bed," I admit.

She hums again, content to be in my arms. "Yes, I can see how you would feel deprived. I am hands down the best you've ever had," she muses.

I smile; there's no point in denying it. "Are you saying it isn't that way for you?" I ask. What we shared last night wasn't possibly one-sided.

"I'm only saying that I may need another session to confirm my stance," she says, sliding her palms up my chest slowly.

"Oh?" I bend just enough to position my hands under her thighs. When I straighten, I lift her body with me. She slips her legs around my hips and locks her arms around my neck. "Is that so?" I question again.

She nods. "Yes. I'm definitely going to need to do some more research before coming to a final decision," she tells me with a sigh.

"Then what the hell are we still doing out here?" I ask, swatting her ass once before turning us toward the glass door. She giggles before gripping my face in her hands and kissing me as I fumble for the door handle to get us back inside and in my bed as fast as humanly possible.

We spend the rest of the morning doing research and making her candied orange peels. When I finally get myself out the door for work, I can't stop smiling. A goofy, over-the-top smile that spending time with Ivy Rutherford causes me to wear like a fucking badge of honor.

Ivy

For the first time all day, I'm not regretting my choice to wear my ski pants and jacket. I was supposed to be outside for most of the day, but instead, it's been a long day of phone calls and emails. I've spent a good portion of the day fantasizing about what I'm hoping is a night full of incredibly hot sex with the man I saw helping one of our elderly guests off the ski lift this morning. The patience and care he has is not limited to helping old ladies, and that benefits me in the best of ways. I'm getting ready to text said man to tell him I'm on my way home when the view stuns me.

The snow is crunchy beneath my feet, and the moon is full, casting light onto glittering snow. It really is beautiful. If you would have told me a month ago, I'd be enjoying the view from the top of this mountain and growing attached to this place. I wouldn't have believed you, but I'll miss it here when my sentence is served and I go back home. Home. That word has lost a little of its shine while I've been in Silverthorne. A place that's welcomed me despite being an outsider to their close-knit, small town. It makes my chest feel funny.

Alder wanted to meet me when I finished for the day, but I insisted I'd be fine. I could tell he was a little reluctant, but he didn't argue. A man in my life respecting my wishes? It's unheard of. I make it to my cabin just as the snow starts up again, fully expecting it to be dark, but there's a glow coming from inside. I halt, almost skidding on the light dusting that's starting to accumulate. My mind instantly goes to Noah. He said he was leaving, but this wouldn't be the first time he's lied. I don't think I could even count all the lies at this point.

I'm getting sucked into a panic when I hear music. I turn my head, and that's when I recognize The Rolling Stones. Alder. I feel myself smile just thinking of his name. I doubt I'm in the minority in that respect. I'm very concerned about how I instantly feel like if he's in there, waiting for me, then I can master my panic. Hell, I think I could take on a Russian spy when he's near. Yes, that's concerning, but I'll concern myself with it later. Right now? Right now, I've got a smokin' hot snow-boarder inside my cabin, and I'm ready to send it. I think I'll use that line on Alder; he'll love it.

I've just thought of the perfect thing to yell when I walk inside, but when I open my door, I'm stunned silent.

I'm fully aware that I'm letting cold air and snow inside, but I'm having trouble remembering how to move, and to be honest, I also refuse to take my eyes off the man before me. Missing one second of this would be detrimental to my health or at least my sexual fantasies to conjure up later. Alder Holloway is in the small living room in nothing but a white towel slung low on his hips, singing. He turns from the fireplace and meets my eyes briefly. His are crinkled at the corners, and he's smiling so big I can see all his perfect teeth, not that I can look anywhere but at his torso at this moment.

The lines of his abs that I'm dying to lick flex as he starts moving toward me. I give the cut V, smattered with dark hair, one more longing look before I shift my eyes up to his again. He's singing about how I keep telling him he's not my kind of man, but here when it's just us in this space. I think Alder may be my only kind of man. I may be ruined for any other after this. He stops singing when he sees my expression. I tend to play it cool, but I can't hide how badly I want him. How this is all I've been looking forward to all day.

He's dancing his way over to me now, and the grin on his face is truly mesmerizing. The sway of his hips is hypnotic. How was it that a month ago, I thought I could hold my own against him? Choose whichever metaphor you prefer; I am a moth to his white-hot flame. He doesn't break eye contact or stop singing when he reaches me. His toned arms reach around me, closing the door. Hands that I am dying to have on me unwind the scarf at my neck, then slide down each of my arms, stopping at my fingers. He grips both of my middle fingers and pulls my gloves from my hands, and fuck, why is that the hottest thing that's ever happened to me? Then the zipper on my coat is next; he drags it down swiftly, but it's too slow for me. I'm suddenly grateful I chose this one and not my favorite with all the buttons. He pushes the offending object off my shoulders, taking the suspenders attached to my ski pants with it. Untucking my shirt, he stares into me with eyes that tonight remind me of ice and how it burns if it's in contact with your skin for too long. *Burn me. Please.* His lips twitch, and for a split second, I'm afraid I've said it out loud. I wet my lips, and his chest expands with a sharp intake of air. We still haven't spoken. The thought solidifies what I already know. We hide behind our words, trading jabs and innuendos, and it's allowed us to feel like we're in control of where this has been heading.

The music is still playing, but it fades to the background around us. He lifts his chin at me in an unspoken request, and I lift my arms without hesitation.

"Good girl." He breathes out. Indignation and something I'm not ready to name flow through me. My cheeks burn, and my mouth pops open, but before I can make a sound, before I can tell him I'm nobody's good girl and he can fuck right off, he whips my shirt halfway over my head, leaving my eyes covered. My arms are still in the air, stuck inside my shirt as he leans into me. I gasp as my bare back makes contact with the cold door then feel his hot breath in my ear.

"Shh, Ivy." The gravel in his voice sets a fire in me. "We both know I love when you're being mean to me. I get off on it." *Oh, god. I'm buying whatever he's selling.* "But I'm thinking tonight we do things a little differently. Tonight, you're going to do what you're told, and we're both really going to enjoy that." He nips my earlobe, and I let out an embarrassingly loud moan, only I'm so turned on I can't bring myself to feel embarrassed. He gives my shirt a small tug, leaving me in just my bra, and reaches around me. I arch my back to give him space to unhook it. He hums when it drops to our feet. I'm now naked from the waist up, my nipples are peaked, and my skin is hot. And the way he's looking at me like I could be his last meal and he would die happy makes me breathless.

"Hands on my shoulders, Ivy," he commands. It's gentle, but I know a command when I hear one. It takes everything in me not to fight him, but he shakes his head at me. He knows I'm biting my tongue. I place my hands on his broad shoulders, and he crouches in front of me. The image has my head spinning. I am good and drunk on this man. He grips my knee and lifts a leg to slide my boot off, and I steady myself on him. He does the same with the other before reaching up to unsnap my pants and drag them down my legs.

His face is level with the part of me that needs him the most, so when he bends his head and kisses me through my lace panties, I almost combust right here in the entryway before he's even really touched me. When did I get so needy?

"Alder?" I plead. I don't think I've ever pleaded in my life, but here I am, ready to beg for him.

"I know." Is his only reply. It comes out a quiet rumble while he sits back on his heels and pulls my pants down to my feet. His full attention is on me. God, why do I love that so much? It's like he can hear my thoughts, and I'm beyond trying to hide them. "You love this, don't you? Me on my knees in front of you, telling you what a good girl you are." He hooks his thumbs into the pants around my ankles.

"Step." I step away from the door. Out of my pants. Closer to him—his mouth. "That's good, Ivy. Really good," he praises me, hot air whispering over my thighs. My insides turn molten. His hands encircle my ankles, thumbs rubbing little massaging circles into them, slowly moving up my calves, and when he reaches my thighs, he grips them tightly and stands, taking me with him. His towel is no longer around his waist—only my legs, and I clench them tighter when the friction of his hard stomach rubbing into me stokes the fire inside me higher and hotter.

"You like it when I tell you how good you are, don't you?" My fingers dig into his shoulders tighter, and I bite my lip. He makes a sound in the back of his throat, letting me know he likes that. Me marking him. "Tell me, Ivy." I shake my head, and that earns me a slap on the ass. I whine. "Tell me how you soaked through these panties when I told you how good of a girl you were being." I don't say anything or make a move to answer, but he's right. So fucking right, and he knows it. I'm a confident woman. I can speak openly about anything.

But this. It feels so intimate. He's looking at me. Waiting for an answer.

"Yes," I whisper. He smiles slightly at my admission. Confirmation that he's right. Fuck is he smug. Or at least that's what I think until he deposits me on the couch in the open living room.

"That's so fucking good to hear, baby. I'm so fucking proud of you." *Baby?* I'm stunned. By how good I feel to have told him and how good it feels to hear those words. *I'm so fucking proud of you.* I didn't realize what those words would do to me. I'm hot and wet. My throat feels tight, but I've never felt lighter.

"God, you're gorgeous, Ivy." He slides his left hand up my body, stopping to cup my breast, massaging. Gently at first, then more firmly. His right hand slides my panties to the side, and he dips one finger inside me. I want to scream.

"Please." I pant. God, I am so desperate.

"Please what, baby? What do you want me to do to this pretty pussy? Should I start with worshiping it with my tongue?" I nod, half-delirious. "Words, Ivy." I glare at him.

"I want your mouth on me, so you'll shut the fuck up," I snap, and he chuckles, shaking his head and tsking.

"Ivy, that's not what we're doing tonight. You said you'd be good for me. Can you do that?" I'm equal parts turned on and ready to kick him off the couch. I start to nod, but he grips my chin with his index finger and thumb. It's gentle, but it stops me and forces me to meet his glassy eyes. "Say you're going to be good for me. I want the words," he tells me slowly. His voice is already thick, and I want him. Badly. I open my mouth, ready to give in when an idea strikes. I stick my tongue out and lick his thumb.

His jaw slackens, and his groan loosens in his chest. "Fuuu-uck, baby," he grits out before sticking his thumb into my waiting mouth. I leave my mouth open, staring at him inno-cently. Waiting for instruction. "Suck." His voice is harsh and rough, and I'm dripping. I wrap my lips around his thumb, flat-tening my tongue against it. Then I suck, hollowing my cheeks. His eyes ignite. I moan, and his lids start to look heavy at the noise. I buck my hips up, needing friction. "Do you want me to touch that pretty pussy now?" I nod and suck harder, groaning. "You look so pretty sucking on my thumb like this baby. Are you wishing it was my dick?" I mmhmm around him and pull his thumb out of my mouth with a loud wet pop.

"I want you, Alder," I demand. He smiles, but not in the way that tells me I'm getting what I want. I whine, and he chuckles.

"What do you want, princess? Do you want me on my knees?" he teases me, pinching a nipple as he kneels before me. I cry out at the sensation.

"I want you to stop teasing me and fuck me." I growl. Alder's eyes are two blue flames now. He grips my thigh, lifting it up, and thrusts inside me. "Yes, oh god, yes," I call out. He continues to pump into me until I can't breathe. I don't remember how to breathe or my own name anymore. I just know that I don't want Alder to ever stop or ever be away from me. That thought scares the shit out of me and has me coming harder than I ever have in my life.

"Say you're mine, Ivy."

"I'm yours, I'm yours!" I scream as he fucks me through my orgasm. I feel like I'm in another universe.

"That's right, baby. *Mine.*" Alder grunts and finishes inside me, calling out my name and landing on top of me. I run my fingers through his still-damp hair. Content to stay here, just like this, listening to his breathing sync with mine and with his arms banding around my back and shoulders, cradling me. Moments like this have me rethinking my plans. Rethinking what I want my life to look like, what it could look like. Who I might want to keep in it.

IVY

I'm...giddy? I've spent the past five nights at Alder's house and have a good collection of cropped T-shirts at mine. I've only been to my place to change for work in the mornings and to grab a toothbrush. My purple toothbrush that is now in the cup by the sink in his bathroom. That thought has me more giddy than is acceptable. I grin, thinking about him putting it in there next to his when he found it left on the counter.

He sent me a text yesterday, telling me where the spare key was and to let myself in. I hesitated, trying to prove to myself that I could spend the night alone. Ultimately, all I proved was that I would rather be with him. I also wanted to know if he was okay. He was getting ready to lead a river rescue. Someone had decided to try ice fishing in an area that was restricted, for good reason, and was stuck out there, too scared to move. It makes me nervous to think of him in these situations, but I've witnessed time and time again that Alder is incredibly capable of the missions he goes on.

. . .

I think back to last night when he brought me chocolate croissants from Thistle and Sage. We were watching yet another documentary about a serial killer who specifically targets people in national parks. I've never met someone who could keep up with true crime like I do. I was telling him about the podcast I listened to. He pulled his phone out and, in seconds, had it queued and ready to go on the TV in his living room. Alder is so straightforward. He says what he means, and he means what he says. I'm not used to it, but I think I *could* get used to it.

"Please never go into a national park by yourself," he begged.

"You either! One of the victims was a single man. It's not just women, Alder," I teased.

"I'm not really single, though, am I?" he asked while dropping lazy kisses onto my neck.

"Hmm...no, maybe not." I could feel his smile against me before sitting up on the couch next to me.

"Now I need you to be honest with me for a minute, princess." He was serious for a minute. I think my exact thoughts were "oh shit" and "not yet" even though I had no idea what he was going to ask.

"Will you..." he started, "watch *Twilight* with me?" He buried his face into my stomach, where it shook with my laughter. A deep, almost painful laugh broke free from me. I love how he teases me.

"Oh, my god. I thought you'd never ask," I wheezed out between laughs and him kissing me.

Of course, after watching the first movie, *New Moon* had to be next, even though it was late. He tried to tell me he'd never seen it, but when Bella gets to the reservation to confront her werewolf best friend, he was saying, "Bella, where the hell have you been, loca?" right along with me and Jacob Black.

We explored each other's bodies and talked about space, which led to an in-depth discussion on which planet we would live on— if it was inhabitable.

When he got home from work, I wasn't sure what kind of mood he would be in. He wanted me in his bed within minutes of walking in the door. I clench my thighs together, remembering the command in his voice. "Bed, Ivy. Now."

The rescue was successful, and I would venture to say that the rest of the night had been as well. I blush thinking about the things he said to me. The things I said back. I don't think I've ever felt like this before.

Sex? I've had it. Not a lot, if I'm being honest, but enough to rate it. At least that's what I thought. *On this side of the chart we have not great and on this side we have good.* That was before. Alder Holloway is now the whole pie chart. Nothing I've experienced before is like what I've shared with Alder. It's all good with him. So good. Everything. Before, during, after. All the time I spend with him is good.

I change out of a big red T-shirt with a sports team logo on it and some sweatpants and add them to the ever-growing pile of Alder's clothing that I'm acquiring. I smile. I like wearing his clothes. I like smelling like him. He told me not to shower this morning so I would smell like him all day. A request that I could easily agree to. I put on a purple sweater and leggings, followed by a pair of thick socks and boots. Not bothering to put any makeup on, I French braid my hair straight down my back. I look in the mirror, and I don't look like myself. Or maybe I look more like myself than I ever have.

The dark edges of myself that I've been clinging so tightly to have brightened a bit. Is this what happiness looks like? What healing could mean for me? It's been so long. I feel lighter. Not weightless. I don't think that's the goal, but like maybe the weight of all that I've gone through, the future I had let myself dream about, isn't something I have to continue to let crush me. Maybe if I let someone care about me, believe that they do, I can let them help me carry the weight of my grief and pain. I won't have to bear it alone anymore.

I physically feel the shift in me. My revelation is so much more than surface level and the way I look outwardly. The reflection in the mirror is only a likeness to the transformation that's been going on inside me. Feelings I bury over and over are coming to the surface, and I let them. I close my eyes and welcome them. Maybe...maybe I can honor Silas...by living a life filled with love. Pain. Love that I will continue to have for him until we're reunited one day. I hear a choked noise and open my eyes to find it's come out of my mouth. From somewhere deep in my gut.

I place shaky fingers to my lips as more emotion barrels into me. I try to avoid thinking about him, my idea of what life would have been with him, knowing that when I do, searing pain comes with it. Anytime I see a little boy around the age he would be, it sends imaginary images to my brain. Letting myself think about him now and be fully immersed in dreams that were stolen, when I didn't feel like I was allowed to for so many years, is painful but also healing.

Noah wouldn't talk to me about it other than to say that my miscarriage at three months pregnant was a blessing in disguise.

I physically recoil, thinking about his callousness during the months that followed. After telling me repeatedly that losing my son was part of a bigger plan and maybe it was for the best since I wasn't ready to be a mom, he took me to that horrible place, saying it would help, but I know now he took me there, so he didn't have to deal with my depressive episode.

I was drowning in grief while he was attending company events, telling people I was at a spa. Most people assumed it was a rehab facility. Somehow, that was more palatable to the social circle I found myself in when I married Noah. How laughable.

But now, envisioning the little boy I never got to be a mother to, I know in my heart I would have been a good mother to him. I know I would have done anything for him. Would do anything for him to still be here with me. For the first time since his loss, I refuse to believe the lies I've told myself. I'm choosing to believe that sharing how my loss has affected me won't make me weak; it will help me keep that love and the memory of Silas alive.

I swipe the tears from my face and smile. I've always prided myself on being capable. If I want something, I'll figure out how to get it, but this may be the first time I feel the strength behind that sentiment. I feel resilient. I don't want to let the fear of that pain stop me from experiencing love in other ways. I look down at the small glass jar I'm holding filled with candy strips. Alder. Alder, with his effortlessly kind and thoughtful nature, is helping me to realize that I don't have to be fully healed to be cared for. I don't think my objective has to be complete healing; I don't think the love I will always feel for Silas requires healing, but maybe with Alder by my side and being vulnerable with him could help me find some peace my way.

It's with this new outlook on life that I walk to the lodge. When I open the door to my office, the feelings of hope I'm getting used to are reinforced by the coffee cup that's waiting on my desk and the absolute heartthrob of a man sitting behind it.

"Good morning, Stormcloud," he says, rising from my chair and coming over to kiss me.

"Good morning, action hero," I respond with his mouth still on mine and his arms wrapped firmly around my body.

"Have we had this conversation before?"

"Mmm...just this morning. And the one before. And the one before that..." I tell him in a singsong voice. He smiles so wide; those dimples I love so much pop. I sigh; I'm in so deep. I don't want to get out.

"I missed you," he whispers, and I grin.

"I left your house less than an hour ago. Obsessed much?"

"Possessed," he says without missing a beat. I blush.

"I know the feeling." Feeling brave, I continue, "What we're doing here...it's..."

"It's everything, Ivy." He finishes my sentence, and I nod.

"I..." I clear my throat. I'm ready to declare myself. I want him. For as long as I can have him. I want his sunshine and warmth, and I want all his late nights, and I want to be his first call when he gets off a shift. "I have a lot of baggage, Alder. Like *a lot* of baggage, and I haven't always been good at letting someone take care of me." He smirks at that, and I glare at him. "If you're going to look at me like that, then we can forget I said anything at all," I threaten.

He pinches his lips between his teeth to stop what I'm sure is a smile and mimes locking them shut before smoothing a loose strand of hair behind my ear.

"With that being said," I hedge. "I like it when you check on me." But that's not exactly what I'm trying to say here. I try again. "I like that you care enough to check on me. I like that you want me to eat a more balanced diet and you like going grocery shopping with me. I like that you sing all the time, and you don't care that you look like an idiot."

"That's debatable. I look good when I sing," he cuts in, and I laugh a little, a tear slipping down my cheek. He swipes it away, and I speak again.

"I like that you've been through something awful and remained the kind of human that people benefit from having in their life." I choke a little. "I like that your family has little picture frames on their Christmas tree, Alder. I think..." My eyes water again, feeling the words before I speak them. "I would like to be on the tree someday," I say, barely able to get it out because I've started breathing so hard, and his answering smile makes him look like light, personified.

"If you want to be on the tree, then you'll be on the tree, baby," he says with a voice that sounds like something contained, but that's about to be let loose. "I'll get seven trees, and they'll all be filled with pictures of you," he tells me before his warm, strong hands thread into me. One at the base of my skull in the messy braid that's there, and the other grips the back of my jacket. This kiss consumes me. I'm filled with fire, and it's spilling out of me and into Alder as we claim each other. I love him. Our kiss is interrupted by a loud ringing. Not a phone, but similar. Alder pulls back and looks into my eyes. His are like blue flames and reflect the heat I feel all over me.

"That's the emergency SAT phone. I have to answer," he tells me, and I nod.

"No, of course." I try to pull back, but he holds me for a

second longer and kisses my forehead before releasing me to retrieve the phone from his coat that's slung over the back of my office chair.

"Alder Holloway" he answers, then he's quiet for a few moments. I wait, reeling from our interaction and also watching his face shift into stone. He's locked in on this call. It's now making me anxious. "Understood. Ten minutes." He hangs up and looks at me. "If it wasn't an emergency—" he starts, but I cut him off.

"I know who you are." I smile. "Go be the action hero I know you to be, and then come home to me." The word home hits us both in the chest if his next move is any indication. He picks me up and kisses me so deeply it makes my head spin. If I'm a flame, then he's pure oxygen. I'm lit up with him.

"I'll be back. We'll talk more," he states, and I laugh. The levity of telling him how I feel threatens to have me floating out to space. He kisses me again, hard. "We'll do a lot more of this too," he demands, and I giggle. The return of the giggle.

"We will."

"I'll be back as soon as I can." He grabs his jacket and walks by me again, pulling me to him once more, and my cheeks have to be fire-engine red at this point.

"Be careful," I whisper.

"Always, baby." He winks, and then he's gone. Leaving me with a goofy smile and enough adrenaline to restart a heart.

# IVY

Noah James is standing in my office. Again. He's supposed to be gone. Far away from here. The sight of him is so unsettling it makes me nauseous.

"We really need to stop meeting like this, Noah. Or at all," I say with as much venom as I can muster. "Why are you in my office?" I ask, then think of a better question. "What are you still doing in Silverthorne?"

"I told you we'd be staying through the new year," he says.

"Yes, and it's January the 6th. Well after the new year," I deadpan. "What can I do for you this morning?"

"It's more about what I can do for you," he starts as I sit in my chair behind my desk.

"I'm listening," I say, motioning with my hand for him to continue. The sooner he says whatever he wants, the sooner I can tell him to get the hell out of here.

"I don't want to marry Margot," he confesses, and I have to will my eyes not to pop out of my head. "I never wanted to marry her."

"That's interesting because you fucked her well before the ink on our marriage certificate had dried, then continued to the whole time we were married, so I got the impression you were pretty happy with her," I say flatly.

"I didn't know you cared." His reply is dripping with sarcasm.

"I didn't then, and I still don't. Which is why I'm very confused about why you're telling me this."

"I know I didn't always treat you how I should have, Red," —I snort at his understatement—"but it wouldn't be like that this time." That's where he completely loses me.

"This time? I'm sorry I'm not following you. We're divorced, Noah," I say slowly, making sure to enunciate every last syllable. He ignores me.

"I've given this a lot of thought, and I think it would be best for both of us to reconcile." The words coming out of his mouth sound like another language to me. He's fully delusional if he thinks there is any possible reality where I go back to the hell that I've barely managed to crawl out of as it is.

"You're missing a very large piece of the puzzle there, Noah." And possibly a few screws.

"I assure you; I've thought of everything. You don't have to do anything. I'll take care of it all. Your father has assured me—"

"My father?" I ask, incredulous.

"Yes, Sullivan and I have talked this through. When you come back to California after your time here, which he and I agree has been extremely beneficial for you. You've proven that the position at Rutherford Industries deserves to be yours. Well done," he rambles. The level of excitement in his voice is unexpected. Like he truly expects me to be happy about this.

"Noah. Let me be clear. I will never marry you again." My voice is unwavering. Keeping my emotions out of it. Inside, I'm raging. He scoffs.

"I suppose your new plaything has something to do with this." He throws at me.

"Alder has nothing to do with this. I will never subject myself to a life with you anywhere near it ever again."

"I think you're forgetting that we're still connected through our business ventures." He smiles, but it's cold. Calculated. "I was hoping we could do this amicably." He sighs and sits in the chair across from me, leaning onto the edge of my desk. I want to scream, but I breathe in through my nose to calm myself.

"What do you mean by that, Noah?"

"It would cause a pretty large scene if word got out about where you actually went when we told them you were at a spa retreat, Ivy. They may even question if you're capable of taking over any position or capable of taking care of yourself at all," he threatens, and I physically flinch as though I've been slapped.

"How would that possibly get out?" I say through clenched teeth. Shame slices at me.

"You know how reporters are these days, and with you disappearing again these past few months—people are asking questions. Questions I have the answers to." My vision blurs. I'm not sure if it's solely from the rage that's brewing inside me or if there are actual tears there.

"Why?" I croak. "Why would you do that to me?" I don't remember much of my time in the psychiatric ward I was sent to, but the flashes I do are not pretty. To this day, I'm not sure if it was actually a licensed mental health facility.

"I don't want to, Ivy, and I won't so long as you see reason," he says gently, like he's speaking to a child.

"I'm not nineteen anymore, Noah. You can't manipulate me anymore," I warn. He sits back in his seat and stares at me.

"Cut the dramatics, Ivy. It's not going to work this time. I think I'm finally past the point of caring if everyone knows about my skeletons. Anyone who truly knows me wouldn't judge, and if they did, then fuck them. I laugh, only it comes out a little hysterical sounding.

"If you think telling whatever struggling journalist you can find that I had to spend time in a mental hospital as a result of the way you treated me, a nineteen-year-old who just lost her baby, then go right ahead, Noah,"—I swallow, unsure if I'll be able to follow through on what I threaten next—"but be ready for the backlash, and be ready for me to tell my side of the story." He sets his jaw and then sucks his teeth.

"Fine. If that's how you want to do this, then I hope you're prepared." His voice lacks all the fake niceties he conjured earlier.

"Prepared for what?" a voice that I wouldn't have expected to hear calls from the hall. "What exactly does Ivy need to be prepared for?"

"Sullivan. Wh-what are you doing here?" Noah stutters out.

"Well, that's going to be revealed very shortly, but first, I would really like to hear what my daughter needs to prepare herself for," he says cooly. Noah opens his mouth, looking for an excuse. A way to weasel out of my father's wrath. He should know by now there's nowhere to run. Threatening my reputation threatens his, and he may not care for me, but he does care about the name Rutherford.

"I...I was just trying to make Ivy see reason. You and I both know she belongs back in California, running the family business, and she should be back at my side." He pauses, then when my father doesn't reply he continues, "She shouldn't be wasting her time here with a fucking snowboarding instructor. There's nothing for her here." He throws, casting a hand out.

My father turns his attention to his hands, and as he speaks, he works on calmly removing them from his gloves. "Noah, I've given you every opportunity to succeed," he says so quietly I can almost hear my heart pounding. "But..." He sighs heavily. "You've squandered all of them. I think it's best if we part ways." His eyes flit up to a shocked Noah. "Permanently," he adds.

"Sullivan. That's...that's not true. Surely we can work something out. I can take on more responsibility. I'm working on something right now—"

"Not for Rutherford Industries." The finality in my father's voice cutting off Noah's sentence is one I've learned you cannot argue with. Pushing off the wall and standing to his full height, he looks incredibly intimidating. I don't think I've ever seen him look like this.

"And if I decide to go to the press and tell them that Ivy here spent time in a psychiatric treatment facility? That she's so weak in the head that she had to spend months wearing grippy socks with drool running down her face just to cope with things that happen to people every day?" I hate how his words slash at my stitched-up wounds. They're bleeding again. The shame is threatening to swallow me alive.

"I'm not sure how that's relevant to this conversation. Does Ivy know that you're here as a last-ditch effort to save your name from ruin?" my father asks, and I blink. *What?* Noah looks like he's been sucker punched for a second before schooling his features.

"I'm not sure where you're getting your information, but I can assure you—"

"I'm getting all of my information from my former business partner," he tells Noah. "I think you both know him." He looks at me and then back to Noah. No. He can't mean... "Alder Holloway." My mouth pops open in shock, and my vision starts to tunnel.

"Your business partner?" Noah and I ask at the same time. Sullivan just nods, like he's bored.

"Former, as of this morning," he confirms, and then he looks at me. My mind is whirling. *Alder knows my father?* He is...er he was my father's business partner? In what? Why wouldn't he tell me? I stare at my father. Stunned. He speaks again, and I hear him, but I'm not sure if I process everything happening.

"As we speak, your office back in California is being audited by the IRS. They got a tip that you hadn't been completely truthful with the income amounts you've been reporting to them. They don't like that, and neither do I. I turned everything I had over to them in exchange for immunity," he states plainly. Noah's face pales, then it turns angry.

"You don't know what you've just done. You just made an enemy out of not only me but my family, Sullivan! All my family's business associates." He's trying to intimidate him, but my father just nods, contemplative.

"Maybe, but I'm assuming they will all want to stay far away from you for the next five to seven years while all this gets settled." No sooner does he get the words out that two police officers walk in, grip each of his arms, and start telling him his rights. I'm shocked. Completely at a loss for words. My emotions have been taken for a ride the last hour and a half, and I'm not sure what I feel. Other than the burn of his betrayal. Alder lied to me. Like every man I have ever trusted has—he lied. I stare at the ceiling while Noah tries to plead with the officers. I don't know how to reconcile the man I'm learning has lied to me since the moment I met him with the man I was beginning to fall for. The Alder I know wouldn't do something like that.

The officers who read Noah his rights have left, leaving just a few investigators to stay back and speak with my father. I'm barely hanging on. My mind won't reconcile what's just occurred. That he knew about it and decided to keep me out of it. I sit in my desk chair spiraling, and when I look up again, I see it's just us now.

"Ivy," my father says, and I look up to meet his eyes.

"A heads-up phone call would have just been too much?" I accuse, and he sighs.

"Let's not get too hung up on the details, Ivy. I'm really in no mood," he dismisses me.

"You're in no mood? Ha." I let out a harsh laugh. "I've just found out you had my ex-husband investigated by the IRS," I say.

"Actually, I didn't have him investigated. Alder Holloway did. He just informed me of his findings, giving me the opportunity to cut ties with Noah before my name was dragged through the mud. Not a good look," he tells me. "I'm sure you're happy to hear this though. All this ensures you'll be appointed the role of creative director at Rutherford Industries," he supplies, clueless to the fact that the man who saved his company has wrecked my heart in the process.

"I don't think I want the job anymore," I say, barely above a whisper.

"Well. I suppose that will be your decision. I need to get

back to the airstrip, so I look forward to hearing from you with your formal answer. The job is yours if you want it. If not, I'm going to need to fill the position soon. With all this turnover, our investors will want a statement." I'm numb to his words. I don't care about the job anymore. I don't care about Rutherford Industries or what Sullivan Rutherford thinks of me, maybe for the first time in my life, as ironic as that is.

"Goodbye, Ivy. Take care," he says with a wave of his hand, walking out my office door, leaving me with the knowledge that the one man I chose to let into my life after years of thinking I never would—is just like all the others before.

ALDER

I'm flying.

I've never been so happy in my life. Ivy's just told me she wants to be with me. She wants me to be hers. And with the information I received this morning from her father, I'll be able to explain my part in The Edgemont and ask her to stay with an offer to run it with me. Indefinitely. As well as riding the emotional high of her confession, I am also piloting the helicopter to our destination. Getting the call that there was an emergency out near Clearwater Canyon came at the most inconvenient time in my whole life, but I guess that's the whole point of my profession.

"Almost there," I relay to my crew, and they move around the cabin of the helicopter, getting ready to pick up our patient. Fifty-six. Male. Fell while hiking. Has a possible broken leg as well as a dislocated shoulder. Someone from the trail above was able to hear him yelling for help and called it in. Thankfully, they didn't try to get to him themselves.

"Landing in forty-five seconds," I say.

"Heard."

"Copy." Ty and Griff confirm they've heard me at the same time.

Once we've landed, I stay in the helicopter while Griff and Ty make the hike down to our patient. Sometimes too many sets of helping hands in a situation like this is not helpful.

"Patient has a broken tibia. I've splinted it, and he's now on the stretcher. He has a confirmed shoulder dislocation. We'll be back to you in two shakes of a lamb's tail," Griff says over the comms.

"Otherwise known as two minutes," Ty adds.

"Copy that. I'll let the hospital know we're ten minutes out," I say into my headset.

I'm anxious to get back to town, and then back up the mountain, back home, back to Ivy.

We land on the hospital roof, then unload the patient, Steve, who was out for a hike and slipped on some ice before falling into the canyon. By the sound of it, it could have been a lot worse, especially if someone hadn't been out on the same trail today to help us locate him.

"Alright, I'm out," I tell Ty and Griff as I walk down the hall of the hospital to the elevators.

"Where are you off to in such a hurry? We were gonna go to AJ's for a drink," Ty asks me.

"I've got something important to take care of," I tell him.

"Ooooo...you got a date, Alder?" Griff calls.

"Something like that," I yell as the elevator doors shut. Date. Locking Ivy down for good. Keeping her forever. Yeah, something like that. I shake my head.

I pull my phone out and see I have a missed call. It's from Sullivan. Sighing, I hit his number and wait for him to pick up.

"Hello," he answers.

"Sullivan. I thought all our business was finished after the transaction this morning," I say.

"Business is all wrapped up. I was calling to let you know that Noah James was arrested on your property earlier."

"He was where?" I ask, worrying for Ivy and struggling to stay in control. "Was he alone?"

"No. I was there as well as my daughter," he explains.

"Ivy was there? Is she okay?" I let the fear into my voice now.

"She's fine. When I left, she was still in her office. A bit confused by our partnership, but physically she's fine," he tells me. She knows. She knows, and it wasn't me who told her. Is all I can think. No. Fuck. "I offered her the job, so she should be out of your hair soon," he comments. "If that's all. I have other business to attend to." He doesn't wait for my reply before hanging up. Shit, shit, shit. I see I have three texts, two are from the family group chat, and one is from Ivy.

STORMCLOUD

I'll be at the office late tonight.

That's all it says. I shoot off a reply.

ALDER

I'm on my way. I'll be there soon.

Please don't leave. Please just give me a chance.

IVY

I'm cold. A bone-chilling cold. It's such an odd contrast to the way I felt this morning. The burn that was searing into my veins earlier is now icy shock. Biting and brutal. I feel like the slightest stumble will cause me to shatter. I've been through worse, I tell myself. It does nothing to lessen the pain, but it does serve to remind me that the pain will lessen. Eventually. Hopefully.

I'm not sure what I'll do now. I had foolishly started to believe that Silverthorne could be my home. Home. I wince. Oh my god. I said I wanted to be on his family's Christmas tree. He let me say that. He let me pour my heart out when he's been lying to me. Alder made me fall for him, and now I'm going to have to dig my way out of this ravine by myself.

Better start now. I start packing my desk up. I don't have a lot of personal items here, so it takes less than half an hour. With nothing else to do, I just sit here. I don't want to go to my cabin. Alone. I don't need the reminder. Pulling out my phone, I make a call.

"Hello, thanks for calling The Holloway Hotel. How can I help you?" A sweet, young voice that I've grown attached to answers.

"Hi, um, do you have any rooms available?" I ask, and my throat burns.

"Let me check on that for you."

"Thank you." I hold my phone away from my mouth and take a breath.

"Of course, so it looks like we have three rooms available. A queen, a king, and a double twin."

"I'll take the queen, please."

"Perfect, have you stayed with us before?"

"I have a few months ago."

"Great, can I get your name?"

"Yeah, It's Ivy."

"Ivy?! Why do you need a room? Is everything okay?" she asks one question after the other.

"No, yeah. I'm okay. Just needing the room."

"Ooohhkay. Well, you'll have one when you get here," she chirps. "Let me know if you need anything, okay?" Tears spill then. I'll miss that.

"Sure, thanks, Florence." I hang up and rest my head against the back of my chair, willing the tears to be sucked back up into my head. I'm not sure how long I sit like that, long enough for my stomach to growl and my head to start hurting.

"Ivy." At the sound of my name, I shut my eyes. Then swiftly wipe them and turn my chair to face him.

"So, you don't actually work here. You own The Edgemont?" I ask. I need to gather as much information as I can.

"Yes," he confirms. I knew that, but it still hurts to hear it.

"Why?" I can't see through the tears gathering again. "Why did you lie?"

"I didn't lie—or I didn't mean to lie. I didn't know you—"

"And that makes it okay to lie? And you did lie. You knew who I was when you heard my name. You let me walk around here and pretended like I was in charge. Ugh. I feel so stupid, Alder."

"That's not how it was. You were in charge. I never would have intervened with anything you wanted to do."

"But you could have," I spit out.

"Everything you've done the last few months is all you. They were all your ideas, and they've been damn good ones, don't let this tarnish that," he pleads. "You're so good at this. Please, I'm sorry for not telling you. This isn't how I wanted you to find out."

"How did you want me to find out?"

"I tried to tell you. I did tell you the first night you came to my house," he says. I reel back, confused.

"No, you didn't, Alder. I would remember that little nugget of information." My sadness is turning into something different now. Something is brewing in me. I'm so angry; I'm so *sad*. I feel so incredibly betrayed.

"I told you on the couch, but you had already fallen asleep." He looks up toward the ceiling as he speaks. I laugh. It's cold and mean, and I'm glad because that's how I feel. I want to hurt him. I want him to hurt as much as I do.

"Well, if you told me while I was asleep, I guess I have to forgive you," I say with as much sarcasm as I can muster.

"That's not what I'm saying—"

"That's exactly what you just said. It doesn't matter anyway, Alder. This was never going to work long-term. I was always going to leave, and this was only ever a fling. I thought —" I stop myself before my voice cracks. He's been so much more than a fling since the moment he told me he made lists. I try to believe what I'm saying. "I had thought I was the problem, that maybe I could be what you deserved—" My voice does crack this time; I can feel my nose stinging and the fresh wave of tears. "But then, I come to find out—it's you. You're no better than any other man I've had the awful luck of knowing." His eyes flare, and I see his jaw flex. Good. Get mad at me. Hate me. Let's be done with this.

"Please, Ivy," he says, and there's no anger in it. Only pain. I don't want to feel bad about making him hurt, but I do. Damn it. "You know that's not true, Ivy. I'm nothing like Noah or your father," he defends.

"Speaking of my father, it seems like you know him pretty well."

"I don't know him. He was just my partner who I had no say in." He sighs.

I hate this. I can't be here. I feel sick to my stomach, and I might throw up, but I will die before I let Alder take care of me.

"I'm leaving."

"Where are you going?" Alder asks quietly.

"I'm leaving Silverthorne."

"Hold on, princess. Just—"

"Do not. Call me that. Again," I reply in a hushed but lethal tone. He doesn't want to mess with me right now. "I'll be gone in three days. I need to see my father and clear some things up, and I can't be here. I can't see you." I rush by him, trying to flee.

"The resort is yours," he calls when I'm a few steps down the hall. I whip my head around back to him. *What the hell?*

"Don't leave. Please," he pleads, but I can't focus on the anguish in his eyes. I can only think about what he's said about the resort.

"What are you talking about?"

He clears his throat before he speaks again, "The Edgemont. It's yours. If you want it,"

"How? That doesn't make any sense," I begin.

"I bought it." His words hang in the air between us.

"You...bought it? How?"

"I bought out your father. I don't want another partner unless it's you," he says earnestly. The awful truth is that I believe him.

"Why? Why wouldn't you tell me? Why should I stay?" My voice comes out barely above a whisper.

"Because I wanted it for you. I wanted to be able to present it to you before I asked you to stay. It's yours now. That last one is a little more complicated to answer," he says, rubbing at his neck. The why I should stay. The question I so desperately want his answer to. I look at him. This man who I have been falling so hard for without even knowing it for the past few months. He's still Alder. He's still here. I'm still helplessly in love with him. But now, he's also a man who lied, and he can't give me the answer I need to hear now. He doesn't know why I should stay, and he doesn't know why he wants me to. I feel my heart squeeze. I didn't even know that I wanted to hear the three words until he didn't say them. I could crumple, but instead, I feed the fire, I feed my anger.

"I don't want it," I spew at him. Then I turn on my heel and leave.

ALDER

I haven't spoken to or seen Ivy in two days, but it may as well have been two years. She told me she was leaving Silverthorne, and all I've really been able to do is sulk over it. I can feel the distance she's putting between us. It's like my heart's being ripped from my chest with every one of my calls that she sends to voicemail and each one of my texts that goes unanswered. I stopped by her cabin, but she wasn't there. I panicked, thinking she'd left, but later, I got a text from Florence telling me that she was staying at the hotel for a couple of nights.

BABY LO

She's at the hotel.

ALDER

Is she alright?

BABY LO

She hasn't really said much other than she didn't really feel like talking.

ALDER

> Okay, thanks, Baby Lo. Please keep me in the loop.

BABY LO

> Nope. Sorry, sweet brother of mine. I'm not going to keep tabs on her for you. I only told you she was here, so you knew you still had a shot. The rest is between you two.

ALDER

> That's fair. Thank you. Love you.

BABY LO

> I love you too. So I hope you can fix this.

ALDER

> I will. I just need to figure out how.

The relief that washed over me at hearing she hadn't left for good, at least yet, was enough to ease the tension in my shoulders. I need to see her, though. To explain myself better. If she would just let me speak to her. She deserves more than my apologies, but I'll beg if she'll let me.

These are the thoughts I'm left with, that and her smell still clinging to my pillow every night as I try, and fail, to fall asleep. Her purple toothbrush sits next to mine in the cup by my sink. She left her ski suit here after our last lesson. I couldn't bear to look at it any longer, so I have it hanging in my closet next to all my clothes; a constant reminder that she should be here next to me too. I decide to head out to the mountain and get a couple of runs in to get my mind clear before attempting to make this right. I will explain, and she will understand because if I can't and she doesn't—I don't know how to move on from this. From her. I don't think my soul can take another hit. Another loss.

The drive up the mountain is long as I try to calm my

thoughts. Gearing up for a run, I know I need to focus, but I can only think about our last conversation. I just asked her to stay. God, I feel like such an idiot. She's been clear on what this is from the beginning. "It doesn't matter anyway, Alder. This was never going to work long-term. I was always going to leave, and this was only ever a fling." I just thought things had been changing between us. She's so much more open with me now. They have changed. I may have handled the situation with her father wrong, but if she would just let me explain, let me apologize. It's only been two months. I need more time with her. I need her. I'm in love with her. So damn in love with her. Did I tell her that? *Oh, god. Why didn't I tell her that?* My house smells of her orange candies. I have a journal filled with her. I don't write about anything else these days. I don't think about anything else besides her.

I'm a man possessed. For so long, I've survived. A silent struggle that I never wanted to share. Sharing my deepest thoughts and dreams with Ivy? It was like if I didn't share it with her, the world might end. I wanted her to know me. Inside and out. I want to be embedded into her skin. Like she's in mine.

Ivy is the only thing on my mind as I weave down the side of the peak. I go over the last month in my head from the moment I laid eyes on her. Things changed on New Year's when she started staying over in my home, in my bed. But if I'm being honest with myself, things were changing before then. Every time she was near, I only wanted to be closer. I only ever want to be with her. I haven't let myself look toward the future since losing Ray. I've focused instead on being the best I can be at my job and the best version of myself for me and for my family.

I'm a good man in a storm. I know my limits and follow protocol. That's how you stay alive when things go sideways. But Ivy Rutherford has me wanting to be reckless. Jump first and see where we land. We could end up with broken dreams and broken hearts, but being with her, experiencing any length of time with Ivy, may never satisfy my need for her. But the comedown after riding that high would be worth the rush that it would bring.

I reach the bottom of my run with renewed determination. I frantically unstrap myself from my board and run to where I have my truck parked. I need to tell her that I'll move to California if that's what she wants. I'll go wherever she wants me to. I'll find a job in California; my resume is decent, and I have enough money to get me by. I'll figure it out as long as I'm where she is. As much as I love calling Silverthorne home, Ivy is where I want to be at the end of a long day. She's where I want to lie down at night. She is my home.

I throw my board into the back and drive down the mountain road. My mind is racing, knowing this could be my last chance to get everything I'm thinking and feeling off my chest, and I'm desperate to see her again. Her, just her. I'm almost there, and my mind gets more and more tangled. I can't lose her, at least not because of distance. I need to lay it all out, every card on the table. I want her to know how I feel, how important she is to me, how precious. How I don't want to change a single stubborn thing about her.

I pull up outside her cabin, barely managing to park before jumping out and running to her front door. I knock five times in quick succession. Then I'm yelling.

"Ivy! I need to talk to you! I know it's only been a couple of months, but you've turned my world upside down in ways I could have only ever dreamed!" I am fully aware that surrounding cabins can probably hear me. Good. "Ivy, if you don't answer, I'll come in anyway because as much as it drives me completely insane, I know you never lock your door." I give it another ten seconds and then open the door slowly. She never locks her fucking door. I'll lock it for her. I'll make sure our doors are locked every night if she'll let me.

"Princess?" I call into the silence. Fully opening the door, I'm shocked at the sight before me. Nothing. There's nothing left here except the faint smell of oranges. I walk into the cabin and in and out of the rooms. Everything's gone. She's left. And she didn't even tell me goodbye. My first thought is to go after her, but maybe she's making a clean cut.

She left. She left. She left.

I knew she said she was leaving, but now that she's really gone? I see how entirely empty it makes me feel. I can almost hear her telling me I'm pathetic. I would give anything to hear her tell me what a love-sick fool I am as long as I could kiss the sass right out of her after.

She doesn't want me. I showed her who I was, and she doesn't want it. I don't blame her, though, I'm not what she signed up for. She wanted fun and charming. I'm good at that. I'm good *for* that. That coupled with keeping things from her, I'm not somebody's bring-home-to-Mom. I can feel my chest starting to get tight. My head is filling with pressure, and my eyes are burning. I haven't felt this way in almost twelve years. I reach my hand up to my face, and it's wet when I pull it back.

Crying in her empty cabin. She would have a field day with this. "Maybe you should try getting a grip, Lover Boy? Yeah?" I close my eyes. I'm not sure what to do. So I do the only thing I can think of: I go to tell the only person I want to tell.

Ray's grave is out past his family's property down at the Silverthorne Cemetery, but that's not where I am now. I'm where I lost him. I don't know if I'll ever forgive myself. I know he wouldn't blame me. It wasn't even my decision, and maybe that's what gets to me the most. Maybe it should have been my decision. That's something that I bear alone. It was his idea to be ice climbing where we were. I wasn't sure about it and wanted to do some more checks on it before starting. He started climbing before I could stop him, and I didn't insist on our safety check.

We didn't know that on the other side of the wall of ice would be a cavern. A cavern so deep that it took a week to recover Ray. That's what my nightmares are about. Him—alone in that cavern that I couldn't pull him out of. I steal my body as memories of that day beat against me. I lost Ray that day because I wasn't careful. I wasn't cautious. That's why I always insist on all safety checks now. It's why I fly a helicopter and why I trained to be an EMS. I don't want to lose anyone again.

"Hey, Ray." My voice is gritty. The wind is stinging my face now because of the tears there. "I met someone," I tell him. I've talked to Ray many times over the years, but never here. "She's stunning and funny. She's so damn smart, and I want to listen to her talk forever. A dream. I'm in love with her." The last sentence is a whisper. Part of my therapy was working through the guilt of moving on in life when he couldn't.

It isn't eating me alive anymore, but it's still a work in progress. "I think she has feelings for me, but I waited too long.

I didn't tell her, and now she's gone," I choke out. "I know. I sound like men we would have made fun of. If you think this is funny, get a load of what she calls me. Lover Boy," I say on a choked laugh. "What's worse is that I love it. I think you two would really get along." I let the words out into the thin mountain air.

"I'm not sure why I came here; I just wanted to tell someone I love that I'm in love." I scoff. "Even though I can picture what you'd say to me and the face you'd make when saying it." He would absolutely be making fun of me, but I also know deep down that he would understand. Ray was deep. Deeper than most people had a chance to see. That has me crying in earnest now. "I'm sorry, Ray. I'm so sorry." I feel a hand on my shoulder and turn to see it's Mr. Thompson. I feel the blood drain from my face. I wasn't expecting to see him here. I avoid the cemetery, usually coming to this spot, so I don't bother his family.

"I didn't...I don't..." I try for a coherent sentence, but I won't be able to make one. I can barely see through the moisture collecting in my eyes.

"It's okay, Alder. It's okay. I miss him too," he tells me, and I collapse into him. Jerry and Sophia Thompson are two people I have avoided at all costs over the years. After being drunk and unable to speak at the funeral, I couldn't bring myself to face them. "It wasn't your fault, son." At thirty-six years old. I didn't expect to be crying into another man's arms like this, but life has a twisted and dark, humorous way of taking your expectations and bending them to see if you'll break.

"I wasn't...I didn't...I'm so sorry, I should've..." I trip over my words, trying to contradict him, but he holds me steady and lets me release so much guilt and pain that I've held onto, whispering words I really needed to hear.

"No one blames you, Alder. You know Ray wouldn't." I cry until I have nothing left. Until the sun has moved further across the sky, and I say goodbye to Mr. Thompson. "Don't be a stranger, please. Sophia would love to see you. She has some photos for you," he tells me, and then he goes on his way. I wait till I see his truck disappear.

I'm not sure how long I've been sitting in the snow now. My pants are soaked through, and I know I need to leave. If I don't, I'll end up sick and in danger of getting frostbite. I stand and watch the sun lower up on the ridge. I think this one's gonna be just for you, Ray," I tell him. Feeling lighter than I have in years. Now, I just need to figure out how to make Ivy see that we belong together.

When I get back in my truck, I text all my siblings and let them in on my plan.

ALDER

I'm going to get her back.

BABY LO

It's about time.

RHETT

Hell, yes!

WINNIE

I approve of this message. I'll go with you if you need backup. I kind of already inducted her into the girl gang, so...I'm going to need you to get her back ASAP.

RHETT

You have a gang, and I'm not in it, darlin'?

I chuckle at that, then see what my older brother has to say.

KNOX

Hazel likes Ivy. Make it right and then be
happy, Alder. You deserve it.

A man of few words, but damn do they hold so much weight.

ALDER

Thank you all. I love you. I leave in the
morning, but I'll keep you updated.

I bought a plane ticket. I leave tomorrow morning at seven o'clock. Which means I have twelve hours until my flight departs. I'm going to California to plead my case. I've never actually been there. I've been to Seattle a few times when Rhett was playing hockey there, but it's been a while. I don't leave town much, but I change that. I have learned skills that help me adapt. Maybe I should put them to use in my own life. Maybe I'll take up surfing. Pull a reverse *Johnny Tsunami*. If some kid from Hawaii can learn how to snowboard, then I can figure out surfing.I can see it. If it means I'm with Ivy, I can see it.

I drive up to my cabin. It's started snowing again. I've always loved the snow. It always reminds me of being a kid, and that feeling is tied to the possibilities of things to come. Tonight, it feels less magical though. I don't see it cling to red hair and a purple coat. That thought actually feels like a physical blow. Will I see her in the snow again? I walk up my steps and put my key in the door. It's already unlocked. Huh, I guess I shouldn't have been such a prick about Ivy leaving her door unlocked when I have all day.

I push open the door, ready to find enough clothes for at least a couple of weeks. I also need to call Jack and let him know I'll be gone for a while. I'm not sure how to start that conversation just yet. The weather is turning, and I hear my radio crackle from the kitchen. I turn up the volume and listen to the broadcast.

"There's been an avalanche breakout in the area. Anyone able, please report. This is an all-hands-on-deck situation. We need all crews on standby."

"Shit!" I run a hand through my hair and race to my bedroom to change into my gear. I toss my shirt onto the bed and hear something crunch underneath it. I pick it up and see a piece of paper. What I read chills me to my bones and sends fear down my spine.

"Fuck!" I yell and pray that I make it in time.

IVY

I didn't expect to be here for very long today. But here I am, sitting on Alder's front porch. In fact, I only stopped by to say goodbye and give him his keys and hat back. I'm supposed to be getting on a plane in a few hours. I'm heading back to California, but I wanted to say a real goodbye. I told him I was leaving a few days ago. He's sent messages and called, but I haven't been able to speak to him. I was too upset, angry. At him, my father, at myself. He asked me to stay. I can't though. He doesn't know what he's getting into with me. I come with a lot of baggage, and I may be mad now, but the depth of my feelings hasn't changed, and his feelings can't be anywhere near as intense as mine. It's freezing, though, so I use the key, not seeing it as an invasion of privacy since he gave it to me, and go inside to wait.

Walking into Alder's cabin, I'm hit with sadness. I expected this, but it's one thing to expect; it's another to experience it. I look at the counter where there's a bag of oranges. A twinge pulls at my heart. I know they're for me. Or they would have been. I go into the back bedroom and let myself breathe him in. I'll miss him. So much. More than I'm willing to admit to myself right now. More than I've ever missed anyone. I can't stay for what we've been doing if there isn't a destination in mind—as much as I wish I could. It's time for me to make myself a priority. Put the things I want in life at the top of my list.

And I want someone to share my life with. I want to build one with someone. After so much soul-searching, I think I want to try and have more babies. Alder played an instrumental part in that emotional shift. I'll always be grateful to him for the softening of the hard edges I present. Even if we can't have it together. I feel the sting behind my eyes. If he could have given me anything more than what he did—maybe I could have stayed. What's waiting for me in California isn't a lot. I'll have to start from square one, but it's a fresh start. Maybe that's what I need. Maybe what Alder and I need is a clean break. I should leave. He isn't here, and I shouldn't be either. I stand and hit my knee into that damn nightstand, and I knock his books off it.

The leather-bound notebook has all my attention. It's open. I've seen him writing in it plenty of times, but I've never read any of the things he's written in there. Curiosity is winning as I pick it up from the floor and read. It's beautiful. Poetic. Page after page, poem after poem. I turn to the last few pages, and as I read, my throat tightens, and my vision swims.

> *And I will go where you go.*
> *Hang my hat by your coat.*
> *I'll follow my soul,*
> *so let it be known.*

Where your heart is,
there is my home.

It's dated five days ago. The one before it is the day before.

She forces me to feel real while
Floating in a daydream
She is as grounding as she is mystical.
She is a tether to my instincts
And a spell cast over my bones.

One after another of beautiful poems, things he thinks but never says. Does he truly feel this way for me? Would he be honest with me about what he wants from me? I guess I'll be missing my flight tonight. I quickly scribble a note to Alder.

If you truly feel this way,
if what you wrote about in here is about me
then I'll wait for you, where two other lovers'
story may have ended,
but I want it to be where ours begins.

I place it on top of the book and put it on his bed.

Driving up the mountain is a little eerie. It doesn't feel like it did the last time I was here with Alder. It's probably just my nervous energy. What if he doesn't come? After I've put myself out there again. That would be mortifying. He'll come through. I know that he will. If he doesn't, I'll deal with that then, but we're going to be hopeful, Ivy. The sky is clear today. I checked the weather for any pop-up storms, and it showed nothing but clear skies. I tried to be as cautious as I could be. As cautious as Alder would be.

When I get to the turnoff, I take one more second to think. Should I really be doing this? Will he think this is as romantic as it is in my head? He may find it odd, and I'll admit it is a little. I mean, the lore of this place is that two people committed suicide here. That's not romantic at all. It's a fucking tragedy. Oh, shit. Maybe I should have thought a little more before leaving the note. I'll just send him a text and tell him to disregard my note and go back to his house. I park my SUV and pull out my phone, but I don't have any service.

"Shit," I say out loud. "Okay, this is fine. I'll just wait here for a little while, and if he doesn't show, I'll leave, and we never have to talk about it again," I say out loud again to no one. I get out of my car and take in the beautiful view. I'll probably only be able to last out here in the cold for another hour or so. Especially because the sun sets quicker here, and once the sun goes down, the temperature will follow. I hop onto the hood of my car, watching the clouds float by, and wait.

ALDER

S hit, shit, shit. Fuck. It plays on a loop in my head. I take a deep breath as I reach the hangar. I cannot panic. Panicking will get me or someone else killed. I walk into the big metal building and see Nate. It's good to see him. I'm going to need him with me out there.

"Hey, Alder," my dispatch organizer calls.

"I need to be in the air as soon as possible," I tell her. Nadine smiles.

"Always eager to help. We don't have any emergency calls out just yet, but I'll make sure you're on the first flight out. Most of the activity has been on the western slope, and it's clear for now. Teams on the ground have set up barricades. No one's getting through. We just wanted to make sure—"

"I'm sorry to interrupt, but I know someone is up on that mountain. I need a team, and I need to get airborne," I cut her off. She looks at me for only a second. I know she has questions, but I thank my lucky stars that she doesn't decide to ask any right now.

"Nate, Griffin, Ty, you're with Alder," she orders, then looks at me. "Be safe out there and stay in contact." I nod at her.

"We will," I respond, and then we're getting in the helicopter, thankful all preflight checks were done beforehand. Nate gets in the pilot's seat. Good. That's where I need him today. I need all my focus on scanning the mountain and finding my girl.

"Where are we headed, Alder?" he asks.

"Lovers Leap."

"Who's out there at this time of day?" he questions.

"Someone who doesn't know the area well. Someone I'm madly in love with," I answer honestly. He whips his head around to me. "I'm serious," I tell him.

"I believe you. I'm just surprised." His eyebrows are raised when he responds to my declaration.

"No one's more surprised than me, Nate. I didn't expect this, and I didn't see it coming, but I have to find her. She could be in real danger."

"Alright, let's go get Alder's woman," he says over the headset, and everyone cheers.

"Focus," I bark. Nate continues to smile, but we all quiet down as the helicopter takes flight, and we make our way to Lovers Leap, to Ivy.

The air is thick with tension, and we can all feel it. We have maybe forty minutes of daylight left, and then we'll be using a spotlight, and even though everyone in the cabin of this aircraft is well-trained in night searches—they're less likely to have a successful outcome. Temperatures are starting to drop, and my adrenaline is rising. We need to find her and soon.

# IVY

I'm thinking again. Something that's typically a good thing for others. but it's hit or miss for me. Regardless, I'm thinking that maybe making Alder dinner or waiting for him naked in his bed would have been the better option than waiting on the top of a mountain range in the middle of winter with the sun starting to go down. The wind whips my hair off my neck, and I shiver. It's confirmed; waiting in Alder's cozy cabin would have been the better plan.

I inhale the cold mountain air one last time and get back into my car. If he's on his way here, I'll meet him on the road anyway. It won't be quite as romantic or dramatic, but maybe I've had enough of that. I crank the heat once I start up the engine and sit in the car for another couple of minutes. With a deep sigh, I let go of my not-so-fantastic idea and turn around; only I don't turn around. One of my wheels keeps spinning, and I can't gain any traction. Oh, shit. Oh, shit. "No, no, no, no, nooo. Don't freak out. It's fine. Alder knows where you are. Unless he didn't get my note." *What if he didn't get my note?*

He wasn't home when I got there, and he may not be coming home at all. "Oh my god, Ivy. You are such a fucking idiot."

I'm going to die up here. No. I'm not going to die because I'm going to tell Alder that I love him. I'm going to live in that little house with him. I hear a sob escape my chest. I'm...I'm going to run the resort, and I want to have his...really beautiful and sunshiny babies. and we're going to be really fucking happy. He'll make sure of it. I won't be so mean...I'll try not to be so mean, I amend quickly.

I remember watching a TV show once where they used cat litter to gain traction. I don't have any of that. I also watched a documentary about a man from Sweden who drank snow for three days and survived. There's plenty of snow around for me to eat so I most likely won't die. Unless there's a serial killer lurking. Stop it, Ivy. There is not a serial killer around. No, I'm the only idiot on the mountain right now.

An idiot who's fallen in love with this town and the people in it. One person in particular. His shaggy hair and easy going smile. That body. Oh, god, that body. I really want to be near that body again. A noise so loud that it makes my car rumble has me looking to the right. Out the windshield, just a little to the right, I see what looks like clouds rising. Odd. They're coming from below the ridge, but it looks like they may be getting bigger or closer?

My SUV is still rumbling a little; I open my car door, and it sounds a little like there's a river nearby. I walk to the nose of my car and look up to see a helicopter in the distance and feel relief. I just need to get its attention. I can barely hear its blades over the sound of rushing water. But why am I hearing rushing water? Movement draws my attention from the sky to the ground. The clouds are definitely closer now. Goose bumps break out over my skin, and I wave at the helicopter when I hear another rumble, this time it's bigger and definitely closer. I look back to what I thought were clouds. Oh, no. Oh, shit. No, no, no. That is a fucking avalanche.

I run back to the door I left open and shut it behind me. I'm going to be buried alive, and they aren't going to find me in time. I see the mountain of snow getting closer and can barely make out the helicopter in the distance. It sounds less like water now and more like a freight train. I close my eyes. "Alder. I love you," I say out loud as tears slip down my face, and then I'm upside down, and I can hear metal crunching. There's a horrible pain in my left arm, and I can hear my own screaming. Everything goes dark.

ALDER

"IVY!" I scream in horror, watching helplessly as the edge of the avalanche hits and rolls Ivy's SUV over until it's barely visible.

"Alder, I need you to stay calm. If you can't, we'll have to go down there and rescue your girl without you," Nate tells me as he flies the helicopter at the fastest speed that's considered safe. I just watched the woman I'm out of my mind for rolled over by a fucking avalanche, and he wants me to remain calm. I think I finally have just a small understanding of why women get pissed when they're asked to calm down.

"I'm calm. I'm ready. Like hell, I'm not going down there."

"Good. We're almost there. We still have visibility on the vehicle, and we have everything we need to get to her. She's going to be fine" Griffin tells me over the comm system. I knew there was a reason I liked him. We approach the spot where Ivy's SUV is half covered.

"Lace up your boots, everyone. Another minute, and we'll be on top of it." Nate signals for us to get our gear and tools all situated. I sit down and give myself just a moment to steady my erratic heart. I need to check my emotions. I do my mental checklist like I do on every mission. I see the men around me doing the same. Touching their gear, physically checking it.

"Here's your stop boys!" Nate yells to us. I stand and clip myself into the system quickly.

"I'll go first. Keep us steady, Nate."

"You got it. Go get your girl, Holloway." He nods, and I start my descent. He got us into a perfect position. We can't land, but he's hovering only twenty-five feet in the air. I land with a thud, having rappelled as quickly as possible. I give the all clear with my hand, and the tether goes back up for the next person to clip in. I run to the overturned vehicle.

"Ivy, can you hear me?" I shout.

"Alder?! Is that you? I can't see anything!" she yells back to me. I feel like I could float away with the relief that courses through my veins at the sound of her voice.

"It's me, baby! We're gonna get you out of there. Is there anything obstructing your view?" I ask.

"You mean besides the upside-down car that's entombed me and buried me alive in the snow? You mean besides *that*?" she snipes, and I let out a strangled chuckle. "Shit, I just said I would be nicer," she mutters.

"Be as mean as you want, princess. Just be okay," I call to her.

"Alder?" she asks as I start digging on her side.

"Yeah, Ivy?"

"Did you get my note?" she asks, voice breaking and hitting me right in the fucking chest.

"Yeah, baby. I got your note. I got here as fast as I could."

"Okay, good," she says. "Alder?" she asks again.

"Yeah, Ivy?"

"I'm feeling a little dizzy," she tells me.

"Just hang tight. We'll get you out of there real soon." I let her know. Griffin is at my side digging into the snow with me in the next second and soon after him is Ty.

"Ivy?"

"Yeah?" she answers, her voice weaker.

"You doing okay in there?" I question.

"I'm okay. My arm just really hurts. I think it might be broken," she tells me. I dig faster. When we get the door uncovered, I ease it open and reach for her. I support her shoulders so she isn't just hanging anymore.

"I've got you, baby. It's alright." She sniffs at my words. I unbuckle her seatbelt and cradle her as she comes down from her seat into my arms. I shift her so she's upright on my lap and can't stop myself from scanning her head and face. Needing the reassurance that she's okay.

"Ah!" she cries out and holds her arm close to her chest.

"I'm so sorry. Let's get you out of here, okay? Did you hit your head at all?" She shakes her head at my question.

"No, no, just hit my arm or something. It hurts, but I'm fine. I'm okay. You're here," she says the last thing like it means more than the rest. My chest explodes. I grab her face and kiss her. Hard. I pour all the adrenaline, all the anxiety, all the worry into it. She matches my frenzy with her own. She grips my flight jacket with her good arm and pulls me closer, moaning into my mouth. I hear a throat clear and smile as I continue to kiss the hell out of her. She smiles back but doesn't break our kiss until she's ready. I'd be happy to die here if this is how I go.

"Okay, you two. It's a good show, but I'm going to need to cut it short. We need to get Ivy to the hospital to get checked out before our next round," Nate says into the comms. Ivy pulls back, blushing, but she doesn't look sorry. I nod and stand with her in my arms.

"I can walk, Alder. It's my arm, not my legs, which might be broken," she teases, but her voice fades in and out a little. There's a slur to her words.

"I don't feel like taking any unnecessary risks with you tonight, Ivy. I'm going to need a full body scan just to make sure you're alright."

"I'm really okay, Alder. I just think my blood sugar is getting a little low is all."

"I'll feel better once we get the okay from a doctor. Better safe than sorry," I tell her as I put the sling around her, careful to mind her injured arm. "I am by the way. So sorry, Ivy. I should have done things differently, and I should have been honest as soon as I knew who you were." I can't defend my actions; I just want her to know that I know they were wrong.

"I know, hotshot. I know who you are. You may see me, but I see you too." I kiss her head gently. I quickly hook us in securely, and then we're in the air. When we reach the cabin opening, I get her in and situated as the others join us inside. She's pale, which could absolutely be because of the ordeal she's just been through, but I'll need confirmation of that.

The ride to the hospital is short, thankfully. When we arrive on the landing pad at the top of the hospital, I pick Ivy up bridal style as soon as we touch down and carry her out to meet Mare. Nate called us in, but he didn't give anyone's name. Her eyes widen when she sees the redhead in my arms.

"Ivy?!" she exclaims.

"Hi, Mare," Ivy says quietly.

"She has an injury to her left arm, and she's weak. She has a history of low blood sugar. She doesn't remember hitting her head, but I'm worried," I tell Mare.

"Mmfinne," Ivy mumbles.

"Get me a stretcher!" she yells to her staff. I look at her, and she meets my eyes before speaking. "I'm checking her out myself, Alder. You have to wait outside." I nod. I know the rules. I fucking hate them at the moment, but I understand. I walk as far as Mare will allow me to, holding onto Ivy's hand in mine, and when they pass through the swinging doors, I drop down into a crouch and lean onto my knees, willing myself to breathe. If she isn't okay, I don't know what I'll do.

I stand and walk to the waiting area. The helicopter and crew took off after they dropped us off, so it's just me and all the other people waiting to hear if their loved ones are going to be okay out here. I sit, and then I pace, unable to sit still. I walk the hall up and down and then get a drink of water from the nurses' lounge. I'm too keyed up for coffee.

"Alder!" I look up to see my brother walking toward me. He grabs me in a hug, and I cling to him. "Is she okay?" he asks. I shrug.

"I think so, but Mare took her back to run some tests. She has a broken arm."

"What do you need?"

"Just for her to be okay." He nods his agreement. I look around him.

"Where's Haze?"

"She's with Mom and Dad, I was the closest, so I got here the fastest. You can expect the rest of us to be here shortly," he assures me, and I smile. I won the family jackpot with this lot.

"Thanks, big brother," I tell Knox.

"Of course." Something catches his eye over my shoulder. I

turn and see Florence, followed by Rhett and Winnie. When they get to us, I'm enveloped in a mass hug.

"We're here," Winnie tells me and holds me tight. This may be the only time in the history of knowing her that she hugs me, and Rhett doesn't drag her off me. I hear a door swing shut and crane my head around to see Mare coming toward us. I spin with Winnie still holding my arm and Rhett with a hand on my shoulder.

"Is she okay?" I practically beg. She nods at us.

"She broke her arm in two places, but it's set for now. We'll cast it tomorrow. She's okay though. She wants to see you," she tells me, smiling. I grin and start for the doors. "Room 202!" she calls to me, but I don't slow down until I reach her door. I knock.

"Come in." I hear her raspy voice say, and when I see her it's like my whole world clicks back into focus. Everything I've ever wanted, things I'm only just beginning to dream about, is right in front of me.

"Hey, Lover Boy."

IVY

"You're pregnant."

The words seem to float above my head. Like I could reach up and touch them. I'm lying down in a hospital bed with my arm in a sling, having just survived being hit by an actual avalanche, and yet this news definitely hits harder. After a basic assessment was complete, an abdominal scan was ordered as a precaution to rule out any internal bleeding. Now, I'm lying flat on my back, getting an abdominal ultrasound.

"I'm sorry, what?" I ask in a bit of a daze.

"You're pregnant. About two months along it looks like," Mare informs me, staring at a screen and running a little doppler over my still flat belly.

"How? I..." I think back to the first night I was in town, and the very long and extremely pleasant time I spent with Alder all those nights ago. I hadn't confirmed protection. I've been reckless with him in that regard. "Shit," I whisper. This isn't at all how I planned the rest of my life to start, but I can't stop the laugh that bubbles out of me. Shock gives way to something new. Something I'm only just now, after years of suppressing, beginning to feel. I'm—happy. I don't know how Alder will feel about this new information, but I want this baby.

"Are you alright?" Mare asks me, and I realize I haven't spoken to her.

"Yes." There's water in my eyes, and I'm sure I'm sporting an unhinged smile. "I'm great." Then happiness is tinged in fear. "Is the baby, okay?" I ask, snapping my eyes to my belly.

"Baby is doing just fine. Strong heartbeat. Do you want to hear?" she asks, and I nod frantically. Then she presses a button on the machine, and I hear it. The strange but beautiful sound of my baby's heartbeat. My eyes well. Is this real? Then fear tries to grip me.

"I...I've miscarried before, I..." I start to feel the panic.

"Ivy. Look at me," Mare says calmly. I lift my face to see her.

"This baby and its mother are both healthy, and we're going to do everything we can to make sure it stays that way. Okay? Now breathe with me. In through your nose..." I do as she says. "Out through your mouth. A few more times." I complete the circuit, and at the end, I feel a bit better.

"Good. If you want a specialist, I can send someone from OB in here." Mare offers, and I nod.

"Can I see Alder first? You can tell him I'm fine and about my arm, but please let me tell him about..." I request, wiping my eyes, and Mare smiles at me.

"I'm your doctor, Ivy. Whatever happens here is confidential. I won't share any of your personal medical information with anyone," she assures me. "As your friend, though, because

I'm really hoping we're friends..." she hedges. "Congratulations." She's smiling at me with such warmth.

I nod and say, "Thank you, Mare. I feel the same way." She smiles at me and wipes my stomach clean from the jelly. Then she removes her gloves and stands.

"Alright, I'm going to go give Alder and your fan club the all clear now."

"My fan club?" I ask, puzzled.

"Oh yeah, all the Holloway siblings will be out there by now," she reports, and I grin.

"That's ridiculous. They barely know me." I snort.

"Alder does, and he cares for you very much. That's enough. You're in the family now, and I don't just mean that because you're having a baby Holloway." She winks and then leaves the room. I place my hand over my belly. A baby Holloway. I chuckle at that. I've already made my decision to stay in Silverthorne, but I do need to iron out some details of my staying with Alder. Like, do I have a job? If he meant what he said, if he wants me to help him run the resort where I can be a part of something there, I might really want that. I'm still mad at him for not telling me about the deals he made with my father sooner. I'm hurt that he wouldn't tell me that he owns The Edgemont, but I made peace with that when I decided to wait for him at the top of a mountain.

I'm smiling at the absurd turn of events when I hear a knock on the door.

"Come in." It's him. He's here, and any worries I have about the future melt away when he grins back at me. Not because they're gone but because I know he'll be there to help me. He's part of my team. He's *mine.* "Hey, Lover Boy."

"I love you." He declares it, and I gasp. That's one way to

start this conversation. "I love you, and that's why I want you to stay. I should have told you that then, but I want to make sure you're fully aware now. I love you, Ivy. I'm in love with you, and I want you here with me. The Edgemont is yours; *I'm* yours if you'll have me." A sob tears out of me at his words. The way they echo what I already know deep inside. I drag air into my mouth. I'm sure I look awful, and now my face will be red and splotchy. "You don't have to say—"

"Shut up! I love you too," I confess, and he's on me in the next second. He slides his hand around the back of my head, burying it into my tangled hair and tilting my head back. He kisses me like he wants to devour me, like he's been starved for me. I kiss him deeply, throwing myself into him. My broken arm protests, and I whimper. He pulls back, and I whimper again at the loss of his lips on mine.

"Shit, princess. I'm sorry. You must be in so much pain here." He starts settling me back into the pillows. "You're alright though? Mare said you broke your arm in two places, but otherwise, you're healthy," he recounts as he pulls the blanket up over me and sits on the end of the bed. I swallow. Well, now's the time, I suppose.

"I am. I'm fine..." I start playing with the edge of my hospital gown. "More than fine actually. I hope you know that I didn't plan for this to happen, but now that it has. I'm really happy."

"I'm really happy too, baby." *Just say it.*

"I'm pregnant." I blurt it out. His eyes bulge, then they move to my stomach. "Only two months. I think some of the times I was nauseous or dizzy may have been because of this, not because of my low blood sugar."

"You're pregnant," he repeats.

"Yes." I steel myself. There's one more thing I need to say. An important thing. "I just found out, and I want you to know I don't expect anything from you."

"Ivy—" he cuts in, but I hold up my good arm.

"Shh. I need to say this. Don't interrupt me." He shuts his mouth and pulls his lips between his teeth, nodding. "If you want to be in our lives, then great, but if this changes things for you, I'll figure it out. I know we've only known each other a few months, and part of that I've been a little hard to deal with." He smirks at my rambling, then slides forward on the bed so he's right next to me.

"Move in with me," he demands.

"What?" I shriek, and move my left arm too much. I wince, then I have to raise my other one to let him know I'm okay. "Alder, I just told you I'm having a baby. We still have things to talk about. That's a lot to—"

"You're having my baby, *our baby*." He halts my words with ones I didn't know I needed to hear. "I'm gonna be a dad." His eyes are full of love. He places his big hand on my belly. "I'm going to be here every step of the way if you'll let me, Ivy. I know I hurt you. I should never have kept things from you, but I'm going to make it up to you, I'm going to be so good to you, baby."

At his words, I feel my nose sting, and I know more tears are close behind. "I'm going to get you whatever you want. I'm going to spoil the shit out of you. Whatever you're craving. Whatever you need. I'm there. I'm yours," he says again. "You're mine too. You've been mine, Ivy, and this baby is ours, and I'm going to take care of you two, Stormcloud. Let me take care of you, please?" he asks so earnestly, so endearing. I'm done resisting.

I nod. "Okay. But I'm not very good at being taken care of. I may not always get it right," I say, sniffing. He reaches for my face, swiping the tears from my cheeks.

"You don't have to always get it right. You just have to let me in."

"You're already in, Alder."

"This is going to be good, Ivy. Really good," he tells me, and as hard as I've fought not to let the threat of pain into my life again, I believe him. I'm choosing to trust him. I believe in the life we're going to have. In the life I was always worthy of. If life this far has taught me anything, it's that even if we were to end in heartbreak, any time I'm gifted with this man and the joy he brings to my life will be worth the rush.

TWO YEARS LATER

How did I get so lucky?

I look out over the mountains. At this view I've loved since I was a kid. It's the reason I added all the windows here. It never gets old to me. It's still just as beautiful as it was a year ago, but it doesn't even compare to the view I get when I look back into our home. Ours. I smile, taking in my gorgeous wife while she chases our perfect daughter around the living room. My girls.

Ivy moved in with me after the avalanche. I was worried she would want to have more time to adjust, but when you know, you know. I love her more now than I ever thought possible for me. She's my best friend and partner in everything, including our business. The lodge has reached an insane amount of success. With Ivy at the forefront of the business, I suspect that will continue to be the case.

She stands and puts her hands on her hips, then rubs her stomach. Round with another Holloway baby. I told her I wanted five more after Raylen. She came up with our daughter's name. She thought it would be a nice way to honor my friend's memory. It made me love her even more. She also said two kids. Period. And I can't really argue since she's the one who has to do all the heavy lifting, so I agreed. Baby boy will be our last.

My family will be here any minute with the other cousins. I think about my life and how I never saw Ivy coming. How if I had gone home that first night or stayed somewhere else, we might not have crossed paths. What a sad life I would have had. *She* is my life now, her and those babies. I would do anything for them, and I will continue to prove to Ivy every single day that taking the chance on me was worth it. Our life together will be worth it.

"Are you just going to stand there smiling, Lover Boy? Or are you going to help me wrangle the little angel?" she asks, snapping me out of my love-fest thoughts. I chuckle. Damn that mouth. That absolutely thrilling and beautiful mouth.

"You keep talking like that, and I'm going to accidentally put another baby in you before this one's here," I tease.

She laughs, loudly. My favorite laugh. "Baby, that's now how it works, and it worries me if you don't know that."

"Dadadadada," Ray babbles and teeters toward me. I scoop her up in my arms and kiss all over her face, making her giggle.

"We need to get you ready, princess, or Mommy's gonna eat Daddy alive." Ivy rolls her eyes at me and walks over.

"Mommy thinks Daddy would like that a little too much," she coos at our daughter, and I let out a surprised laugh. Life with Ivy will never be boring. I'll always be kept on my toes. That's fine by me as long as I'm kept.

"I love you, Stormcloud." She leans in and kisses me tenderly.

"I love you too, Alder. In this life and the next."

The End

Acknowledgments

I published another book! That feels amazing, and truly surreal to say. This story was challenging, and incredibly rewarding to write. A lot of what I wrote about are things that we don't talk about enough. I hope everyone who reads one of my books feels seen in some way, but if one person does then that is enough for me. With that being said, I have some people to thank.

First of all, I would like to thank *you*; the readers. Thank you for taking the time to read my book and this story that I hold so dear. Your support means the world to me. Thank you!

To my husband Joe, your support at bedtime, mealtimes, and all other times of our life together is what allows me this creative outlet, and you help me strive to be a better version of myself in all ways. Thank you for your unwavering love. I love you, more than I can say.

To my parents, being happy with the person I am is in no small part to how you raised me. Having been encouraged, and supported by you my whole life is such a cornerstone for my confidence to publish a book. I love you both so much. Thank you.

To Ginsa, thank you for being my friend, my soul sister, my twin flame. I am forever grateful, and in awe that we've found each other on this journey. You are a safe place for me, and a rock when I need stability. I love you.

To Bailey at Wildflower Fiction, thank you for taking a chance on my debut all those months ago. It gave me hope and confidence that I can actually do this even though I'm still such a new author. I'll forever be grateful for you reaching out to me and your continued support of not only me, but all indie authors.

To Ingrid, thank you for all the hard work you have put into helping me discover a brand and style I love. Thank you for being the ultimate hype-girl, and always making me feel like my stories are worth writing.

To the bookstagram community, the arc readers, I will never forget how you have shown up for me and how so many of you have taken a chance on me and my books. The beautiful edits and the messages I've received have encouraged me to keep writing.

Thank you all,

Xo, Bea

About This Author

Bea Borges is a romance author living out her small town love story in the Ozark Mountains with her husband and two magical children.

She enjoys trash TV, baking treats, and hosting friends. Most days you'll find her reading, writing, or watching a romance, but if not, she's probably hiking.

She writes love stories with flawed characters that are still so deserving of love.

Follow her on Instagram or TikTok to keep up with new books she's writing, and the parts of her life she's sharing.

@beaborges.author

www.ingramcontent.com/pod-product-compliance
Lightning Source LLC
Chambersburg PA
CBHW030150310726
48970CB00005B/1671